Pauline is a mum to a wonderful son. She lives in Werribee in Australia's south-east. Moby, her rescue Border Collie, often interrupts her focus on writing and work as an editor, demanding walks and cuddles and lots of ball time. But she doesn't mind.

Also by Pauline Toohey

Historical Fiction:

Pull of the Yew Tree – Book I of the Chronicles of Crom Abu
Published by *Indigo Dreams Publishing*

Contemporary Crime:

My Rickety Metronome – An Anna Murdoch Crime Story
Published by *Indigo Dreams Publishing*

Melting of the Mettle

Book 2: The Chronicles of Crom Abu

Pauline Toohey

First Edition: Melting of the Mettle
First published in Australia in 2015.

Pauline Toohey has asserted her right under the Copyright,
Designs and Patents Act 1988 to be identified as the author of
this work.
©2013 Pauline Toohey
ISBN 978-0-646-94449-4

Designed and typeset in Minion Pro

Cover design by Jaya Abela

A CiP catalogue record of this book is available from the
National Library of Australia.

To my veranda-ites
For your love and support, all my thanks.

Remember, oh remember
Pain before beauty
Chill before the blossom
For but a time, then colour will brag

Melting of the Mettle

Cast of Characters

Fitzgerald Family

Ainnir Fitzgerald:	*daughter of Hugh O'Byrne, and wife of Jarlath Fitzgerald*
Alice Fitzgerald:	*wife of Gerald* *
Anne Fitzgerald:	*daughter of Earl Thomas* *
Conor Fitzgerald:	*son of Jarlath and Ainnir*
Donal Fitzgerald:	*cousin of Earl Thomas*
Eleanor Fitzgerald:	*daughter of Earl Thomas* *
Ellie (Alice) Fitzgerald:	*daughter of Gerald* *
Elizabeth Fitzgerald:	*daughter of Gerald* *
Gerald Fitzgerald:	*eldest son of Earl Thomas* *
James Fitzgerald:	*son of Earl Thomas* *
Jarlath Fitzgerald:	*nephew of Earl Thomas and nephew of Esmond O'Toole*
Joan Fitzgerald:	*Countess of Kildare, wife of Earl Thomas* *
Margaret Fitzgerald:	*daughter of Gerald and Alice* *
Maurice Fitzgerald:	*son of Earl Thomas* *
Siobhan Fitzgerald:	*daughter of Jarlath and Ainnir*
Thomas Fitzgerald:	*7th Earl of Kildare, Justiciar of Ireland* *
Tom Fitzgerald:	*son of Earl Thomas* *

O'Byrne Family

Bradan O'Byrne:	*son of Hugh O'Byrne*
Brigid O'Byrne:	*wife of Hugh O'Byrne*
Eamonn O'Byrne:	*eldest son of Hugh O'Byrne*
Hugh O'Byrne:	*Gaelic Chieftain of Wicklow* *

9

Eustace Family

Manus Eustace:	*nephew of the Baron Roland Eustace*
Margaret Eustace:	*wife of Roland Eustace* *
Meg Eustace:	*wife of Manus Eustace*
Roland Eustace:	*Baron of Portlester* *

Agnes:	*servant to the Fitzgeralds*
Barnwell, Barnaby:	*nobleman of Meath* *
Baron, Robert:	*nobleman of Howth* *
Bellew, Richard:	*nobleman of Louth* *
Butler, John:	*Earl of Ormond* *
Butler, James:	*nephew of John Butler* *
Claire:	*daughter of Glendalough's blacksmith*
Dowdal, Robert:	*nobleman of Dublin* *
Edward IV:	*King of England* *
Emma:	*servant at Manor Kildea*
Ferghal:	*blacksmith of Glendalough*
Francis:	*servant to Prior of Kilmainham*
George, Duke of Clarence:	*brother of King Edward* *
Gretel/Grace:	*Harry's female companion*
Grey, Henry:	*Lord of Codnor* *
Harry:	*friend of Gerald Fitzgerald*
Keating, James:	*Prior of Kilmainham* *
Marared:	*maidservant to Ainnir Fitzgerald*
Mrs. Mulhearn:	*housekeeper at Kildea*
Nell:	*inn servant*

O'More, Dorothea: *Thomas Fitzgerald's first wife* *

O'More, John: *son of Thomas Fitzgerald* *

O'More, William: *son of Thomas Fitzgerald* *

O'Neill, Conn Mor: *Prince of Ulster* *

O'Neill, Henry: *King of Ulster* *

O'Neill, Sean Buidhe: *cousin to Conn Mor* *

O'Toole, Esmond: *Gaelic Chieftain of Wicklow* *

Patrick: *gardener of Manor Kildea*

Plunkett, Alexander: *nobleman of Meath* *

Plunkett, Edward: *nobleman of Meath* *

Richard, Duke of Gloucester: *brother of King Edward* *

Sherwood, William: *Bishop of Meath* *

Taaf, Lawrence: *nobleman of Drogheda* *

Woodville, Elizabeth: *wife to King Edward IV* *

Ussher, Arland: *past mayor of Dublin* *

Veronique: *maidservant to Meg Eustace*

Those marked * are recorded in history

Part One

Prologue

Solitude no longer calls my name nor begs my presence. No longer does it entice me to run. No longer does it lure me to hide, bid me retreat to the high branches of the mighty yew trees along the River Lyreen and there conceal myself behind spindly leaves that hang above gnarled roots clawing at the earth like the talons of my son's eager hawk.

Time has played tonic. Courage has eroded my childhood ailment.

Time too, has worn thin my initials. My initials, JF, a crude inscription once made in my yesterdays in those high yew branches by a young boy's knife, now blur. Or perhaps the carving is worn thin by children climbing and playing and scuffling, or perhaps by the wind and rain, the snow and sleet, or the wood-warblers that nest in the tree's arms each year. Time alters much, but often, not enough.

Now impatience plagues my days. I watch greed and power and prideful mettle bring discontent to my land, my home, my Ireland. I await accord. I await peace, no matter how frail my hope.

I mourn the loss of many and know I will mourn more. I shout the war cry of the Fitzgeralds, 'Crom Abu', as my blade takes lives, and know I will soon take more.

The warm breeze that stirs often at my boots tells me

so, the sweet breeze that speaks to me without words. It is a heart I once knew. I know so, for the breeze dances as lightly as that heart once did. And I am not the only soul to feel her touch.

Yet no matter my antipathy, I must endure, I must obey. I am loyal and steadfast. I am a man of Kildare. I am Jarlath Fitzgerald, nephew to Thomas Fitzgerald, the 7th Earl of Kildare, and my story continues.

⊠

Chapter One

Castle Maynooth – Ireland
Summer 1475

Brooding. His mood was dark.

Tapestries interrupted the grey-blue stone of the castle walls. Images of epic battles, golden fields before harvest, an Italian winter's countryside, French terraced gardens, unicorns feasting on bluebells, and to the end of the hall a recently hung piece depicting what appeared to be undernourished angels caught in thundering clouds. If his wife insisted on expanding their collection of woven art, Ireland's looms would weep with exhaustion.

Thomas sat at the dais drumming fingers on the wooden table, and studied that last piece again. Angels or slaves? A closer inspection would be required, a task best left to an occasion when his home held less distraction, and he a better mood.

The trestles and benches below spared no room. His guests ate and chatted, gorged and purged, scoffed and ranted and little else. With their brocades and laces, the women granted a picture no less an event in thread than his walls. And to the men, Thomas gave over the discriminating attention usually afforded a game of chess. He spied men of power, men of affluence and men wanting both, and then pondered which of the flesh and blood game pieces were sincere in their joy at this occasion and which were parasitic.

Knights, Pawns and Bishops, he branded the minions. Knights for their loyalty, Pawns their expendability, and Bishops their cunning. Despite his religious ethos, Thomas did not favour Christendom's Bishops and their facades of righteousness, their trinkets of gold and tongues as sharp as a Flemish blade. Pretenders all of them.

Yes, brooding and sombre.

The sounds beyond the walls were the next to suffer the Earl's scrutiny. The night wind played eerie notes, each sounding above the music in the hall. Shutters knocked and doors shook. It was summer, and the weather was not as it ought to be. Why?

Thomas almost laughed. Could he not let it all be?

He knew the answer. Impossible! To incessantly suffer suspicion was an unavoidable binding bestowed to the most powerful man in Ireland, and it dragged like an anchor. Be gone, he ordered in silence, and made a magnanimous effort to still his busy fingers.

Thomas felt eyes directed his way. Close eyes. Beautiful eyes.

His wife gently placed a hand upon his arm. 'Is it such a chore to be here, my love?'

Thomas slanted Joan a look, vying for something between cryptic and perplexing.

Not hoodwinked, the Countess gave a hint of a smile in return. 'Our son is to marry the Baron's daughter at week's end, and I would think you'd find it an occasion to celebrate.'

'You know me too well, Joan.'

'And that is why you love me so.'

Thomas nodded then frowned. His fingers may have stilled, but his tongue did not, and it played at an aching tooth.

'I think it past time you had that tooth attended.'

Thomas looked to those misty-grey eyes. 'I would prefer the pleasure of having my nails pulled.'

At that very moment he would have given his purse and more, even have his nails truly pulled, to take his wife above stairs and collapse into peaceful slumber. Every corner of Castle Maynooth had proven insufferably busy this past week. Every guest, every archway, every corridor, every discussion, whether in shadow or sun, all demanded his time. Sleep seemed to be his only reprieve, and what came was all but destroyed by his damnable tooth.

But he knew none was her making and to appease his beloved wife, Thomas shifted in his chair and looked back to his guests with fresh eyes. Brooding be gone.

Musicians filled the hall with melody. Shrill laughter offered a cadence of cheer. Skirt folds swayed. Silver and gold thread caught flickering candlelight. A rainbow of hues floated across the floor like windblown clouds, and as gowns rustled and settled, they offered their own accompaniment to the music. Servants scampered from trestle to trestle removing empty platters, making way for smoking meats, tureens of spiced vegetables and lashings of sauces. Rosemary and cloves wafted and duelled with scented oils and sweat and flea-ridden dogs.

The music ceased on a trill from a flute. The castle bard took his place at the centre of the hall, and dressed in a jacket of yellow, and boots that climbed higher than his knees, retold a well-known tale of love. Thomas managed a smattering of plausible laughter, for the ending was not as expected. It appeared the fabled forgiveness of the Goddess Rhiannon was not to be portrayed this evening.

> 'The Goddess's hand of pardon was but pretence,
> Her smile a lure to a false finale.
> Her nails transformed to talons,
> And Pwyll yelped like a hound.
> Bloodied slash marks appeared upon his cheeks and

neck,

> Crimson flowed without cease.
> Dear people of Kildare, a keepsake of warning,
> For within each woman a shrew awaits in ambush.'

Faces spoke approval. Wide genuine grins, some thin-lipped, some overly animated by the indulgence of wine, others more smirk than smile. The crowd cheered for more. Thomas added his voice to the calls. It would please him equally to enjoy another diversion. But his stay of guarded suspicion lasted no more than a modicum of time. The sounds of dogs snarling over discarded bones came to his ears, and then a distant clamour from the inner bailey.

Before the hounds could further dispute the ownership of bones, the doors of the great hall burst free. A gust of wind entered and an intruder, leading a small band of men, followed. The man's march toward the dais parted the crowd with little effort, yet his gait possessed an almost imperceptible bias, an inclination to favour his left leg. Murmurs from inquisitive guests rose above the stir.

Thomas noted the silver brooch fastened at the neck of

the intruder's dirtied mantle. The symbol of a beast, half boar-half lion, crafted with emerald stones at its centre. Not the normal attire of a mere messenger. Then Thomas recognised the man. James Butler. Nephew to John Butler, the Earl of Ormond. Thomas' eternal nemesis.

Courtesy was needless. At the age of fifty Thomas was long accustomed to asserting authority and he held no desire to indulge Butler with any degree of sufferance.

'So, it is a Butler such an ill-wind brings to my home. I do not remember dispatching an invitation in your name.'

Some of the guests braved laughter. The wise remained silent.

Positioned at a point between wise and brave, or perhaps foolish and more foolish, James Butler sneered. 'The King has entrusted me with a message, my lord, to be delivered directly to your hands.' The sneer transformed to a conceited smile, one which lasted too long. Butler produced a scroll with the royal seal and did not wait for a reply, spinning on his heel the moment the missive left his hand.

'Butler!' Thomas bellowed.

James Butler stopped mid-stride.

'You have my leave.' Thomas used an easy tone, more venomous for its simplicity.

With nary a glance, James Butler continued his way, the hem of his mantle billowing and waving. There could have been a litter of fox cubs playing beneath that material for all its movement, or a troop of wrestling sprites.

Of a sudden Butler's progress was again interrupted. His regard snapped to one side. Thomas watched Butler's angry eyes catch another's – those of Gerald, Thomas' eldest son.

Words were exchanged, words not heard by most, but Thomas read his son's lips with little difficulty.

James Butler restruck his gait, the thud of his boots sounding more an escape than an exodus.

With a nod Thomas gave silent orders to two of his captains to follow Butler then turned his focus to the missive. Impatient fingers ripped at the wax seal. A message from across the Irish Sea, delivered by the hands of a Butler would hold naught but unwelcome tidings. He could not remember the last time a Butler ventured into his home. Too much blood had been spilt for civilities to resume. How did it come that a Butler left the shores of Ireland without his knowledge? And more perplexing, how did a Butler gain an audience with the King? He cursed on a single grunt. Did he not have in his employ more spies than a haystack has mice? He would address such a slight in good time. Someone would indeed bear his wrath.

Ornately-penned lettering lined the pages. The missive was curt, accusatory and Thomas felt no surprise. He pitched a cursory glance across the hall to his good friend Roland Eustace the Baron of Portlester, and moved promptly toward the stairway. Thomas gave thought to the question of Butler's nature. Which chess piece? Only a Rook could perform double manoeuvres with a King.

A new game had just begun.

He barked orders for his two eldest, Gerald and Tom to follow. They could come, listen and possibly absorb – possibly.

'Out!' Thomas ordered the servants from the solar and moved to pour drinks for himself and the men. He reached for the spicy hippocras and hesitated, settling for the ale. Bitterness suited the occasion.

The men took their cups. Quiet filled the room for a prickly moment before Thomas joined them at the table. Cup in one hand, the King's letter in the other, he held the missive high.

'The King wants near on all our coin to finance his march upon Louis and France. He demands to know our reasons for the poundage we take from merchants. And to add further royal insult, he again entreats me to accord peace with Butler.' One hand came down fast, spilling wine to the floor. 'Has the King lost his wits?'

The other hand moved just as quickly. The letter slid across the table's surface and Roland Eustace grabbed at the pages before they took flight.

'Butler! That man is foe, and was no less to the King's dead father.' Thomas turned to Roland. 'See the exact words His Grace uses to speak of our foul neighbour.'

The Baron scanned the pages and read, 'If good breeding and liberal qualities were lost in the world, they might be all found in John Butler, the Earl of Ormond.'

Thomas knocked at the table with his knuckles, then turned and stalked the length of the room. His thoughts raced. This news was unwelcome to say the least. For five glorious years, as Earl of Kildare and Justiciar of Ireland, Thomas had ruled his beloved lands. For five glorious years in every way possible, he brought laws and decrees to his lands for peace and prosperity, had consigned his closest confidantes and most trustworthy of allies to positions of importance and power, had raised an army, the Guild of Saint George, to protect the good

23

people of Ireland from its rebellious natives and enemies to the crown. And it was no easy achievement to bring a form of primogeniture, one made certain by written dictate that his eldest son was his heir in every sense of the word. Gerald would inherit his estates, his wealth and all titles.

In all of this he had indeed achieved his greatest desire – the Fitzgeralds of Kildare held Ireland firmly in their grip. For five years they had done so without castigation. For five years there was little interference from the King; none that bandied concern in any event. None until now.

Tapping toes and a clicking tongue followed. The rhythm mimicked a lively tune. Thomas turned to the self-styled musician. Gerald rested his booted feet on the table, hands clasped behind his head; a lizard basking beneath a summer sun.

Thomas caught Gerald's eye. The sounds ceased. He regarded his son in uneasy silence. No stranger would ever believe this young man to be the heir to the greatest Earldom in Ireland. Forever attired informally in riding garb and interested only in pleasure, he was more likely to be mistaken for a huntsman, a blissfully contented huntsman. It brought to mind words Joan often counselled – Gerald's only fear was boredom.

Roland broke the quiet. 'By my reckoning, Thomas, the Butlers are the source of the King's sudden bout of curiosity, and for all of James Butler's show, his hasty exit suggested he feared the devil was at his back. I fear little.'

'Butler's exit may have more to do with my son's words. Testicle breath, was it not, Gerald, you called young Butler?'

'You did not, brother?' Tom's tone was high.

A small lift to Gerald's lips hinted at his infamous mischief.

Roland spoke. 'No matter the anatomical irregularities of our unwelcome visitor, I suggest His Grace need only hear a well-penned reply as to the state of Ireland and your plans, and a few blunt reminders that Butler is not to be trusted.'

'I suspect Butler has concocted more schemes than you surmise, Roland,' said Thomas.

'You may be correct. Therefore as your Chancellor I will allocate coin to be sent across the sea. An amount not to drain our coffers unnecessarily, yet an amount not to insult. To appease His Grace to some degree, we must.'

Thomas held two fingers to his jaw and grimaced. 'Goose feathers may appease the King.' He closed his eyes in an attempt to wipe all problems from his mind, including the growing ache in his mouth.

'Goose feathers?' questioned Gerald.

Roland stood from the table, the rare occasion of a smirk appearing upon his face. He seemed the only one present to understand Thomas' quip, and took it upon himself to explain the witticism to the two younger men. 'Sixty years gone, King Henry ordered every goose in his realm be deplumed of six feathers for the making of arrows. All were used at the battle at Agincourt, another battle on French soil.'

Gerald shifted in his chair. 'Therefore another offering from our birds would not seem so impudent. I suggest a cargo of parson's noses.'

Roland's eyebrows arched. It wasn't in question.

'Bird arses,' Gerald said, as if an explanation was needed.

25

'For Christ's sake, Gerald,' said Thomas impatiently. 'You are here to learn statecraft and offer intelligible options. We face a serious threat.'

Gerald grabbed at two apples perched atop a platter on the table, pitched one to his brother, tossed and caught with the adroitness of youth. 'The missive is nothing. And besides,' Gerald paused, uncrossing and recrossing his ankles, and chomping into his apple, 'it was cock breath I called Butler.'

Tom laughed. Tom always did. He loved his elder brother.

Thomas said naught, moved to the sideboard and refilled his empty cup. He swallowed wishing for the ale to have some effect, and quickly. And refilled again.

'Your father is right, Gerald,' Roland said with his usual calm. A predictable manner, for Roland was not one to cosset impertinence. 'May I suggest, Thomas, that in your reply to the King we speak of the need for our army to expand if the Gaels of the east are to be controlled, and, we speak of the Prince of Ulster's betrothal to your daughter. Such will no doubt illustrate that we continue to make inroads with some of the native Irish, if not all. The King's interest is sure to be roused at this, and douse what Butler has set.'

Thomas turned at the sound of legs swinging to the floor. Gerald stood from his chair. Thomas noted the usual steel-blue eyes had taken on the colour of smoke.

'More,' said Gerald. 'We should raid and bring the eastern Chieftains to heel. Perhaps then you would not receive chastisement on paper.'

Thomas measured his reply before he spoke. He knew to pick his way carefully through conversations of the eastern

Chieftains with Gerald, for too often they started and ended awkwardly.

'There is not the need. But some of what you say holds merit. To mention such a plan in my reply, no matter the truth of it, will serve us well.'

'There is great need! The Wicklow Chieftains are in the north courting our enemies. If we refuse to take action …' Gerald grasped for appropriate words. None came.

'I agree with Gerald, Papa,' said Tom.

'Two of you? Two antagonists?'

'Is that what you think us?' said Gerald, indignantly. 'Rivals?'

'I don't think Papa meant—' Tom was cut off by a sure look from Gerald.

Thomas had two choices. To come down upon his eldest with a torrent of censure, or give the usual litany of reasons why an attack upon the Gaels of Wicklow was not an option. He chose the latter.

'The O'Toole and the O'Byrne have stayed their hands, albeit with unsteadiness for the past five years, and as much as I am certain it aggravates them unto pain, they have cunningly done little to incur the end of my sword.'

Gerald made to say something.

Thomas raised a stiff hand. 'And do not doubt I know their every move, know of all their intrigue and schemes, even before they know it themselves.'

'They plan and they plot.'

'Yes, they plan and they plot. I know all.'

'So we leave them to their scheming? Allow them to laugh at us? Think us vague? Think us idiotic?'

'There is a purpose.'

'Vengeance is mine saith the Lord.'

The night wind played at the windows. Candlelight flickered as a draft stole in through the chimney. A fire-worn log rolled in the hearth. Thomas felt a wry scowl come to the fore. It was aimed at Gerald. Why did his son believe patience sinful?

'And you are not the Lord, son.'

'The O'Toole is overdue for Nil-fine and I will avenge your cousin's death, Papa. Donal took that arrow for me five years ago, and before I take my last breath the O'Toole will come to taste the end of my sword.'

'I was there, or do you forget?'

'Forget? I relive that moment every day. You refuse to act, all because of Jarlath. Yes?'

The shuffling feet of Roland retreating to the far wall was the only sound to be heard.

Then Thomas said, 'You have a fool's mouth.'

'Gerald,' Tom said quietly in warning.

'No. It is time our father hears this. We all know you favour your nephew above your own. Jarlath, Jarlath Fitzgerald, the bastard son of your dead brother. And you stay your hand because his wife is the daughter of the O'Byrne.'

'That is enough!' Thomas' words erupted with rage. Such an accusation bore no amount of truth and he would not tolerate any to assume such. 'Ainnir is not the enemy.'

Gerald threw his hands in the air. 'Ainnir will always be an O'Byrne. And it seems I will always be no more than a nuisance. I doubt you would throw your precious wine upon my burning carcass?'

Thomas swept an arm toward the hearth. 'Here is an abundance of flames. Let's see, shall we?'

'See shall we?'

'For the love of Christ, Gerald, let your unfounded insecurities vanish. What do you want from me? My care for you inscribed in blood upon a piece of parchment.'

'And place it in my pocket to be burnt along with my carcass?'

'I will hear no more of your foolishness!' Thomas gave the room his back.

Silence came – a long length of silence.

Tom interrupted the quiet. 'I for one would like to know what Nil-fine is.'

Thomas gave the room his profile. 'Yes, Gerald. I too, am intrigued.' He knew the answer.

Gerald straightened his jacket, composed himself. 'Nil-fine is a Viking's darkest of Hells, something akin to what our heads are bound to feel on the morn, brother. I wish to drink in the village. Do we have your leave, Papa?'

Thomas knew it would do no good to continue conversing of the King's orders. Best the young men find oblivion in ale. He faced his sons. 'Go.'

Gerald accepted the abrupt dismissal and marched out the door. Tom offered Thomas a look of meagre apology before following Gerald's exit.

Roland's voice came from the shadows. 'They will be arriving tomorrow.'

Thomas stared at the door and swallowed roughly from his cup. 'Who?'

'Jarlath and Ainnir.'

Thomas made no move to reply.

'You know, Thomas, Gerald is not unlike Jarlath?'

'So you believe as my son does?'

'That James Butler has cock breath? Possibly. That feathered arses will appease the King? No. That you favour Jarlath? That is not for me to say.'

Thomas spied a look of sympathetic censure. He pondered what Roland did not voice. 'My son's guilt for Donal's death bakes a poisonous tart.'

'And cooking is a skill best left for the women.'

Thomas laughed. 'Never change, Roland. Your banal manner is endearing.'

'And yours may differ from Gerald's, but that does not make his wrong. Your son will prove a fine leader when the time comes. You should not doubt that.'

Thomas twirled the empty cup in his hand, his thumb tracing the intricate etchings of vines and leaves. 'I'd wager all the coin in Ireland Jarlath knows how to interpret scripture, and how to pronounce Niflheim.' He grimaced as the tooth gave more pain.

'Well, Niflheim it will be for you for some time if you do not have a barber attend that tooth.'

'I would rather—'

'Yes, I know,' Roland interrupted. 'You would rather have your nails pulled.'

Chapter Two

Manor Ballymore

From the bedchamber window Meg looked down to the steps of her home. Servants laboured beneath an endless line of heavy coffers while her four spaniels yapped, dodging busy booted feet. Her husband shouted orders demanding speed. Meg thought Manus quite irritated. Even from this distance, she knew his eyes darkened in their shade. He was tall, uncommonly handsome, with hair as dark as hers was light. A shame his patience did not equate his good looks.

Two servants became inattentive to their duty and Meg breathed in sharply as their burden almost fell to the ground. The more inquisitive spaniel, Blanchette, came close to injury and Meg's concern was equally for the contents of the coffers. Utter necessities. Silks, furs, laces, rubies, pearls, perfumes, creams. She could still smell the lingering scent of the now-removed creams; exotic and spicy. All were the latest fashion wants from Spain, France and England, modes which ostensibly rooted their demand into society's exorbitance – and Meg's. It would not do for a woman of her lineage to travel with less.

Not for the first time Meg lamented how life's erroneous path brought her to be the mistress of a small manor in the bordering lands of County Kildare and County Dublin, and wife to a mere nephew of Roland Eustace, Baron of Portlester. May her father's soul rot in Hell. It deserved no more for his dim-witted arrangement. His measure of ambition was unforgivably lacking. She was a De Burgh, deserving of much more than what her pallid life bestowed, and she was related, however distantly, to the Earl of Kildare's wife, for she too, hailed from the De Burgh line, not that the Countess publically acknowledged their bond with any fondness.

How had a woman of such lineage come to be here?

This marriage won her a diminutive estate with a none-too-lofty tally of eight bedchambers, one cook, twelve servants, no outer or inner bailey, no thick castle walls, no opulent courtyard leading to a magnificent hall, and no dais with a grand high table for the hosting of great feasts.

Trapped. Nothing more than an unappreciated possession. A mare, and not even a brood-mare at that, for no child had come of the six years of their marriage. How could they for the number of times Manus sought her bed?

Meg returned to her seat at the night table and mindlessly shifted rows of empty trinket boxes. She looked to her reflection. The gilded mirror framed a well-groomed woman, hair the shade of shimmering moonlight, petite features, cheeks splashed with the perfect hue of peach, and emerald green eyes. A gown of green, woven with a sparkling thread, was a perfect choice for this day. Its square neckline, low yet decent, flaunted unblemished skin, skin as pure as snow. Yes, may my father's soul rot in Hell.

Meg applied the last of her powder. 'Are you certain all provisions have been packed, Veronique?'

'Oui, madame. Barely a garment remains.'

Meg arched an eyebrow. Veronique too, was a luxuriant accessory. A French maidservant with a French name and a heavily accented French tongue, and one who brought unexpected pleasantries, for a friendship of sorts blossomed between the two women. It was perhaps the only positive relationship Meg had ever experienced.

'Ridicule in disguise all you like but a lady should always be prepared, and on this occasion I refuse to be ill-equipped.'

Veronique laughed quietly. 'It is not mockery I intend. I know you well and the telling signs of excited nervousness are revealing themselves. Look at your fidgeting and that cloud of powder. 'Tis as if fog has fallen within this room.'

The unmistakable stride of Manus hammered up the stairs, accompanied with growls of, 'Get out of my way, you ball of useless fluff.' The bedchamber door flew open and the entrance of Blanchette the Spaniel tapped a tune on the floor. Manus' steps were a little more brutal.

'Why do you find it necessary to travel with so many fripperies, Meg?'

Meg sent her husband an oblique look of bemused indifference. 'We are to be guests of the Earl of Kildare, are to attend the wedding of his heir to your cousin. Can you not imagine the litany of power and affluence we shall be company to?'

'We are not to meet with a King.'

'I see no harm in ensuring we present ourselves in a way to improve our standing, all for the recognition of the De Burgh family, Manus.'

His silence intimated a peevish displeasure, and Meg refused to appear chastised by the void.

'What?' she asked with feigned innocence, lifting a

simpering Blanchette onto her lap.

'Do you not mean the Eustace family?'

Meg sniffed. 'As always you are right, husband, and have corrected me on a menial faux pas. It is of course for the recognition of the Eustace family, your family.'

Not duped by the pretend apology, 'I intend to depart within the hour. You will have yourself ready. And that dog stays.'

Meg gave one short tut. 'I swear, Manus, if the great flood of scripture swelled at my feet, I do not think I would take you onto my ark.'

As Manus turned to quit the room, his voice floated above his pressing footsteps. 'Then lucky it is for me, dear wife, that I can swim.'

Chapter Three

The journey from Ballymore to Castle Maynooth progressed in the expected fashion – eventless. Eyes kept to the scenery, exchanges kept to necessities. Minutes were counted as hours, and therefore what felt like days of monotonous travel finally came to a welcome end.

Manus and Meg entered Maynooth's hall. Their entrance could not have differed more from their journey, for lively movement and jovial banter greeted them from every corner. With his familiar grin and wearing a jacket fashioned of red velvet, Manus weaved a path through the crowd, toward the hearth. Meg followed with the poise of a flamingo, the glide of a swan.

'Mayhem has arrived at Maynooth,' Thomas Fitzgerald bellowed, employing his usual affectionate welcome. Seemed Manus and mayhem were thought to be synonyms of sorts.

'My lord, your habitual wording in that greeting grows tiresome. Is it not past time you pose another form of welcome?' Manus lowered his voice; perhaps not low enough. 'Why not invoke, *and here comes the great Manus Eustace, bravest of the brave, with ballocks big enough to evoke envy amongst the most endowed of his time*? A more fitting tribute I could not implore.'

The Earl roared with laughter. 'It is always a pleasure to

35

have you in my home. You are a welcome change to the pace of ceremony, Manus. I've had more than my fill of these guests and their styled conversations.'

'What is this I hear about ballocks, Manus?' a feminine voice whispered from behind.

Thomas choked on his drink and spat wine onto his tunic.

Manus turned to Joan Fitzgerald and gave a gracious bow, bending lower than necessary. He rose with a conciliatory smile. 'My lady, Countess, short of a pathetic apology for my ill-timed manners, I can only say how delightful it is to mark your company and how regal, as always, you look.'

'Ah, Manus, such eloquent praise. You are absolved of all sins. It is glad we are to have you here.' Joan took Manus into a warm embrace and whispered, 'None more than I, for your company will do well to distract the Earl from his moods.'

'Unbearable, intolerable, impossible or grumpy?' Manus whispered in return.

'All those and more. But today he grumbles a little less for he finally succumbed to having a bad tooth pulled.'

'Then he has my sympathies.'

'Manus, welcome.' Gerald's voice was as loud as his approach.

'The man about to be shackled. How does it feel?'

'If my wife-to-be was as beautiful as yours,' said Gerald, inclining his head without discretion, 'I would be thrilled beyond words.'

Manus turned to see that his wife had halted at an unnecessary distance. 'Some butterflies bite.'

'Some say pain gains entry to Heaven.' Gerald winked.

36

'I have matters to attend. I will see you later in the day.'

'You will,' said Manus.

Gerald's eye wandered to Meg again. He looked back to Manus and threw a loud laugh to the air. 'That butterfly's nip would be memorable.'

'Ignore my son's boldness, Manus.' Joan studied the figure of Meg. As always, Manus' wife appeared not too dissimilar to a keenly attentive canary: polished to perfection, not a hair out of place, impeccable deportment. The canary looked perched and ready to fly as soon as etiquette allowed. Joan summoned fortitude. 'Meg. Welcome, dear. Your husband has just gifted me with a great compliment, for no reason but his munificence.'

Manus cleared his throat, a gravelly sound.

Joan remained straight-faced. 'And may I say from one as beautiful as you, any such similar comment on my appearance would curry favour to no end.'

It was intended as a jest, but the canary, in her green shimmering gown, took flight, landed at Joan's feet and began to stammer, seemingly clutching for suitable compliments – to sing. Words found, Meg trilled awkwardly of the grandeur of Castle Maynooth's grounds and the beauty of the summer weather to herald such a propitious alliance in the form of the impending marriage. Joan silently thanked the Lord for small blessings, for so far, Meg refrained from talk of their shared ancestry. She wanted no reminder. Joan cared neither for Meg's mother nor the woman's obscenely precocious attitude toward the Gaels or toward most people for that matter. Nor did she care for Meg's long-dead father and his violent and devious ways. She often wondered what evil spell was cast all those years ago to have any person believe the marriage of Manus and Meg a favourable idea. They were as suited as an otter and a one-legged rooster.

The prattling of the canary ran its course.

Thomas pitched Manus a teasing glance. 'Your uncle the Baron will join me soon in the solar, Manus. I wish for you to be present. We have much to discuss of the King's demands and your counsel is needed.'

Meg's eyes betrayed her surprise at the last comment. Joan knew Meg thought Manus beneath her station and therefore his counsel unwanted, and Joan hid her amusement.

'Is it true,' asked Manus, 'the O'Byrne has acquired a sudden friendship with our enemies in the north?'

'True. But my son gives me more angst than that alliance,' answered Thomas.

'All for the Wicklow O'Toole?'

'And the O'Byrne.'

'I heard Gerald bakes a rancid pie to poison the masses, or was it bakes a tart like a woman?'

'Hah. Your uncle talks too much. And how do you hear of such things so quickly?'

'That is why you appreciate my counsel. Has Ainnir arrived as yet?' Manus inquired of their favourite Gael.

'She and Jarlath are in the gardens with their children. Join them before we adjourn to the solar.'

Joan caught a fleeting frown on Meg's forehead. 'You have not yet met our Ainnir, have you?'

As was expected, Meg's eyes widened almost imperceptibly. The use of *our Ainnir* made its mark.

'No, my lady. I have not.'

Joan gave thought to whether Ainnir's kind-heartedness and generous smiles could diffuse this one. Yes, she decided with little contemplation, and almost laughed at the fervour with which Ainnir would approach this project, this challenge.

'Ainnir is a delight and very much loved by the Earl and I.' Joan ensured her smile said much. 'Enjoy your turn around our garden for the blossoms are at their utmost splendid.'

'Thank you, my lady. You are too kind.'

There was a slight blush to Meg's face.

The message was understood entirely.

Meg tried to keep pace with her husband's steps. 'Manus, I would prefer that we retire to the guest chamber.'

'You will not shame me?'

'You know my thoughts.'

'Jarlath and Ainnir are my dearest friends.'

'I simply do not possess the acquired liking for the natives of Ireland. She is the daughter of a Chieftain, and Jarlath is not only the son of the Earl's bastard born brother, but his mother was a Gael. It is beyond my sensibilities—'

'And you will keep your sensibilities beyond that cold heart of yours.'

She offered no further argument.

Climbing rose vines framed the entrance to the private garden. Balls of yellow petals with sweet scents peppered the green. Meg caught sight of a family joined in a game of quoits beneath a poplar tree. Two small children struggled with the task of tossing horseshoes. She recognised Jarlath. He bent and whispered words to the children.

A little girl turned their way. 'Uncle Manus, Uncle Manus,' she shrieked, running into the open arms of her husband. Long, curly, honey-gold locks bounced around the child's shoulders, dishevelled and unconfined, and the bluest of eyes, as if they caught the sky, bore an emotional welcome.

Manus swung the girl high in the air then pulled her down into a tight embrace.

'Well if it isn't the Princess of the unicorn world,' he said in a playful voice, one which Meg found unfamiliar.

A second small body jumped into Manus' arms, a young boy of about three with the darkest of hair and brownest of eyes. His display of pleasure at seeing Manus was no less dramatic than the young girl's.

'My two favourite frogs.' Manus wriggled his nose into their sides. The children exploded with laughter.

'Not frogs, Uncle Manus,' the young boy said.

'I cannot keep up with what either of you are nowadays. You both change so quickly. The last time I saw you I could have sworn you were turtles.'

Their laughter spliced the air again like the scent of peonies in their first bloom.

Meg regarded the commotion, not sure what to make of it all. The man before her seemed a stranger. He tickled the children, feigned tricks and magic, and gave warm unconditional attentiveness, the likes of which she had never seen.

She did not know how long she stood staring, but of a sudden, a woman she suspected to be the daughter of the

O'Byrne Chieftain, stood to her side.

'You must be Meg. I am disappointed it has taken so long to make your acquaintance.'

Meg's eyes wandered back and forth between this woman and the small girl in her husband's arms for it was like seeing a replica. The same hued hair, the same blue eyes. Everything about them announced they could only be mother and daughter.

'Oh, please forgive me. I am Ainnir Fitzgerald, Jarlath's wife.'

'Yes, I assumed as much,' Meg replied, finding an acceptable balance between graciousness and passive rebuke. 'The Earl informed us you wandered the gardens, and my husband insisted we attend.'

Ainnir's smile grew and one eyebrow arched.

Meg tilted a defiant chin, a movement made for Ainnir's eyes only. What did this woman expect? A friendship? She stood in her presence under sufferance, nothing more. An attachment of any kind was impossible.

The two men embraced in their own warm welcome. They could be mistaken for brothers, so alike were they in colouring and build. Manus' curls and Jarlath's slight advantage of height were the only variances.

'It is a shame our homes are so distant,' said Ainnir, 'for if not, we would now be better acquainted.'

'It is, as you say, a shame.' Meg lifted her hand to check her coiffure.

'And you are a distant cousin to the Countess?'

Was this woman trying to cozen her into conversation? 'Yes. Yes, I am.'

41

'That would make us kin of sorts.'

'No. Certainly not—'

No more could be said on that point for Ainnir was swept off her feet. Manus swung the woman up into his arms and placed a kiss on her laughing face.

'The Wicklow Princess still bedazzles me every time I look into those eyes. I have missed you, Ainnir.'

'And I you,' Ainnir answered a little out of breath.

'Meg, it is good to see you again,' Jarlath said joining the conversation. He was polite, his tone courteous.

'Jarlath,' Meg greeted with a nod and a flowering smile, and assumed the civil movement to thwart any accusation from Manus that she indeed intended to cause embarrassment for anyone.

'May I introduce my children? My daughter Siobhan, and my son Conor,' said Jarlath.

Two sets of eyes stared intently at Meg.

'She is very beautiful, Papa. Like the merrow in our stories.' Siobhan's words erupted as an exclamation of awe.

Five sets of eyes suddenly studied Meg. She stammered sounds, nothing forming a decipherable word. Receiving compliments from any but Veronique was an alien occurrence to Meg.

Jarlath gave Manus a fleeting look of pity.

Ainnir's reaction was of a different measure. She continued to stare, with little movement to her stance or expression. 'My daughter is honest to a fault, Meg, but she indeed has an eye for God's work. The merrow she speaks of is a mermaid, and last night's storytelling was of the most beautiful of the merrows, one who took to land in a gown of green, a gown which sparkled silver in the sun's light, just as yours does now. And she also had eyes of green, said to be as alluring as a cat's.' Ainnir seemed to study Meg more intently. 'Just as yours,' she added, again.

Meg blinked and her hands fidgeted.

Manus stepped forward. 'It is just a tale Siobhan speaks of.'

'You are not their uncle,' Meg said matter-of-factly.

'It is a term of endearment, Meg.' His voice was low, his tone laconic. 'To them I am like an uncle, and I love them no less in return.'

'Something you expect I would not understand?'

Manus did not reply. He turned to Jarlath. 'Our rooms are being prepared. Give me an hour and I will join you in the solar.'

The garden grew quiet.

'But she does, Papa. She does look like our merrow.'

Jarlath winked at his daughter. 'Indeed, Siobhan.'

Ainnir stared at the backs of Manus and Meg as they disappeared behind an apple blossom hedge.

'Leave well enough alone, Ainnir.'

'She cannot be as bad as you say. I know she presents herself in a pretentious way but surely—'

'If the animal looks like a duck and quacks—'

'It could be a goose.'

'A goose honks. Meg quacks. She is a painful hag. And that is for Manus to deal with, not you.'

'Is that a challenge, husband?'

'It is not a challenge.'

'I believe it is.'

'Then I withdraw my words.' Jarlath's hands brushed the heads of his children as they chased around his legs.

'That, I will not allow.' Ainnir's hands flew to her hips and a smile threatened to betray her feigned huff. After five years of marriage she knew her blue eyes still possessed a power.

Laughter broke Jarlath's serious face. He threw his arms around Ainnir's shoulders and hugged tightly. Small bodies joined in the carousing, climbing upwards, shrieking with their own laughter.

'Children,' Jarlath said to Siobhan and Conor, 'I am deeply and unashamedly in love with your mother.'

On the eve of the wedding day, the guests enjoyed a great feast in Maynooth's hall. Honeyed pig, eel and fish pie, pike stuffed with chestnuts, and rabbit and onion stew were the earlier courses. And now servants busied themselves clearing trestles to make way for the next.

Meg studied the men and women seated at the dais. Her silent inventory included titles, power, influence and suspected wealth. Heading her list of prominence, the Earl and his wife. Affluence at its best, she thought. They smiled as they chatted. Hands touched. An enigma of sorts to see a wife and husband content in each other's company.

Next, the Earl's eldest son, Gerald, and his betrothed, Manus's cousin. Alice was a sweet girl. Meg always thought her kindly. Not beautiful as per the dictates of the day, but handsome in her own way with a roll of chestnut hair. She would do well to sit straight, refrain from speaking, and tighten that childlike cackle of hers to a demure sound. But this night Alice possessed a smile that could best a blinding sun, and why not? She was soon to marry the heir to the most powerful man in Ireland. Gerald's hair shone dark with the slightest hint of copper, barely noticeable until caught by light. Alice's eyes did not leave Gerald's face. Yet Gerald's regard lay elsewhere. He seemed deep in thought. His eyes jumped back and forth to the guests at the far end of the dais, as if giving a moment to measure or perhaps judge, no less than Meg herself was doing.

Next to Alice sat her parents, Roland the Baron of Portlester and his wife, Margaret. He, an aging man sharp and clever, and she, a woman perhaps once attractive. It was not time that pilfered beauty, but an unrestrained penchant for sugared delicacies. Yet the puffy Baroness looked no less thrilled for the morrow's event than did her daughter.

To the left sat the Earl's other children, and as if time tired dark to light, their hair altered from the mother's shade to the father's in order of age. Tom, a burnished brown. James, lighter again. Maurice, a fallen autumn leaf. Eleanor possessed the most glorious shade of red, luminous and shimmering. Then the youngest, Anne, a glowing gold.

None could deny the similarity of their eyes. Wide and round, very round. These siblings put Meg's mind to a group of wise birds, lively and alert, like owls, and she suspected the Fitzgeralds missed naught.

Maurice's autumn-coloured head tilted to the side and his eyes speared high, his thoughts not in this room, perhaps with the stars, perhaps with the stable cats, perhaps with yesterday's sunrise. Meg knew this son to be slow-witted. He rarely spoke, and always fell in behind his siblings, preferring the shadows. The Earl gestured to Maurice, who seemed not to be aware of his father's request. Eleanor took her brother by the hand, leading the boy to the centre of the dais. Earl Thomas lifted the boy onto his lap and selected morsels of food, inviting him to eat, then pointed to the line of servants carrying covered platters to each of the trestles.

Further along, Jarlath and his Gaelic wife sat to the far end of the table, the two who held Gerald's attention.

'Why is Jarlath invited to sit at the dais?' asked Meg. 'He is only the Earl's nephew is he not?'

Servants placed one of the many covered platters before Manus and Meg.

'Jarlath was raised by the Earl and is considered a true son to a great extent.' Manus swallowed deeply of his wine, then waved to a servant to have his cup refilled.

Meg's focus returned to the Earl. Sir Thomas spoke animatedly to Maurice, encouraging the boy's attention to remain with the newly arrived platters.

'Tell me of Ainnir's first husband,' Meg prompted.

'Donal Fitzgerald? Why?'

'I thought you would be pleased with my attempt to create conversation. What meal do you think is before us?'

'My guess is frog custard.'

'Frog custard?'

In unison, servants lifted lids.

Meg screamed.

Frogs, large frogs, lots of them, jumped across the trestles. Many of the guests laughed. Many applauded. The Earl roared his enjoyment. His son's eyes seemed to follow the darting creatures. Eleanor captured one and placed it into her brother's hands. The boy smiled.

Frogs flew left and right. One landed on Meg's shoulder.

'Manus!' Meg screeched.

'Yes, Meg?'

'Remove the creature!'

The frog leapt again, its front legs clawing at Meg's hair, its back legs fighting for purchase.

'Manus!' she screeched again.

Manus plucked the flailing frog and threw it back to the trencher.

'We are not expected to eat them alive, are we?'

Manus laughed. 'There, on the smaller trencher, is the custard. A mixture of frog, almonds, pomegranate and spices. Those smaller pieces of meat alongside,' he said, reaching for one, a piece that resembled a tiny goose leg, 'are cooked frog legs. And they're dead.' Manus sucked the meat from the small bone.

'My appetite has waned.' Meg flinched as another frog hopped across the trestle, and then another. 'Answer my earlier question,' she requested, holding up her hands to thwart another attack from slimy legs.

'Of Donal?' Manus flicked the bone to the ground.

'Yes, of Donal.'

'Donal was the Earl's cousin, and widowed. Thomas was keen to forge an alliance with the O'Byrne Chieftain of Wicklow. A marriage was made, and soon after, Donal was killed fighting the O'Toole and the O'Byrne's men. He took an

47

arrow that was meant for Gerald.'

'The O'Byrne is Ainnir's father is he not?'

Manus nodded and picked at another cooked frog leg.

'Why was the Earl so keen to have Ainnir passed to another of his kin?'

'Donal and Ainnir's marriage was made for an alliance, but Jarlath and Ainnir's was not. It was for love. Surely you can see that?'

More laughter came from the middle of the hall as children chased frogs, some mimicking the awkward leap.

So, Meg thought, the talk was correct. Those two had loved before Ainnir was betrothed to Donal. How quaint. She would reflect upon that ripe piece of information later.

To the other end of the dais sat Henry O'Neill, the King of Ulster. A weather-worn man, bearing the demeanour of a seasoned fighter. Beside O'Neill sat a surly man, quite ill-favoured in his looks, almost scary. He wore his hair cropped short, his dark facial hair similarly cropped, futile in its attempt to conceal an unsightly scar stretching from lip to chin. His large build and irreverent slouch lent Meg to believe him too confident. She supposed if he stood to walk it would be with an arrogant swagger. He devoured frog leg after frog leg after frog leg.

'Who is the brusque gentleman to the end of the dais?' Meg asked as a platter of dry cheeses rolled in herbs was placed before Manus.

'Beside Henry O'Neill? His son, Conn Mor O'Neill, the Prince of Ulster.'

'He does not look too pleased to be here.'

Manus gave a humdrum laugh and reached for a piece

of cheese. 'Conn is at his happiest on a horse, swinging a sword. And, it does not help that his young betrothed chases his attention.'

'He is what … twenty and one, perhaps twenty and two? Certainly of an age to have been married for a time.'

'Conn's first wife died recently, leaving him with three children.'

'Sad,' Meg said spuriously, wasting no time to glean further gabble. 'So which unfortunate lady possesses the honour of being his second wife?'

Manus speared another piece of cheese with his knife and offered it to Meg. She shook her head.

'The young red-haired girl wandering to his side,' he replied. 'The one about to give him an earful of chatter. The Earl's daughter, Eleanor.'

'Oh, to be betrothed to such a beastly man, let alone one who is a Gael. It is regrettable.'

'Eleanor would disagree. She's keen to become a Princess, and at the age of eleven she measures the wait in weeks not years.'

'And the reason he is seated at the dais?'

'King Edward gives little support to keep order here. Thomas now nurtures relationships with the native Kings to achieve his goal, and O'Neill is the strongest on that list of allies.'

Meg had no time to pose another question. The men at the dais began to move. So too, did Manus. He signalled for more wine.

'I am to join the men. You look weary, Meg. I suggest you retire. Have Veronique select your finest night gown.' He emptied the fresh cup. 'I will not be late.'

Meg understood she had just been dismissed, knew too, what was expected of her this night. Her husband would choose to find his bed sport in their own chamber. The small muscles along her jaw tightened, and not from a sense of repugnance.

Before Manus moved away, he said, 'The creatures fear the cook's pot more than you fear their touch, Meg.'

Meg followed his line of sight and jumped. A frog sat not a hand's width away, eyeing her gown with particular relish.

The nightly chore of one-hundred strokes with the brush kept Veronique busy. Meg toyed with the powders and creams lining the sideboard. She shuffled the order of the pots, stacked, unstacked, removed lids, replaced lids. Her nervousness knew not how to still.

'We do not even have the comfort of an antechamber,' Meg complained to the air.

Before Veronique could add an opinion, Manus entered the bedchamber.

'Veronique, you are dismissed,' he said, not unpleasantly.

Veronique squeezed Meg's shoulder ever so gently then hurried from the room.

Manus sat on the bed and removed his boots. His level of balance confirmed he had indulged in many drinks. But as Meg often learnt, his liking for wine had its advantages. Her nervousness shifted to excited apprehension.

'An agreeable evening?' she asked.

'I am in a somewhat affable mood, Meg.' His tone was

deep as tolling bells. His eyes wandered the length of her body. 'Where is that scented cream of yours, the one with jasmine? I would like it to fill my nostrils this night.'

Meg fumbled with the pots. Where is that cream? 'If Veronique were here, she would know.' Where is it? Her tongue grew loose, too loose. 'It astounds me, Manus. Why are we relegated to such a small room? And to have my maidservant pallet down in a place almost as distant as the moon. What am I to do if I need her as I do now?' She continued to fossick. That cream? 'Your friends are sure to be enjoying the comforts of a more privileged room, and we are stuffed in here like ... like ... like fish in a small pond. There is no room for all my coffers. That Gaelic woman could have no more than one. I am sure of it, and here I am—'

A grunt interrupted the tirade. 'You can be such a self-interested, spiteful—'

'And I am wrong?' Meg offered her best look of annoyance.

Manus pulled his boots back on, stood and gave Meg his back.

'Where do you intend to go at this late hour?'

No answer came.

'Off to find yourself a whore, husband? Why you would waste our coin when we are given one room and one bed and forced to share is beyond my understanding.'

Manus swung back and shot Meg a disdainful glare. 'Forced to share, Meg? Your choice of words does little to encourage my stay.'

'It is of no consequence to me, Manus,' Meg hissed. 'No consequence at all. Appease your carnal yearnings with a filthy, scratching thing if it is your will.'

'I know, Meg. I know only too well you find me and my things of no consequence.'

The door slammed.

Still and poised, chin angled unnaturally, Meg stared at the closed door. Her hand swiped at an errant tear. 'No consequence at all,' she repeated. It was uttered in the palest of whispers.

Chapter Four

Like a forest of trees plagued by whipping winds, the raised hurling sticks raced back and forth across the clearing. The direction of the small skin ball dictated their sway. Running at a good speed, the now-married Gerald shouldered his way through the pack and jumped over a fallen opponent. He dodged left then right, with eyes fixed on the ball. Of a sudden a great shove came to his side, catapulting him through the air.

Gerald fell harder than he'd first realised, and remained prone catching his breath. His audience responded with a mixture of oaths and badly disguised laughter, and the reactions from two of his brothers were also singularly at odds; a shaking head with soundless laughter, and tight lips which loosened on a sigh.

'I'll hear nothing from you two,' Gerald warned.

James looked to Tom. 'Our brother wishes our silence,' he said with good humour. 'That does not bode well.'

'You're right,' said Tom. 'Gerald does not take to loss with any measure of charm.'

'We have not yet lost,' said Gerald, but was ignored.

'Does he do anything with a measure of charm?' James asked of Tom.

53

'Nothing that I know of. But there's always a first.'

'Grab my stick,' Gerald ordered.

Tom obliged, but was not quite ready to give up the tease. 'Do you remember the story of the Battle of Moytura?' he said to James.

'No, but I suspect you are about to instruct me.'

'Let it be, Tom,' said Gerald lifting himself from the ground.

'Not a chance. More than a thousand years ago the Fir Bolg and the Tuatha De Dannan readied for battle, and declared that a contest of hurling would suffice.'

'A game instead of blood?'

'I haven't finished.'

'I think you have,' complained Gerald.

'Oh, continue,' said James.

'It was a bloody match. The Fir Bolg was victorious, and cut the throats of the defeated. There were twenty-three competitors on each team.'

'Hell's Gate,' James almost sang. 'Gerald has twenty-three players lined up on both sides.'

Tom's mouth stretched sardonically. 'Our brother is ever provocative and perhaps a little perverse.'

'Perverse. An excellent word for our brother, brother.'

'Enough at my expense,' said Gerald, then turned and looked beyond the playing field.

Maurice, sat among the grasses clapping his hands. He looked to Gerald with a smile of excitement, his childish grin concealing his true age. 'What do you think, little brother?' he yelled.

More claps.

54

'Just as I thought. Maurice says the two of you are idiots.'

'I interpreted those claps differently,' said James.

'Come on,' said Gerald. 'Let's go and win this game.'

The players moved back to the field. Gerald's focus travelled to the giant wall that had sent him to the ground. His opponent returned the stare with a sharp turn to his lip. An oversized monster of a man with unfashionably long hair, light in colour and plaited to his rear. He was a sight which put Gerald's mind to a Viking warrior, and his opponent's hurling stick a battle axe. No wonder this man's companions called him Beowulf.

Gerald gave a tight smile in spite of himself and Beowulf returned a similar expression, but the man's eyes flared wide. A dull-blue danced on large plates of white and he finished with a quick flash of teeth; a look of madness. The giant wall gave Gerald his back and pitched a laugh of sorts to the sky. It was like one sharp clap of thunder. Yes, mad, Gerald thought again, then his focus turned to revenge.

The game resumed, the ball travelled the length of the field with speed. Bumps and more bumps. Elbows and hips collided, none too lightly. Tumbles and more tumbles. Blood came, bruises and abrasions, too many devious attacks to count, and injuries aplenty to be nursed on the morrow. Gerald's eyes rarely sought the ball. Instead, they slanted obliquely too often to the giant wall, Beowulf. If he had only looked with eyes not so intent on vengeance he would have seen his adversary mirrored his own thoughts.

Gerald saw his chance. The ball came close. Beowulf appeared at the ready to swing. Gerald ran at his target, hurling stick held high. He could not say how, but once again he found himself sprawled on his back. A searing pain burned through his left shoulder. He closed his eyes to the pain, rolled to his side and clenched his teeth. No laughter came. Nothing came. He opened his eyes to be greeted by the wide grin of the Viking warrior and wondered cynically if he perchance was in Nil-fine. He heard that thunder-like laugh again, one quick burst, and Beowulf walked away.

'A litter,' Tom ordered.

'Not if you value your life,' groaned Gerald, trying to rise from the ground.

'You cannot lift yourself,' said Tom.

'If I see a litter within a mile of this clearing, you will wish our lady mother had not birthed you.'

'Suit yourself.' Tom folded his arms across his chest and stood back.

With great difficulty Gerald sat himself up. Shifting left then right he tried to find leverage, but got no further.

'A litter?' asked Tom, with smiling eyes.

'No,' said Gerald with a stifled gasp, and finally succeeded in pushing himself from the ground, his right arm doing all the work. 'See. Not a difficulty at all.' He looked to his horse, and blew out a heavy puff of air. 'But I may need help with that. I think it's time I withdrew from the game.' He cringed as the pain hit again.

James grabbed the reins and guided the horse to Gerald's side.

Gerald managed to climb into the saddle with little help. He fitted his boots into the stirrups. 'I'll meet you back at the castle. Watch that Maurice stays from the river.'

One hand on the reins, Gerald turned his mount and headed toward the gathered opposition, voices boisterously claiming their victory, a victory awarded by forfeit to their way of thinking.

The giant wall stood with hands on hips, no smile, but the dull-blue balls dancing on white held their own grin. 'You have come to congratulate us then, my lord, all in the name of good sportsmanship?'

'The game is not complete. You may consider it adjourned until I can grow a new shoulder.'

'Hah! Hah!' The man they call Beowulf laughed his thunder-like laugh, this time in two short bursts. 'Then I look forward to meeting you again on the field.'

'I would have a word with you, before we part. Take to your saddle and ride with me a distance.' Gerald gave no room for refusal.

Beowulf hesitated then spat on the ground. 'As you wish, my lord. Anything for you, my lord. May I shine your boots, my lord?' and he offered a deep bow, bending low to the ground.

Their horses walked side by side at a slow gait, and followed the line of beech and yew trees back toward Maynooth Castle.

'You are either very brave or a very foolish man,' Gerald began. 'There are not many who would goad the heir to the Earl of Kildare as you have.'

'So, it is a reprimand you intend? A sulking son of an Earl? That would make you a shrivelled Flemish turd, my lord.'

Gerald snorted a half-suppressed laugh. 'A shrivelled Flemish turd?'

'Deaf as well as dumb?'

'I hear well enough.'

'Good,' said Beowulf. 'Then you will hear this. It is you that is either brave or foolish, Fitzgerald, to have tried me a second time.'

'They aptly call you Beowulf. What is your true name?'

'My name? Harry to my friends. And you, you can call me Beowulf.'

Gerald smiled. 'How do you make your way?'

'As best I can.'

'You are a native mercenary?'

'A native, yes. A mercenary, no. However,' Beowulf looked to the sky, 'if there is coin to be earned, I know only too well the discomfort of an empty belly.'

'I would have you in my employ ... Harry.'

A condescending smile found light upon Harry's face. 'Your employ? And what is it you would have me do?'

'You seem big of heart, big of courage, big of strength, big of—'

'I am proportionate. Hah!'

'Are you mad, Harry?'

'When it suits.'

'When it suits?'

'When it suits.'

'Well then, for a start, you would captain my hurling team.'

Harry seemed to contemplate the offer. 'A worse job I could think of.'

The horses continued at a slow walk. The wind picked up and played at the treetops.

'And your kin? Are they from these parts?' asked Gerald.

'You ask too many questions.'

'And answers usually follow.'

'I am warming to you, my lord.' Harry sent more disjointed laughter to the air. 'I have no kin to speak of. My mother, Maebh of Breifne she was known as, was a hearth mate to a righteous swine of the cloth, and discarded before I was born. She died when I was still a young'un and I was placed with a good farmer and his wife in the west. They raised me as best they could with the little they had. Now it is just me.'

'So you have not turned your mind to follow in your father's footsteps?'

'Do you refer to the righteous, the swine, or the cloth?'

Gerald pulled his horse to a stop. 'My offer stands, Harry, and I pay well. I may need a day of self-pity.' He gestured to his injured shoulder. 'I will expect you at the castle gate on the morrow. We can discuss your terms of employ then.'

'I will see what the weather brings, my lord, and my mood.'

'You have better plans?'

'A foundling of no rank or standing, and no possessions save a horse and a knife?' His knife hissed on the throat of its scabbard. Harry raised the point to his tongue. 'No.'

'You are mad, then.'

'When it suits.'

'On the morrow then, Harry.'

'On the morrow then, my lord.'

Edward Burnell, trusted physician to the Fitzgeralds, conducted his examination of Gerald with few words. Burnell was a man of years with a voice as smooth as steel in velvet, one that did not suit his appearance. Spikes of coarse grey, pointing every which way, formed eyebrows of sorts. Hands soft and untainted, wore rotund fingers that seemed too short for their purpose. And he was rather squat and more than wide, allowing a large circle of pink scalp where hair no longer grew, to be viewed from all angles. His form made good fodder for jocularity.

'No breaks,' he announced in that smooth tone. 'I predict a profusion of bruises over the next few days, but with rest your arm will be well. A wrenched shoulder and overstretched muscles is all you suffer.'

'See, Mama. You overreact.'

'Nonsense. And what was your mischief, Gerald?' Joan fluffed the pile of pillows at her son's back, straightened the bed's coverlet, eyes not leaving Gerald's for one moment.

'Mama, you are the only one who instils fear into my very soul.'

'Then I have acquitted myself well as your mother. For the now, make an aging woman happy and give her one consolation. Do not whine and speak true.'

'To me you will never age,' Gerald answered with a sly grin.

Joan flashed a smile, but saw the compliment for what it truly was. Her look returned to expectant.

'I will return in a day or two,' said Burnell, 'not to check your injury, but more so what tales are evoked in this room.'

'Best you stick to your profession.'

'Gerald,' scolded Joan.

Burnell's shoulders lifted with his silent laughter, then the physician walked from the room.

Gerald turned back to his mother. 'Was just a game amongst the lads. Hurling.'

'And let me guess. Twenty-three a side and you thought you were the Fir Bolg?'

'Perhaps.'

'And was it your temper which led to this?'

'Perhaps.'

'You should try for a more evocative response if you want me gone.'

'You know me well.'

'And it is good that I do. Your passion burns as the white heat of a flame, and someone needs—'

'Gerald!' The shrill voice came from the corridor. Alice ran into the room, halted at the sight of her husband propped up by pillows.

'I am fine. You need not concern yourself.'

Alice jumped onto the bed with little care, and showered her husband with kisses. 'Dear Lord, but you had me worried.'

Alice smelt of apple blossoms, a scent that seemed to dull the aggravation as her shoulder met his.

Joan sent her eldest a wink. Gerald thought the gesture odd. He gave a quizzical frown. His mother returned her own – comically – so he returned the first gesture. A wink. With not another word said between the two, Joan ushered the remaining servants from the room and followed their exit.

'Are you truly fine?' Alice plucked at his shirt, as if preening a cat.

'I will mend.'

'I was so frightened. All I could think was our child would not have his father.'

'It is nothing … you are with child?'

Alice nodded and lowered her eyes coyly.

'An heir for Kildare?'

'Yes,' Alice said. 'An heir for the man who will one day be Ireland's greatest leader.'

'You have more confidence in me than my father.'

'And that is the duty of a wife, no?' She snuggled in closer. 'I will stand at your side and provide you with … five, yes five sons.'

'Five?'

'Do you want six?'

'Seven sons and four daughters.'

Alice's laugh was that of a young girl. 'Seven and four. I promise.'

'Do you really believe I will be a great leader?' Gerald surprised himself with the question. Never before had he dared voice the doubt he suspected his father nursed. It seemed nothing he did appeased his father's sense of right and achievement, and he would give anything to see pride reflected in his father's eyes. Just once.

'What a strange question. Why do you ask such a thing?'

He thought to answer, but refrained. Perhaps it was a blessing that his trusting wife possessed a measure of naivety.

Best she remain ignorant. After all, he was the husband and the protector, and frailty in a man was weakness. He placed his hand onto Alice's stomach. 'This will be the first of many. We did not waste any time did we?' His tone was suggestive. He pulled his wife to his body with his good arm and kissed her deeply. 'You are a very clever wife, Alice.'

'And you are the sole beneficiary of my cleverness, husband.' Her voice was no less cheeky.

'A celebration is warranted, a private celebration. Maybe I will show you just how clever I can be.' He pulled pins from her hair to have chestnut locks cascade to her waist, just as he liked.

'Oh, but you are injured.' Her reply was riddled with mock concern. She ran her hand along his thigh. 'Allow me to check your bindings.'

'Is it safe?'

Alice looked intently into his eyes. 'You mean the babe? Of course it is safe.'

'How do you know?'

'I asked your mother.'

'You asked my mother?'

'Yes.'

'You asked my mother if we could …'

'Yes,' she giggled.

That wink! 'So my mother knows?'

'Again, yes. Now shush, beloved.'

But their frolicking progressed no further. Shuffled noises echoed along the corridor outside the room. Neither could mistake the sounds of alarm. Ignoring the sudden return of pain to his shoulder, Gerald jumped from the bed and flew from the room.

Tom with his face tear-stained, carried a limp Maurice in his arms. James led the way, his face wearing fear. Maurice's clothes were dark with wetness, his face a sickly blue, almost grey, his eyes wide, staring fixedly to nothing. Edward Burnell walked at Tom's side, holding fingers to Maurice's neck and wrist feeling for a pulse.

'In here,' said James, nodding to a closed chamber door.

Servants ran ahead unbarring the door.

'What happened?' It felt as if a tight fist thumped at Gerald's chest.

'The river. He went to the river,' sobbed Tom.

Tom placed Maurice onto a bed, the younger's head flopped heavily to the right.

'He's cold. Get his clothes off.' James tugged at the sodden boots.

Thomas rushed through the crowded doorway, Joan not far behind.

'What happened?' roared Thomas.

'The river, Papa,' Tom explained again. 'He went into the river.'

Thomas knelt onto the bed, his large hands feeling Maurice's cheeks, his forehead. 'And who was to be watching him? You know Maurice likes water.'

Neither Tom nor James answered. They looked to their older brother for instruction.

'Who?' Thomas demanded, more forcefully.

'It was me,' said Tom.

'And me, Papa,' said James.

64

'No,' Gerald interrupted sternly. Gerald lifted his shoulders and straightened his arm concealing his injury from his father. 'Maurice was my responsibility this morn. It was I.'

'We shall speak of this later,' Thomas seethed.

At the sight of Tom's mouth readying to throw argument to the air, Gerald shook his head, an indiscernible movement to all but his two brothers; a warning to remain silent. Gerald was adamant, resolved. Better that one wear their father's wrath than all.

'Oh, my darling,' cried Joan. 'Wake up. Wake up, dear one. Your mama is her.' She rubbed Maurice's cold white hands between her own.

Edward Burnell stepped from the bed, his head low, bowed with reverence.

'No!' Joan screamed. 'No!' and threw herself onto the small body.

The deeper sounds of male-grieving suffocated the room.

Maurice Fitzgerald, the forth son of the Earl of Kildare, was buried in the grounds of the friary near Cill-Dara in the shade of two mighty oak trees. His body now lay alongside Donal Fitzgerald. A young Maurice had loved Donal well. It was only with Donal that the boy ventured to sit astride a saddle, secure in the large arms wrapped around his smaller frame. Not even Thomas was given that honour. Maurice trusted Donal, did not fear any horse when in his capable hands.

Thomas was now forced to again entrust his son into Donal's keeping, and to the Lord's.

Chapter Five

Manor Kildea – County Kildare
Winter 1476

The wheels of the carriage bounced unforgivingly along the rambling roads. Not for the first time, Meg returned her eyes to the page in her book.

> *The reeve replied and said: 'Oh, shut your trap,*
> *Let be your ignorant drunken ribaldry!*
> *It is a sin, and further, great folly*
> *To asperse any man, or him defame,*
> *And, too, to bring upon a man's wife shame*

How many times was she to read the reeve's outburst without truly reading? Any earnest endeavour seemed futile. She snapped the book shut and turned her thoughts to the predicament plaguing her mind, their imminent arrival at Manor Kildea. She could not decide what irritated more; that she be expected to attend Jarlath's home or that her husband found as much displeasure in her inclusion in the invitation as did she. Silence stood as her protest on both counts, yet fortitude did not hold fast.

'I would have remained at home with little argument, Manus.'

The carriage swayed with a jerk, and Manus' head

bumped at the sidewall. His mouth took on a look of annoyance. 'And ignore their invitation?'

'I did not wish to accept. You have kidnapped me.'

'Kidnapped, Meg? You flatter yourself. I will leave any commandeering of your person to road bandits.'

Meg gasped and her hand flew to her throat. 'You tease. There are none so along these roads.'

Manus shrugged.

Meg moved her watch to the forest edges, wondering. The arms of the trees held snow, and the trunks hid who knew what. 'Manus, tell me you jest.' She looked back quickly to see a grin replace his annoyance. She straightened the skirts of her gown. 'I do not find you amusing.'

Not all was to be unpleasant, Meg reminded herself. There was one consolation to this trap. The Earl's eldest daughter would join their company. Meg would use this occasion to cozen herself into Eleanor's circle. The girl would one day be influential, and to cause familiarity would surely improve her own standing. As mistress of the humble estate of Ballymore, it would be rash to forgo such an opportunity. Yes, she must focus upon the prospects.

Manor Kildea came into view. A building of three floors, constructed of grey brick almost the shade of blue. Vines grew at each corner, climbing to the roofline, with flashes of yellow and orange peering through glossy green foliage. To the left of the home lay a pond, more a small lake, hemmed by water reeds. Ducks and geese plunged along the shallows, sounding their unmistakable throaty squawk over and again.

The grounds simple, the building uninteresting, the home's entrance was neither. A doorway of arched stone with ornate pillars to each side framed a large wooden door. Meg thought the two pillars Romanesque in their embellishment, yet above the peak of the archway sat the Fitzgerald crest, finely carved into bronze; scrolls of floral vines climbed the sides of a shield and a helm, and above that, a monkey. She had sighted the Fitzgerald crest at many of the family strongholds and buildings, but had never come to understand the significance of the monkey, and if Meg wasn't so determined to continue her silent protest, she would have queried her husband on the matter. It would have to wait. Her stubbornness demanded it so.

After settling into the guest rooms and enjoying a short rest, the evening meal was served in the dining room. Conversation was kept to reminiscing of past events, none of which involved Meg. She endured the chatter, nothing more.

Eleanor recounted the day she believed she lost Jarlath's wolfhound, Hunter. 'I was very brave that day and summoned the courage of Eleanor of Aquitaine, the past Queen of both England and France.' Theatrical hand gestures flew through the air as she said to Siobhan and Conor, 'Did you know Queen Eleanor and I share the same name?'

The children looked to each other with blank expressions. The adults hid their grins – all except Meg.

'And what a great lady she was.' Meg pulled her lips into a pretty pout. 'Queen Eleanor is ancestor to me.'

'How so?' asked Ainnir.

'Paternally.'

The room quietened, expectant of further. None came. Nor did any particular interest in Meg's revelation.

'By my recollection, Eleanor,' said Jarlath, 'you cried

tears enough to fill a barrel. And it was I who spoke of the greatness of a queen who shares your name. It was all I could do to have you loosen your grip around my neck.' Before Eleanor could deliver her argument, Jarlath continued, 'You were four, I was twenty. I wager my memory to be more reliable than yours.'

Eleanor's eyes pleaded for some margin of embellishment, and when none came, 'Jarf!' she chastised playfully, employing an abbreviation of her cousin's name, a version she deferred to in her childhood. 'We found Hunter, did we not? Jarf?'

The aging wolfhound in question lazed in the corner of the room, one of his ears lifting at every mention of his name.

The room laughed at the flicking ear. Meg too, however, hers was a coquettish pretence.

In the next recount of history, Jarlath spoke of Manus' sickness when at full sail on the Irish Sea five years ago. 'Your colour altered from white to yellow then to green, all in that order.'

'You are wrong, Jarlath,' Manus protested. 'You forget the hue of violet.'

The children joined in with the entertainment.

'And blue and red,' said Conor.

'Green like cats' eyes,' added Siobhan, slanting a look along the table toward Meg.

'Papa already said green.'

'Then purple,' Siobhan countered.

Meg's eyelids fluttered. Her purple gown became the centre of attention.

'Ah, yes, there was definitely a shade of purple. 'Tis

true,' Manus sang.

'But that story has nothing on my friend's reluctance to make acquaintance with a barber some weeks earlier during a stay in Bristol,' said Jarlath. 'So paining was his tooth it had to be pulled, but to have him stilled required the strength of two dragons, four goblins, two angels and one Jarlath.'

Siobhan scrunched up her face, hands lifted to her mouth, imagining the pain of having a tooth pulled. Conor mimicked his sister.

Again Manus pleaded falsehoods. 'There were seven dragons assisting the goblins, angels and you, for how could a mere party of eight, no seven, hold me down?'

Meg thought the scene odd. Manus the entertainer. Manus the lark. Manus the humourist. She could not recall the last time she witnessed his laughter. The recounts and good-intended accusations continued one after the other, none offering her anymore enjoyment than the previous. And no one seemed overly appreciative of her presence, not even the Earl's daughter despite Meg's endeavours. There seemed only one option. Attempts to slither into the girl's confidence would be deferred, and tried again another day, and Meg excused herself from the company declaring exhaustion.

Manus and Jarlath gave little attention to her announcement.

'Goodnight, Meg,' said Ainnir.

'Will you stay tomorrow?' asked Siobhan.

Meg looked to Manus. His eyes dared her to answer.

She looked to Eleanor. 'Of course. More pleasant company I could not imagine. Good night.'

Wandering the corridor of the second floor toward her

allotted room, a maidservant rushed from an open door almost collecting Meg in her haste.

'Oh, my,' Meg exclaimed, inserting a little rancour to her tone. Meg knew the servant's name to be Marared for she heard it uttered earlier by the children. 'You should take more care, Marared.'

Marared bore unfashionably dark hair, was tall of stature, possessed little curve to her body, and a sprinkle of freckles touched her cheeks. Yet when she raised her lids, a hue of violet – perhaps the same shade spoken of by Manus only minutes earlier – translucent in its exquisiteness, caught Meg's attention.

'I am sorry, my lady,' Marared apologised with a short curtsey.

The young woman's focus passed over Meg's shoulder, and a faint smile flashed upon her lips. Meg turned to learn the source of Marared's amusement.

Nothing.

The corridor was empty.

Not a solitary movement. Not a solitary sound.

'Who do you smile at, girl?'

'No one, my lady.'

'You smiled at someone.'

'I assure you I did not.'

'Do you always look to walls and smile?'

'I am said to smile an awful lot. Perhaps it is just that.'

Meg scrutinised the girl's face. There was little innocence. Deceit and conspiracy were obvious, but not enough to hang a man – or a woman – or a servant. 'As I said, you should take more care.'

Marared repeated her apology before continuing on her way. Meg noted that the lack of curves did little to hinder the sensual movement of the maidservant's hips, for her skirts swayed like a church bell. Meg pondered an unpleasant thought. Was Marared another of Manus' whores? She suspected he had them everywhere. Why not here? Why not this woman? Was Marared the reason he visited Kildea so often? Was Manus lurking at the end of the corridor, awaiting a dalliance? Meg strained her ears, and caught distant laughter downstairs. Manus' sound was easily identifiable. She gathered her composure, lifted her chin and turned once again to look the length of the corridor.

Again – nothing.

Meg glimpsed through an open door. Spheres of candlelight blessed the far corner leaving the rest of the room in variances of darkness. The scent of paper and ink met her senses. Writing utensils were packed neatly into a box on a large table, whilst piles of paperwork sat untidily to the side. An entire wall boasted bookshelves, each seemingly bursting with endless rows of worn covers. She ventured in. With the little light available, her long slim fingers wandered along the faded spines, her head tilted, eyes squinted to catch each title. She would find something that did not include the ranting of a reeve, nor the colour of her gown.

Fingers stopped at a bound book, bulky in size and obviously well-loved for its edges were frayed and the corners sported the stains of endless use. *Tales of the Moruadh* was inscribed in a cursive script. Black lettering, thick and bold. Meg had no idea of the meaning of Moruadh. A Gaelic word she assumed, yet she was inexplicably drawn, lured like a sailor to the song of a siren.

She felt more than heard another's presence and whirled to see Siobhan standing behind a chair, a pretty smile upon her face, and flicking errant wisps of honey-gold locks from her eyes.

'I did not hear you, child.'

'I can be quiet as a mouse.'

Siobhan stared openly. 'If you are looking for your mother, she is not here.'

'I am looking for you.'

'For me? Why?'

Siobhan stepped closer. 'Will you read it to me?'

Meg looked to the book in her hands. 'This? Oh, I do not think so.'

'Mama and Papa read it to me. It has the tale of the merrow, the one with the green gown and green eyes.'

Meg closed her green eyes for an inordinate time. She did not believe in coincidence or chance but this was certainly a strange quirk of fate; the merrow holding the tale of the merrow. How was she to avoid this quandary? The last thing she wanted was to read to the child. She opened her eyes.

A beckoning blue returned her stare.

Meg gave an audible sigh, something that rang true to a huff. 'A few pages, no more.'

Siobhan smiled at the partially generous offer, and Meg sat down onto a cushioned settle close to candlelight. She searched for the index. Meg stopped short, feeling Siobhan climb up and nestle into her side.

'The second story,' Siobhan explained.

Meg raised her brow, looked down to the child then

flicked through the pages to find the requested place.

'Mama says the merrow has a gentle, modest, fectionate and bevlant position.'

'I think you mean to say gentle, modest, affectionate and benevolent disposition.'

'Do you?'

'Do I possess all those traits?

Siobhan nodded.

'Indeed.'

'How?'

'How? You need not hear a litany of evidence.'

Siobhan sat still, looking up, seemingly not placated by Meg's attempt at avoiding the question. This girl was insistent.

Meg surrendered. 'I am all of those.' Her words were quick, and the continued silence of the child brought her to contemplate each quality. She grasped for examples.

'I am gentle when petting my spaniels. I am modest when … bragging of my latest acquisitions, particularly when Manus grows scolding of my expenditure.' She almost laughed at that one. 'I am affectionate … again with my spaniels. Benevolent when I give unwanted gowns to poor houses, and …' She was sure there was more. 'Perhaps we should begin the story.'

Meg's tone was flat at first, then a singsong rhythm developed of its own accord. She came to the word Moruadh. Her tongue stumbled.

'More-uh-agh,' Siobhan explained plainly.

Meg suspected it was not that at the age of four Siobhan could read. The child simply knew the tale by rote.

'That's how Gaels say merrow.'

'Mor-oo-arga.' A slight improvement, but Meg's subsequent attempt ensured that Siobhan giggled.

Meg felt the touch of a small hand to her fingers. She recoiled. 'What are you doing?'

'If you are a true merrow you will have white webs between your fingers.'

The suspected mermaid hesitantly held out her hand for inspection.

'No webs,' Siobhan declared. Her hand remained atop Meg's whilst her eyes returned to the page.

Meg continued with the reading, not at all concentrating upon the words, her mind attentive to the soft touch of the child, an intimate contact she found strange. So distracted was she that the reading of the last words was completed before she comprehended their implication. 'And just as the rest of her like, the Moruadh was promiscuous with all mortals. Dear Lord, this book is not appropriate for your young ears, Siobhan.'

'Are you?'

'Are my ears appropriate for these words? Of course. I am an adult.'

'No. Are you promiscuous?'

'Heavens no, and I doubt you are acquainted with the meaning of such.'

'Is your mama really a queen?'

'My mama a queen?'

'Queen Eleanor.'

'Oh no, no, Queen Eleanor was my great grandmother, well, my great, great, great grandmother. More greats really.'

'May I call you *Aunt Meg*?'

Meg closed the book. 'I am not your aunt.' It was the simplest of replies and dealt plaintively.

'You are married to Uncle Manus.'

'Well, yes, I am. But—'

'Then you are my aunt.'

'No, it is not that simple.'

'Uncle Manus is Uncle Manus, so you are Aunt Meg.'

Meg made a small movement, shifting from Siobhan. 'To be a true aunt—'

'Uncle Manus is a true uncle.'

Unruly. A waif. Doggedly obstinate. Meg thought to set free a flourish of chastisement, yet the sparkling blue orbs, patient, beckoning and untainted all at once, stilled her tongue. Those eyes seemed to possess a mystical influence, and she knew a *no* would not finish the matter. She pursed her lips in defeat. 'Well, I expect that would be fine.'

'Do you know that cousin Maurice is dead?'

Meg hesitated. 'Yes. Yes I do, child.'

'He died in the river. Mama says I mustn't go near the river or the pond by myself.'

'And a wise mama you have.'

'Will your eyes see me when you die?'

'What do you mean?'

'Mama says her eyes will always see me and Conor even when she goes to Heaven. She promised.'

'You are a strange little creature.'

Without warning the little girl knelt and placed a kiss upon her *aunt's* cheek.

Meg blinked heavily. The cherub's display evoked a stirring, a commotion, and a twist of fiery balls that threatened to sit tight in Meg's throat. She looked away, brushed at her gown then opened the book again and flicked through the pages searching for nothing in particular.

Unseen, Ainnir moved from the open door, careful to make no sound. She too, could be as quiet as a mouse. Her smile beamed, so proud was she of her young daughter's small yet astonishing achievement. In truth, it should not have been so surprising, for she always suspected Siobhan to possess something magical.

She would send word to Joan of their progress in the morning.

Manus stood by the tall windows, eyes to the dreary sky. He had refused to indulge Meg her protests, and decided they would stay a few more days at Kildea. Inclement weather turned the few days into five, and Meg's impatience into irritating slights. Dark clouds raced along the sky. A blast of thunder sounded in the distance. Manus predicted the five would turn into ten, and Meg's slights into an irksome temper.

'If I were a cynical man, I would accuse the sky of being sinister. How many more days are your skies to keep us tethered?'

'My skies?' Jarlath closed his book with a quiet snap. He hung a hand lazily across the arm of his chair and petted the dozing Hunter.

'My idle legs cramp.'

'I am pleased to hear it is just your legs.'

'That is all I will admit to.' Manus looked higher. The

grey seemed inexhaustible. He looked to the east, and along the stone pathway. A solitary bird braved the heavy deluge. The teeming rain turned the trees to blue.

'Ainnir believes the weather is conspiring for good,' said Jarlath.

'She does?'

'She does. It gives her time to work on your wife.'

'My wife?' Manus laughed. 'An abundance of patience is needed for that cause.'

'Aunt Joan too, is confident. Apparently in a world where a Jewish carpenter can walk on water, anything is possible, and she believes if anyone can save you two, it is Ainnir.'

'The Countess too? So all the womenfolk of Kildare aspire to miracles?'

'So it seems.'

'Then advise your wife all I require is blissful peace, an active bed, and commonplace love.'

'In that order?'

'In that order.' Manus caught a slight movement in the distance. 'Jarlath, I believe we have company.'

Jarlath joined Manus at the window. Hunter followed, the slow unfolding of his four long legs preceded by a wide-mouthed yawn.

'See? Before the road,' said Manus.

A muddied horse, possibly white on any other day, galloped across the green. The faceless rider held one hand to his hat. His mottled cloak caught the wind and mud flew through the air in tempo with the pounding hooves.

'A messenger?' suggested Manus.

'If so, I fear we are to receive dire news.'

Kildea's thin-shouldered gardener, Patrick, appeared from nowhere and ushered the soaked rider through the door and rid him of his heavy cloak. The messenger's teeth chattered fit to break, whilst Jarlath and Manus read the missive destined for their hands. Within minutes Jarlath ordered horses to be readied.

Manus leapt up the stairs, taking three at a time. He rushed into the bedchamber. The scent of jasmine followed from behind.

'Is it unwelcome news?' Meg's tone seemed to strive for pleasant.

'I must ride for Maynooth.'

'When?'

'Now.'

'Now? That is ridiculous.'

Manus agreed. 'Ridiculous or not, I must.' He ripped off his shirt and threw it to the floor.

'You will catch your death in this weather.'

Manus smiled. 'A disappointment?'

Meg's face soured. 'If you wait a few days the skies may clear.'

'There is not an hour to spare, Meg. Fetch servants to me.'

'You are not the only one shackled by the rains. If you wait one day, perhaps two, the delay may also offer me the opportunity to return to our home. Lord knows I could do with better company.'

Manus laughed soundlessly. 'Is it my company you find so deplorable?'

She lifted her chin. 'A little more attention would be appreciated.'

He ignored the poke. 'Jarlath and I are required for a meeting of counsel.'

'Surely it can wait.'

Manus pulled on fresh riding pants. 'The King has stripped Thomas of his position as Justiciar. The Bishop of Meath stands in his stead. No, it cannot wait.'

'I should accompany you.'

'There will be no festivities at Maynooth, Meg.'

'That is of no consequence to me.'

Manus regarded her intently. He remembered the last time she said those words, and suspected Meg remembered too, for her eyes lowered.

'You would not be welcome.'

'When am I ever welcome? It is a tiresome happenstance that my husband prefers the company of others. I am but a neglected bird in an iron cage.'

'A peacock with your multitude of colours and strut,' Manus muttered under his breath.

Meg's round eyes suggested she caught part of his remark, but perhaps not all, for the peacock began her infamous strut. 'And how long can I expect to have you absent this time?'

Manus shrugged, walked to the table and rifled through papers. 'To guess would be just that.'

'I cannot stay here.'

'It seems you must.'

'Manus, I beg you. I do not even have Veronique to call upon.'

'Beg all you like.' Manus did not look to his wife immediately. He imagined a fidget and a frown and readied for some foolish retort. None came. Curious, he turned and studied Meg with the interest of an artist. No fidget, no frown, the strut had ceased and hands sat propped at her hips. Green eyes levelled his, whether speared with a sharp blade or a heated iron, he could not decipher, but her glare lacked any hint of affection.

'Am I so intolerable to you, Manus? You think me arrogant, snobbish, conceited?'

'You are a perceptive wife.'

'I have patiently endured the company of your friends for almost a week. And now I am expected to remain here and idly await your return?'

'You could busy yourself and act the part of Aunt Meg, or make further pitiable attempts to befriend Eleanor.'

Meg sniffed. 'Enjoy your journey, husband. Take care not to catch your death,' and she left the room in a flourish of skirts.

Manus yelled for servants, his voice more forceful than usual. Storm or no storm, he would be grateful for the escape.

Chapter Six

'Comical.' Thomas' one word fell unheard as he noted the sheen on the Bishop's top lip.

William Sherwood, the Bishop of Meath, stood in the chambers of Naas before a vast crowd to declare the opening of his first parliament. Jeers from the men-of-rank awaiting his address alluded to the opposition he would face, and his sizeable retinue of one-hundred men-at-arms indicated he expected no less.

The men sitting to the Bishop's side looked no more at ease. John Butler, the Earl of Ormond, shadowed Sherwood's every move like a dog awaiting petting. To Butler's left sat his nephew, James Butler. The nephew's appearance bore a remarkable improvement since paths were last crossed, for on this day, although worry still etched his brow, he did not seem to exhibit the inclination of a man perilously close to losing control of his bowels. Thomas wondered with slight amusement what droll imagery his son would conjure to describe James Butler's breath this day. And not disappointed, her heard Gerald say, 'Dung breath.'

Arland Ussher perched near the end of the long table. Once the Mayor of Dublin some five years afore and no more a friend to Thomas than Satan was to the Good Lord, Ussher was an extremely ill-favoured looking gent, and hunched with age.

To the casual eye he appeared a web of misaligned angles. Ussher was craven, and it was fitting that he sat to the side. A brave warrior he was not, but a dangerous enemy he was, for coin and a conniving intellect branded him so.

These men were anti-Geraldine, had been Thomas' enemies for too many years, and would do all in their power to see to the fall of the Fitzgeralds. Their jutting chins and sinister glares chorused conceit. It was with surreal feelings that Thomas now sat in the same room with such hated adversaries. Let them leer all they desired, Thomas thought with strained patience. They would soon prove themselves to be imprudent imbeciles. Soon they would find they erred enormously, erred in their decision to dare the Earl of Kildare.

As much as it rankled, Thomas could not disregard the King's order. He was compelled to stand aside and leave Ireland in the hands of Sherwood. But by all that was Holy, he would soon ensure things were set to right. Flanked by his most trusted confidantes, Thomas knew patience would prevail. 'All in good time, all in good time,' he whispered to no one in particular.

The Bishop signalled for silence. With beady eyes following the curve of his aquiline nose he looked out over the crowd. 'Shall we begin, gentlemen, with a point for which His Grace the King displays much interest, or should I say, possesses a strong desire to rectify?'

The room fell as silent as a chilly church, save for one man to the rear suffering a coughing spasm.

'I am sure,' Sherwood continued, rising above the phlegm-gurgling throat, 'there is not a man among us who would call me foolish when I say the prosperity of Ireland rests for the great part on commerce. Ireland's coffers are lacking. It is obvious the enactment of poundage has deterred wealthy merchants from bringing trade to this great country. Therefore to continue such an ill-conceived legacy would only cause further obstruction.'

'Before you continue, Lord Bishop,' said Thomas in a raised voice, 'may I ask, are you aware of the reason such poundage is demanded?'

The coughing spasm seemed to run its course, the man giving one final cough before ceasing.

'You speak of the Guild of Saint George?'

'I do. And in the absence of such poundage, how do you propose to pay the army we employ to keep the King's peace?'

'I thank you kindly, my Lord of Kildare, for you bring me to the next point. From the Tuesday after the coming feast of the Purification of the Blessed Virgin Mary, the Guild of Saint George will no longer be levied.'

The Bishop could not continue. His attempts to utter further were drowned by the wave of voices.

'We fought to have that army,' yelled one man to Thomas' left.

'It was doomed from the beginning,' yelled another from behind.

The Bishop waited a time for the clamour to recede, but an end to the shouts seemed a mythical notion.

'You're not wanted here, Sherwood,' came a gruff voice.

'Go back to England,' boomed another.

The Bishop's next words bellowed across the chamber

and returned on an echo, a skill no doubt perfected from much practise at the pulpit. 'It is at the order of the King such a venture will cease.'

The room quietened.

'Pray tell me, Lord of Kildare, if the following is correct.' Sherwood raised a sheet of paper, and looked up and down its length. 'The guild provides its captain with one-hundred-and-twenty archers on horseback, forty horsemen and forty pages. Each archer is paid six deniers by the day and each horseman five deniers for himself and his page.'

'That is correct,' replied Thomas.

One man stood from his seat, pointed his hand like a sword. 'Possibly not as much as you pay the men-at-arms here with you today, Bishop.' Many in the room laughed.

The Bishop spoke over the noise. 'And merchants are ordered to pay twelve deniers from every pound of all manner of merchandise, entering or leaving Ireland, all for the purpose of financing such a force of arms.'

Thomas nodded, one slow movement. 'True.'

'And all captains of the guild are your closest of allies, many of whom I see sitting before me this day.'

'Your facts are correct in every manner,' Thomas stated with confidence, looking to some of those men of the guild: Roland Eustace, Sir Laurence Taffe, Richard Bellew and Sir Robert Dowdall.

'A mighty expense one would—'

'A just expense for an essential service.' Thomas stood and opened his arms gesturing to the remainder of the guild, seven men seated behind him. 'And as to your concern for my acquaintanceship with the members of the guild, each has indeed become my closest of allies and equally Ireland's most trustworthy men. All for the better I submit, for to achieve its aim of protecting our lands and our people from enemies and rebels, how could such a force be successful if led by men not in agreement, nor of similar moral standing, nor equally loyal to the cause?' Thomas did not wait for an answer. 'My Lord Bishop, surely you are aware the guild was implemented only after requests were submitted to His Grace to provide us with a force of arms for this same purpose. Surely you are aware the reply was in the negative on each and every occasion. And surely you are aware we noblemen of Ireland found ourselves in a position where the only course left to us was to be self-sufficient in this matter. Self-sufficient, my Lord, just as you are with your one-hundred men-at-arms. Or perhaps, are your men provided by His Grace?'

Thomas knew Sherwood's men were provided him by the King and so too, it seemed did all the room for muffled laughter rose to the chamber's corners. 'Our coffers substantially emptied failing any assistance from our King, therefore another strategy was required, and as such, poundage was imposed. A request was carried directly to His Grace for affirmation of those plans and no objection was made ... none until now.'

'Ah, but what of a commission to your liege's coffers?' The Bishop spoke with all the grace of a calm politician, and held the grin of a fisherman about to net a school of fish. 'What amount of coin was ferried to the King from this poundage?'

The coughing erupted again to the rear of the room. It sounded grievous.

'None,' Thomas answered easily. 'To fill His Grace's

coffers, this poundage was not exacted. Has Ireland not ferried enough coin to assist the King in his alliance with Burgundy, an alliance to defeat the French?'

'That coin in truth belongs to your liege, not to you, Kildare. As Justiciar you were simply His Grace's representative, not his replacement.'

'How can I disagree with you, my Lord Bishop? For in using this poundage, I did in fact save His Grace an uncountable cost. Am I now to believe His Grace has had a turnabout of thought, and now intends to draw on his own purse to raise an army for our lands?'

'No he does not.' A flash of triumph shone from beady eyes. 'I intend to enact that all merchants previously charged with the order of poundage, now defend the country in person or by proxy.'

Shouts of ridicule speared the walls.

'I see,' said Thomas with a laugh. 'Proxies provided by wealthy merchants. An untrained army of half-starved children. For that is the quality of proxy you can expect. What merchant wealthy or otherwise would raise a sword himself, or send valuable men to appease such a dictate? None is your answer. None. And then of course you invite another problem. Who will pay for the soldiers and men-at-arms required to enforce this law you plan to enact this day? Will it be your one-hundred here?' He gestured to the Bishop's guards. 'As sure as the sun rises each day, our merchants will not abide by your proposed laws. What an extraordinarily ill-conceived law you have tabled at your first parliament, my Lord. I expect every man in this room would agree with my summation.' Thomas's eyes moved to John Butler. 'If not, I would have no other course left to me than to accuse them of being supercilious mules.'

With this last the room erupted in laughter. Thomas well-enjoyed the mirthful sounds of disrespect, the sounds of repugnance to the newly appointed Justiciar. And more so, he enjoyed the vibrant colour of crimson painting Butler's face a mottled explosion of rage.

'Your acid tongue, for all the mockery it attempts to mete, does not have the power to alter the King's wish, Kildare. His Grace's demands are final and I as his representative will ensure they are done.' The Bishop looked to his written agenda. 'Now we shall discuss the current edict which allows for the Justiciar's heir to take his place and perform the proclaimed duties in the event of death.'

'Why bother? How many heirs do you have?' Richard Bellew shouted from the floor. More laughter reigned.

'This ruling seems to be,' the Bishop continued ignoring the jibe, 'the bold ask of a man who would see himself as King of Ireland. It is therefore enacted this date such law be removed forthwith.'

In truth, Thomas wholly expected such an announcement, but for all his control his face darkened.

The Bishop's brightened. 'It is of concern to His Grace, the Justiciar of Ireland be utterly aware he is his representative, not his replacement. For to be thought of otherwise would be,' the Bishop looked to the ceiling before spitting his venom, 'treasonous.'

'Spawn of a maggot,' Gerald said none too quietly, drawing silent eyes his way, curious eyes waiting patiently for the Earl's response. None came and Gerald's one curse was the only utterance heard.

Thomas forced a pleasant smile to his face. He gave the Bishop his due with that last. Touché he quipped silently to himself, a nice parry, but not one to cause severe bleeding.

Thomas held his tongue for the remainder of the sitting. Faith possessed incredible power and of this he had plenty. He did not doubt he would see the demise of this farce before too many months passed, and trusted the King's interest in France would soon wane, so too his need for more coin, so too his interference in Ireland's affairs.

The coughing spasms continued spasmodically, and intriguingly followed foolish announcements delivered by the Bishop. Thomas turned to identify the source.

Gerald's new man Harry gave the Earl a gritty smile, then his eyes danced.

Parliament complete, walking from the hall Thomas said, 'Gerald, gather the men and do what you do best. Make mischief and a damnable amount.'

'Never have I experienced a prouder moment. My father believes my greatest skill to be affecting trouble.'

'Be grateful for small gifts.'

'And one is that you age every day,' Gerald said with mirth in his tone.

'I'm not too aged to throw you across my knee and paddle you with the blunt side of my sword.'

'Ah, fond memories from my childhood.'

Thomas did not respond, but his stride increased.

'Humour, Papa. You do remember what humour is?'

Both men stopped, faced each other.

'I have no time for your absurdity,' Thomas snapped. 'Do as you are tasked, and no more.'

'Absurdity? Do as I am tasked? What do you allude to?'

'And I ask the same of you. You are speaking in a foreign tongue.'

'You do not speak of my current mission, do you? Will you never forgive me for Maurice's death?'

'Maurice's death? I made no mention of his death. Seems it is you who harbours ...' Thomas halted mid-sentence, silently admitted to a churning anger that refused respite. All those months ago, his eldest should have been more alert, more attuned to Maurice's ignorance to danger and the boy's love of water. To this point, Thomas found forgiveness and pardon an impossibility. Joan, to the contrary, seemed to have made peace with Gerald's recklessness, and pleaded blame to cease. He had promised he would try. And he would do so this day. He began again, this time with a different direction. 'If you cross paths with any O'Tooles or O'Byrnes, leave them be. They are not the target of your mission. Is that understood?'

'Precisely,' Gerald said with a bland tone.

The men restruck their path. Tom stepped alongside, between the men, stepped too closely to Thomas.

'What is it, Tom?'

'Papa, it is past time Gerald and I tell you of—'

Gerald elbowed Tom. 'Did you hear our orders, brother? We are to play scoundrels, base and unschooled, the scraps of society. An easy task for you.'

'Tell me what, Tom?' Thomas said with little interest.

Tom's reply did not come immediately. 'Oh, 'tis nothing, Papa,' and to his brother he said, not kindly, 'Your perception of reality is peculiar.'

'Because I can ably pick a man's strengths?'

'Because you are an ass, dear brother.'

'My sons are indeed strange animals.'

Gerald and Tom fell behind the men.

With no one to overhear their words, Tom said, 'You must let me speak the truth of Maurice's death one of these days.'

'No.'

Chapter Seven

Wearing rounded helmets and padded jackets with curved collar pieces, Gerald and Harry wandered unrecognised along the streets of Dublin. Hand-drawn carts full of firewood moved along the narrow street. Frost dotted thatched roofs. An elderly man preached vociferously to a small crowd of the virtues of worship.

'Give to the Lord the glory due His name. Bring an offering, and come before Him. Oh, worship the Lord in the beauty of holiness.'

Nearby, a plump woman huddling beneath a tattered shawl held out a dirty hand to disinterested passers-by. Wood smoke filled the air. Any eyes slanted Gerald's way were quickly averted. Dressed as Scottish mercenaries, none dared look too intently at the men, for to do so would invite trouble from the infamous men-for-hire.

Gerald casually smiled. The plump woman lacked not for courage. Unlike the rest of the crowd, her eyes squarely met his and she spat a tart word when he made no offering.

They rounded a corner and met with a marketplace. The pungent stench of sewage hit the air, and the duelling sounds from merchants hawking their wares ebbed and rose to fever pitch. Gerald pushed aside the flapping feathers of a pullet held upside-down then stepped into a muddied puddle.

'Shit,' he cursed.

'Elf shit,' added Harry, pulling at his chaffing collar. 'How long do we need to play at this scabby-pawed charade of yours?'

'For as long as it takes,' answered Gerald.

'You still haven't told me why we're dressed this way. None of this does anything to improve my looks, you know.'

'Would anything?' Gerald asked, then answered Harry's question. 'My father requests we cause as much discomfort as possible.'

'For who? If for me, we have already achieved our aim. My neck feels as though it has been wrapped in nettle for a week.'

'For the Bishop of Meath.' Gerald's interest piqued at the lack of a retort and he looked to the man expectantly. Silence was not Harry's way. 'And?'

'And what?' said Harry, noncommittally.

Gerald stopped at a stall, threw a coin to a peddler and grabbed at a bun covered with sugar and treacle. 'And where is your usual sharp tongue?'

'Can a man not keep his thoughts to himself?'

'Since when do you?' Gerald muttered with his mouth full.

'I am admiring the sights.'

Gerald was not duped. He could almost smell Harry's irritation; a difficult task considering the pungent odour of city life. He looked to the sky. Grey clouds moved fast. They seemed to merge and twist, jumping from one building top to another like children at play. A clap of thunder sounded, and it was not one of Harry's laughs. 'And what sights are you pretending to focus upon?'

'What do you mean?'

'What are you hiding?'

'You have rancid turnips for brains, Fitzgerald.'

Rain began to fall in earnest. Puddles formed and pooled until they found momentum trickling like a creek. Peddlers and customers ran for cover. So too, did the plump woman in the shawl. Gerald felt an ever-so-slight touch at his purse as she moved to rush by. He snatched at her wrist. The woman's eyes flew wide, and she stole a quick look backwards. The elderly man who had entertained with his preaching watched on intently then fled when he caught Gerald's glower.

'Bring an offering, and come before Him, hey?' Gerald yelled to the fleeing man.

The woman whimpered then cowered as if readying to be flogged. Rain darkened her hair and droplets ran in lines down her cheeks. Her shawl moved. A set of eyes popped out from behind the sullied cloth and blinked in the rain. The woman was not plump. She merely hid a half-starved urchin.

He placed a coin into her palm, and gave the child the remaining piece of his bun. 'Go. Get out of this rain.'

The astonished woman wasted no time before melding into the throng.

A shred of cabbage floated by at Gerald's feet. He suspected it would make it to the north of Ireland by the end of the day if the downpour kept up. All thoughts of the conversation with Harry and the slow-handed woman followed the path of the leaf. He looked further along the roadway, past the marketplace, and spotted a familiar sign. Two yellow swords painted on a piece of driftwood hung over a doorway.

'The men are in there,' he said to Harry then led the way to the Cross Swords.

Tom raised a hand in greeting to Gerald and Harry. He sat at a trestle in a corner with Jarlath and Manus, and Conn Mor O'Neill, the Prince of Ulster. Conn Mor was a few years older than Gerald, a few inches taller, and possessed a few bushels less tolerance. It was not here in Dublin that Conn Mor wished to be, but rather, in the north fighting his cousin.

'More cheerful this day, Conn?' asked Gerald.

'Don't stir the dozing monster,' said Manus. 'We've just settled him.'

'Too late,' said Conn Mor, slamming his empty mug on the table. 'Another,' he yelled.

Gerald knew the tavern well. It boasted some of the cleaner and more value-for-money whores in town, and from their shadowed corner he watched his favourite set of hips sway provocatively through the crowd.

Manus' eyes were set in the same direction. 'And the name of that one?'

'Nell,' answered Gerald.

'She's beautiful,' said Tom, eyes all agog.

Buxom, flaxen-haired, all her teeth still in place, and a voice to rival a lark welcoming spring, Nell was a popular attraction. She possessed a beautiful face, one not yet marked by disease or disfigurement; a rarity in her trade.

Nell busied herself refilling mugs, bending low, offering an enticing glimpse of the fair skin available to anyone willing to part with a robust manner of coin. Her eyes met Gerald's and they widened brightly. She had a pretty nose. It lifted with her smile.

'And what does this tartlet taste like?' asked Manus.

'Delicious,'

'I bet she's like baked apple drizzled with burnt honey and butter churned by the hands of the Lord himself,' said Tom.

'I like my women bitter,' said Harry, his knife making short work of a plum. 'Makes for a sharp bite.' He gave one short laugh then returned to the business of cutting and chewing.

Eyes turned as the delicacy named Nell headed their way.

'Good to see you again, my—'

Gerald raised a finger to his lips.

Nell frowned then looked to his garb and that of his companions. A seductive smirk replaced the frown. She filled a fresh mug for Gerald and leaned in close. 'You are the image of a young man I once knew. But you could not be him, for he is not a mercenary. He is a fine gent, dresses per his station and carries a large purse near his bodkin.'

'My taste in fashion may have changed, but my purse is still of an admirable size.'

Nell manoeuvred around the trestle and stood to Tom's side. 'You are drooling, my handsome one.' She cupped his chin with a finger and lifted his jaw. Tom's mouth closed. 'Now isn't that better?'

Nell filled their cups and continued her way. The inn's doors opened. A blast of cold wind stole through the room.

Patrons rubbed hands together and pulled coats closer to their bodies. A group of men followed on the heels of the gust, bold in their swanker and boisterous in their talk, settling themselves on trestles lining the far walls. In the reaches of flickering candlelight, Gerald spotted a brooch fastened at the neck of one of the mantles. A symbol of a beast, half boar-half lion with emerald stones. Gerald smiled a childish grin, full of devilish intent.

'I sense we are about to imbibe in a bit of fun,' said Harry.

'No. Havoc can be achieved from a distance on this occasion,' replied Gerald.

'A man of God-like powers, are we?'

'Nell has uttered those exact words to me on many an occasion.'

Harry's face gave over no emotion. 'Is it not the role of a whore to speak shit?'

Gerald whispered his discovery to the men then sent a low whistle across the room. He caught Nell's eye and beckoned her back to their table. 'I expect your fine establishment still holds a store of special spices for unwanted customers?' He remembered the meals served to the unwelcome, meals that caused an abrupt need for the body to expel the stomach's contents, and the body was never particular as to what orifice it used.

'We do.'

'The new arrivals,' Gerald said, looking directly into her eyes, willing hers not to turn and betray the subject of their conversation. 'Enemies to the Lord of Kildare.'

'And your payment?'

'Will be admirable.'

Nell nodded and returned to travelling the room. The men watched as her swaying hips led her to the new arrivals. Drinks were poured and Nell recommended the inn's mutton stew. 'Full of freshly-harvested winter vegetables, is our stew, gentlemen.'

A curly-haired fellow with a bulbous nose and toothy grin dropped his pants to the pretty Nell. 'And I've got something for you, darlin', full and ready for harvesting.'

Nell smiled at his vulgar attempt at humour as was required, but her eyes fell dark. 'The last time I saw something that small, it was squirming from an apple.'

The room roared with laughter.

Gerald turned back to his men. 'A letter was received from Maynooth this afternoon.'

'Of good or bad?' asked Tom.

'It depends.'

'On?' prompted Manus.

Gerald took his time, enjoying the waiting looks, and emptied his mug in one slow swallow. He raised his eyes to Conn Mor. 'My sister wishes me to pass on pleasantries to her betrothed and asks if I have any inclination as to when their union will be blessed?'

Conn Mor crossed his arms. 'Your sister is still yet a child not much older than my own.'

'My sister is twelve, almost thirteen.'

'A child all the same.'

'Wyrd bid fool ark,' Gerald said with a smirk. It was a line from an Anglo-Saxon poem, *The Wanderer;* a line his father recited more than once, many years ago. Gerald had liked that poem. Or more so, the valued time the reciting of that poem brought. He and his siblings, Maurice too, would sit at their father's feet, lost in the large man's company as his words were for his children, and his children only. Thomas was understandably a busy man, and those moments of intimacy were infrequent and to be treasured. 'They say fate remains wholly inexorable,' Gerald translated unnecessarily, for Jarlath had also sat alongside him all those years ago, at his father's feet.

'Wyrd bið ful ãræd,' said Jarlath, offering the accurate pronunciation.

Gerald shrugged off the correction.

'Get used to the none-too-subtle reminders, Conn,' Jarlath said. 'Eleanor will corner you until she gets what she wants.'

'A new conversation,' ordered Conn Mor.

Gerald looked to Manus. 'Eleanor also tells me your wife still enjoys her company and that of Ainnir. She remains in Kildea.'

'And that was in your letter?' asked Manus.

'Not the enjoyment part.'

'I never doubted it. The roads must be impassable. But now, I agree with Conn … a new conversation.'

'Does no one find pleasure in marriage vows?' asked Tom.

'Jarlath,' the men laughed in unison.

'An enigma,' added Manus, and raised his cup. 'And one lucky son of a bitch.'

'And one lucky son of a bitch,' the men chorused, raising their own cups.

'You'll find out soon enough the blight marriage can bestow, Tom,' said Manus. 'When are you to marry the daughter of Robert Preston?'

'Two months. January.'

'Then you have two months of joy left. Perhaps Nell may see to your pleasure,' Manus suggested with a crooked smile.

'You may have the right of it.' Tom returned the smile.

'I expected you would be married to Eleanor Fitzgibbon,' said Manus.

'James will marry the Fitzgibbon lass. I get Katherine.'

'Fair?'

'Fair enough.'

'And James is billeted with Fitzgibbon now?'

'He is.'

The chant of *sing, sing, sing* interrupted their conversation. The out-of-tune refrain accompanied the sounds of mugs thumping on wood. A trestle was quickly cleared and hands lifted Nell high up onto the table.

The room fell silent. Nell began with a familiar melody. A mournful tune, a song of lament, laced with longing for home, and longing for peace. Gerald had heard the tune many times, but on this occasion Nell sang it in her native tongue, Gaelic, making the song even more beautiful than he remembered.

Her voice was that of a weeping angel. All eyes were fixed Nell's way and not a sound was uttered as she swayed, hands behind her back, a pining look covering her sweet face. To Gerald's surprise, Nell changed some of the words. In her cunningness she paid homage to his father, extolling the virtues of an exiled emperor destined to return to his throne. She sang of the Ari of Maigh Nuad, The King of Maynooth, and of Crom Abu, the war cry of the Fitzgeralds, deliberately mispronouncing some of the words in subterfuge. Clever girl, Gerald thought. By God he was proud of Nell for her daring. She was fearless.

The song finished, a silence sat heavily in the room, every man in awe of the performance. The applause began slowly at first and then grew to a loud cheer. She bowed deeply, demanded she be released to continue her duties and was lifted by hands keen to touch her body in places that would normally be accessed at a cost. She smoothed down her stained apron and carried trenchers of hot stew to James Butler and his companions. The first to be served was the curly-haired fellow with the large nose, and worm-like appendage.

Gerald read Nell's lips.

'Enjoy,' she said with that pretty smile that pulled at her nose.

He thought to wander above stairs with Nell and thank her personally, but looked to his brother. The mouth was again agape. Gerald decided to allow Tom that privilege. Besides, he recently discovered he had fathered two more illegitimate daughters—two more that he knew of—and his mother would not take too kindly to news of another, especially to one such as Nell.

'Close your mouth, Tom. It drips love,' Gerald accused. He would find time with Nell another day, and ask which brother she thought more God-like.

It took not much time for Butler and his companions to scamper for the door.

Well done, Nell.

Chapter Eight

Manor Kildea

Meg stood beneath the Fitzgerald crest at the doors of Manor Kildea. Another day without rain, and no heavy clouds to indicate the reprieve was to be short-lived. A pair of black swans flew overhead, their wing-beats a lonesome sound in the cold air. The wolfhound Hunter threw a harmless bark to the sky. Meg pulled her shawl tight. She could have left Kildea four days ago when a morning brought a clear sky, but refused the opportunity. She would prove her husband wrong, he and his persistent accusations of snobbery, and relish his look of disbelief when told of her extended stay. And so far it proved less agonising than anticipated.

The thin-shouldered gardener toiling at the fence line with a pick, looked up. The man's top lip jutted slightly to accommodate too many teeth, and sat awkwardly below pellucid eyes which hinted his preference for work more than mischief. He was said to be a man ever-loyal to Thomas Fitzgerald, had spent more time at Manor Kildea than anyone could remember, had hunted with the Earl, and accompanied the Countess Joan on her walks during their infrequent visits to Kildea, and, declined an appointment to the position of Castle Maynooth's head-gardener, giving way to the assumption the gardener favoured quiet. The man motioned a short nod in greeting and continued with his digging.

An abrupt voice broke from a distance. 'What are you doing, Emma?'

Meg moved along the front of the home and past the gardener to unearth the source of the noise. Beyond the long-as-it-was-wide kitchen garden a red-haired servant, her hair a mop of tightly wound spirals, struggled with the task of hanging wet linen out to dry.

'I thought to catch some of the fine weather, missus,' said the servant.

'Fine weather? Fool of a girl,' said the housekeeper Mrs. Mulhearn, marching toward Emma. 'My knees tell me the rain is playing a game of hide-go-seek. The skies will weep within the hour.'

'But it'll never dry inside.'

Mrs. Mulhearn waved off the argument with an impatient gesture. She appeared a portly woman, large breasted, a button nose, and fire in her duck-like stride. 'What will I ever do with you, girl?'

'Well, you could see to me getting better wages.' The servant girl Emma bit at her bottom lip as soon as the words were out.

'And a mouth on you too,' Mrs. Mulhearn accused. 'You'll never last in this home if you don't mend your ways.'

'Sorry, missus.'

A slow chortle sounded from the gardener. He mumbled something unintelligible.

'And that's ample stick from you, old Patrick. Back to your digging, you hear me?' ordered Mrs. Mulhearn.

Old Patrick chortled again and followed with more indecipherable ribbing.

Mrs. Mulhearn piled Emma's arms high with the wet laundry. 'On your way now. You've more chores needed done.'

'Yes, missus. I was only meanin' to do good.' Emma bobbed an apologetic curtsey.

'Well, do good inside.'

Emma headed back inside with the teetering load and Meg could have sworn she caught a smirk on the housekeeper's face. It was gone in a heartbeat.

Mrs. Mulhearn looked to Meg. 'Can I help you?'

Meg felt mildly chastised. 'No.'

'Good then.' Mrs. Mulhearn turned toward the house and took to her waddle. 'The family's under the tree near the water if you're looking,' she announced more to the air, than to Meg. 'Mad they are. Will catch their death of cold out in this.' Then with a louder voice, 'You best have that laundry in order, Emma.' And she was gone.

Meg followed the line of muddied puddles, which she assumed usually made for a well-worn pathway. The swans had settled onto the pond.

'Meg,' Ainnir called.

On a rise some distance from the water's edge, Ainnir sat on a garden seat beneath the wide-reaching branches of an aged oak. She was wrapped in a saffron shawl – the colour of the Gaels. Her maidservant Marared, played nearby with Siobhan and Conor. With sticks in hand they chased a ball round and round in circles. Eleanor sat on the tree's lower branches, or perhaps it was more correct to suggest that Meg assumed it was Eleanor, for all she could see was a pair of stockinged legs and dark boots dangling midair.

'Come join us,' invited Ainnir.

Meg looked to the stretch of water-sodden ground.

Ainnir pointed to the south. 'Go further around. You'll find steps.'

Near the edge of the pond a patchwork of bluestone formed a winding pathway to the top of the rise, the steps wide and spaced generously.

'The branches have kept much of the ground dry,' said Ainnir, as Meg reached the top step.

A gust of wind played at the bracken. Meg wrapped her shawl tighter. 'But it is so cold here.'

'Do you not find the cool invigorating?'

As invigorating as a graveyard, Meg thought to say. She settled with, 'No.'

'We've been tethered to the house for too long. You too.' Ainnir patted the seat in invitation. 'We won't stay out long.'

The ball hit Meg's boots. She pushed it away with her toe. Siobhan hit the ball back, and looked to Meg expectantly. Twigs and leaves caught at the child's loose tresses.

'She wants you to play,' came a voice from the tree. A gentle thud followed.

'You are like a cat, Eleanor,' said Ainnir. 'How did you land on your feet from that height?'

'My brothers push me too often. I've had to learn quickly.' Eleanor brushed at her skirts. Meg had not moved. 'Don't you want to play with her?'

'Well ... I'm not too sure—'

'Then I shall.' Eleanor grabbed Siobhan under the arms and swung the young girl in circles. 'This is how you play.'

Siobhan giggled and giggled.

106

'Don't you like children, Meg?' Eleanor inquired artlessly. 'Is that why you have none of your own?'

'Eleanor,' chastised Ainnir.

'I cannot ask?'

'Course she likes children.' Siobhan was back on her feet. 'She likes us.'

'Well, it is certainly not that—' Meg tried.

'I will have lots of children,' Eleanor continued, flopping onto the bench between Ainnir and Meg, 'when I marry the Prince of Ulster. Oh, I almost forgot. He already has three children. Does that make me a mother?'

'Perhaps things may—' Meg tried again.

'Do you think they will love me, Ainnir? How silly of me. Of course they will.'

Meg tried no more.

Ainnir smiled. 'You will make for the most beautiful princess and a wondrous mother, and live in a castle on the ocean's edge. You will learn of the northern clans' heroic stories and you and Conn will come to make your own. And you may just learn a few more manners.'

'Manners are for children. And I have not decided where my husband and I will live.'

'*You* have not?' said Ainnir.

'No, *I* have not. Conn does not talk to me overly much. He is shy. Oh, Ainnir,' she said, suddenly excited. 'You could help me write a letter to Conn. In Gaelic! That will ensure a reply for he is yet to return a message of any type.' She did not wait for agreement or criticism, was on her feet climbing again.

'Would you like to answer that question now?' Ainnir suggested to Meg.

'Question?'

'Children.'

'You have the curiosity of Eleanor.'

'But better manners.'

Meg looked to Conor and Siobhan and contemplated the query. Both children had lost interest in the ball and stick game, and followed Eleanor's lead up the tree. Conor did his best. Holding onto Marared's hand he seemed content to conquer the wandering raised roots.

A loud bark sounded from the water. A splash followed, and then the squawking of swans. At the front of the home, old Patrick abandoned his chores and carried pick and shovel over his shoulder disappearing from sight.

'Look at me, Aunt Meg,' said a proud Conor.

'Your children smile a lot.' Meg surprised herself with the softness in her voice, still contemplating. 'It's not that I dislike children. I once assumed … well Manus and I have been married six years now.' Meg fidgeted with the ends of her shawl. Her eyes moved to Eleanor. 'Eleanor's betrothed is such a harsh looking man.'

Ainnir laughed aloud. 'Do not let Conn's surly exterior deceive you. There is a good and honourable man beneath those scowls.' She paused. 'You do not like the Gaels, Meg, do you?'

Meg summoned a look of disbelief. 'Whatever encouraged that idea?'

Ainnir smiled, and Meg daringly held her eyes for a long moment.

A high voice came from the house, breaking their silent exchange. 'Come. Come quickly.'

'What is it, Emma?' Ainnir yelled.

'There be a gentleman ridden in asking for you by name.'

'And his name?'

Emma panted, her feet slipping half their gain as she climbed the rise forgoing the steps. 'Bradan. Says he's your brother.'

'Bradan?' Marared gasped.

'Uncle Bradan,' squealed Conor.

'Shush, Conor.' Ainnir abruptly stood from the garden seat. 'Siobhan, take your brother to the house.' Her eyes then turned to Marared. But before any look could be returned, Marared hitched up her skirts, and taking the same path as Emma, ran down the rise. Her heels slipped in the mud yet she gave little time to succumb to falling. She rushed past Emma without a word.

'Mama?' queried Conor.

'Siobhan. To the house with your brother,' Ainnir ordered again.

'Emma!' Mrs. Mulhearn yelled from the house. 'Get back here, girl.'

Meg thought everything about the moment unsettling. Emma looked from Ainnir to Meg to Mrs. Mulhearn and back to Ainnir. The women spoke volumes without wagging a tongue.

And then, 'Marared and your brother?' It was more an accusation than a question.

'It could not be. The girl has heard wrong,' Ainnir said too quickly. If Ainnir's glare breathed flames, the servant girl would be scorched. 'Back to the house, Emma.'

Emma dropped her head, and turned back to the

house. The housekeeper meted a swift clip to the girl's ear before throwing a nondescript glance to the top of the rise. The two women disappeared behind the large wooden door.

'Is something amiss, Ainnir?'

'No. All is well. Children, inside now.'

In her hasty departure, Eleanor kicked the ball. It hit at the back of Meg's legs. Meg did not turn, but looked past Ainnir's still frame. Light rain began to fall. The pond's surface danced with gentle movement. A mist tumbled down from the wooded hills like pale gauze. It seemed the housekeeper's knees were to prove reliable.

And … the brother! The brother and the maidservant! How delightful! Manus' arrogance would curdle when told the all-too-perfect Ainnir hid and condoned a tryst between her maidservant and her brother, the Earl's enemy. She could almost smell the predictable satisfaction.

Ainnir started down the rise, but stopped suddenly and looked to Meg, her chin tilted upward. The women stared at each other again, both with impassive faces. Nothing was said for a prickly length of time. Meg was the first to move. She shifted awkwardly.

'I can pretend, Meg, but I suspect you to be too wise.'

'Wise, yes. And wise enough to know—'

'And wise enough, I am sure, to know love is a gift blessed by God.'

'There is a point to which—'

'There is a point, yes. But here and now, we are just two women, two women who know what it is to love a man, no less than Marared does right at this moment.'

Meg opened her mouth, yet strangely held back her

110

words. Perhaps from a niggling sense of bafflement, for her own thoughts created an unexpected and sharp sense of melancholy. Perhaps because she knew not how to counter Ainnir's contention. Two women who know what it is to love a man? Nonsense!

'So I trust you can keep a secret?'

The black swans flew from the lake, their wing-beats heavy in the air. The wolfhound let out a despondent bark.

'Of course,' Meg replied demurely.

'Good,' said Ainnir, her smile sceptical. 'Never forget what it is to love, Meg. And never underestimate the splendour of being loved.'

Chapter Nine

Dublin

The alleyways of Dublin's south stretched like eerie grey tributaries, and at this late hour outside the city's limestone walls, only the brave or foolhardy ventured alone. Most folk settled behind doors, seeking warm hearths, warm beds, safety from cutpurses and drunks. But not Gerald and his men. There was trouble aplenty to be caused.

During the past few months the unleashing of havoc filled their every waking hour. Saddles mysteriously disappeared. Doors became barred. False cries of 'fire' dragged many from their pallets, and of course, a good portion of the Bishop's men met with Nell and the special herbs at the Cross Swords. Trouble not too noxious, but terribly dreary – to some. And this night was to be no different.

Gerald could not believe his luck, for as he turned from Francis Street toward St Nicholas' Gate, he spied an opportunity too marvellous to ignore. With Harry and Tom at his side, he slid into the night shadows and followed his next victim at a distance.

Wrapped in a cloak of fine wool, a lone figure crossed the street ten paces ahead. His head atop a hunched back, swivelled left then right. His was not the manner of confidence.

'Go, Harry,' whispered Gerald.

'Why me?'

'It's the Feast day of Saint Brigid.'

'And what has Saint Brigid got to do with anything?' Harry whispered back.

'Not much.'

'You have the sense of a goat's belly,' said Harry.

Tom chuckled. 'My brother means to say, that gentleman up ahead knows our faces but he doesn't know yours.'

'His name?' asked Harry.

'Arland Ussher,' answered Tom.

'Ally to William Sherwood?'

Raucous laughter drifted down from the heights of the city's walls. Two cats squealed and hissed.

'A *friend* of the Bishop.'

'Cabbage-farting dwarf,' Harry spat, not unlike the hissing felines.

'You dislike the Bishop more than I, Harry. Are you ever to tell me why?'

'Can a man not hate for the sheer purpose of finding pleasure in abhorrence?'

'He can.'

'Do you want blood?'

'No.'

'No?' Harry sounded disappointed.

'No.'

'The Earl's son has a prune for a heart. Well, blood or no, I'll have this man dancing a jig in no time.'

'A wager on his game?' Tom whispered to Gerald. 'Two coins Harry plays a leper.'

'I say he preaches of the transgressions of sin,' Gerald

113

whispered back.

'Och, yoo both are wrong,' said Harry.

'You're a Scotsman now?' asked Gerald with mild surprise.

'Do I no' soond like a Sco'? Yoo insist we dress like a Sco', so I might as well sound like a Sco'.'

'He does sound like a Scot, Gerald,' Tom confirmed with another chuckle.

'Then on your way, Scotsman,' ordered Gerald, and both he and Tom slinked further into the night shadows.

Harry hastened his step and moved into the path of the unsuspecting Ussher. The small man stopped abruptly.

'Ya fare?' Harry asked in a straight forward manner. His large frame towered above his victim.

'My fare? For what?' Ussher took one step backward.

'Don't yoo go playin' coy with me ma little turtle dove.' Harry, with his unconvincing and new-found brogue of a Scotsman, placed a large weather-worn hand on Ussher's shoulder.

'We both know wha' people like yoo and I come to this street for a' this hour, and it certainly isn't for a game of dice.' Harry leaned in close and sniffed at Ussher's shirt.

'Dear Lord, no,' Ussher whined. 'You have me wrong, sir.'

'Och, little man. Do no' let the size of me worry yoo o'er much. I am certainly more than yoo can imagine, but can be gentle too. I must admit though, I have ha' ma share of men who are … how do I say this withoot appear'n impertinent?' Harry paused casually and looked up to the night sky. 'More eye-catching than yoo. So I would expect your fee reflect aptly.'

114

Ussher took another step backward and met with the wall. 'I assure you, sir, you have me mistaken. I am an old man.'

'Och, the pretence of unwilling. I like tha' game. Turn around. This will not take long.'

Harry grabbed at the man's shoulder and spun him around.

'No! No!'

'Well, well, will yoo look a' tha'. Here's a sign tha' reads *vacant* hanging from your arse, and my boot is looking for lodging.' With a half-hearted kick Harry's boot sent Ussher to the ground. 'Now be on your way yoo baseless fool.' It was said none too quietly. 'Tell your eel of a friend, that horse shit, maggot breath, prune-hearted Bishop of Meath, tha' Ireland does not welcome him as its Justiciar, and yoo and yours should leave before I find yoo again and decide to fill tha' vacant arse with something bigger than ma boot.'

Ussher shuffled to his feet and stole a quick look back before he ran.

Trouble complete.

'Christ Almighty, Harry,' said Gerald coming to Harry's side. 'I'm damn sure I'll sleep with one eye open the next time we're billeted together.'

Harry gave Gerald a shove. 'Hah. Your no' pretty enough, boy.'

Woken townsfolk shouted their annoyance from open windows, and the foul contents of a chamber pot followed, splashing up Harry's leg.

'Bitch of a thing,' Harry yelled, all signs of the Scotsman gone.

'Move along you depraved fools.' The voice came from

115

an upper window.

'Your mother should have kept her warty-legs closed,' Harry yelled back.

Another chamber pot rained their way, and the men didn't bother to wait for the next.

'Let's find the others,' said Gerald.

Jarlath squatted in muck on the stable floor. A full moon hung high in the night sky yet only feeble light seeped into the stall through the splintered walls. It mattered not, for his hand confirmed his fear; a bulbous swelling at the horse's fetlock.

'She won't be travelling anywhere soon,' he said, wiping his dirtied hands on a cloth.

'Nor are we,' Conn Mor said with a good measure of irritation.

'Come now, Conn,' said Manus, slapping a friendly arm on his shoulder. 'You mean to say you wish to be gone from our company and Gerald's endless games?'

The men were keen to be back by their hearths; Kildea, Ballymore and Ulster. Months of enforced fun in the form of street fights and mindless pranks had quickly lost its lustre, and they tired of the city people's cold mannerisms and the dank stenches of the places they temporarily called home.

'The north is where I should be, not here playing games in this smutch of a place.' Conn Mor looked up to the boarded windows of the building adjoining the stables; their latest lodging. 'And if I have to spend another night on that flea-ridden mattress I'll rub the skin clean off my arse.'

The men spent no more than four days at any one

place, moving from inn to boarding house to squat-room to tavern floor and to inn again, only to be followed by the pungent fumes of fell-mongers and tripe-scrapers and putrilage, and more often than not, pesky fleas. Luxury was not an option. Their masquerading prevented any acquirement of the usual comforts from the rich merchants of Winetavern Street—those loyal to the Fitzgeralds and generous in hospitality—and their three-storey homes with slate roofs and high balconies and down beds. Nor could they visit the Fitzgerald townhouse in Thomas Street, lest their disguise be discovered.

'We could billet down at St Stephen's leper house,' suggested Manus with a smirk.

'Rotting flesh or rats? A choice,' Conn Mor grumbled.

'We stay until the Earl orders us elsewhere,' said Jarlath.

'And where is the Earl?' queried the Prince of Ulster.

'In apartments at the Priory of Kilmainham.'

'He lives in lavish luxury while we wallow like swine in sludge?' Conn Mor finished his complaint on a fractious grunt.

'Here comes the one man who seems not to mind a base existence.' Jarlath inclined his head to the far end of the street.

Gerald was heard before he was seen, Harry's distinct frame bobbed a head above the thin crowd, and Tom sauntered alongside. Unlike the streets outside the city walls, this part of Dublin never slept.

A flash of alarm heated Jarlath's very core. Not fifteen paces ahead of Gerald, two cloaked figures spilled onto the cobbled street from a building used to store coarse wool and hides for export.

'Trouble,' Jarlath said for Manus' hearing only.

'Trouble?'

'Is that John and William O'More?' Jarlath had not seen either man for near on ten years. Matching red hair, tall frames, long noses, square jaws. They looked very much like Thomas. If he was correct it would not do well to have Gerald cross their path. 'If so, they are with Eamonn O'Byrne,' Jarlath added looking to a third man stepping from the same doorway.

'John,' Eamonn O'Byrne shouted, unaware he and his companions were being watched. 'Wait up.'

The man named John slowed his step, William O'More slowing with him. As if sensing Jarlath's stare the suspected-to-be-William looked up. Jarlath could not be sure their eyes met, but with the sudden push of the crowd the night swallowed the three men.

'Let's hope Gerald doesn't—' Jarlath started.

'Conn, stop them.' Gerald's yell travelled close.

'More games?' Conn Mor complained.

'Christ. Where did they go?' Gerald's elbows met with growls as he hastened to make a clear pathway. 'That was Eamonn O'Byrne. Wicklow ass,' he hissed. 'Come on.'

'No,' Jarlath grabbed at Gerald's arm. 'Your father has given orders.'

Gerald shrugged off the hold a little too violently. 'And you take yours from me.'

'I take orders from your father.'

Gerald faced Jarlath squarely and shoved roughly at his shoulders. 'I have authority here.'

Jarlath looked down to where Gerald had pushed. His

118

fists grew tight.

'Jarlath, no,' whispered Manus.

Gerald pointed to the air. 'One of those men was Ainnir's brother. Who were the other two?'

'I have no idea,' Jarlath lied.

'Was one Bradan O'Byrne?'

'No.' One truthful reply.

Gerald frowned his suspicion. 'Are your loyalties to your wife or the Earl?'

'Foul words, Gerald,' said Jarlath, none too politely. 'You know where my loyalties lie. For Christ's sake, we have to put up with this Godforsaken town, filth for beds, and now your childish insecurities.'

Tom moved to stand between the two men. 'Jarlath is right. We'll be breaking from orders if we chase Eamonn down.'

Gerald closed his eyes and his face tightened. He threw a curse over his shoulder.

Further exchanges were interrupted by a welcome diversion in the form of a young boy at their feet.

Filthy from head to toe and scratching with little pause at lice-ridden hair, the boy was as thin as a water reed. His clothes were mere rags and his shoes, toeless. His height and gait suggested he was eight, perhaps nine.

'I've a message for your leader,' the boy squeaked eagerly.

'We have no leader, boy.' Tom stepped forward. 'We are mercenaries. What business would you have with the likes of us?'

'Nell sent me,' the boy said quickly.

'Nell?' queried Tom.

'Nell from the Cross Swords.'

'And what would Nell have you say?'

'Nell said if you didn't believe me I was to tell your leader his brother was too quick and his candlewick short.' For all his youth, the boy's telling smirk hinted that he understood the mischief such a message held.

Tom grunted. 'A joke mistress Nell has sent you armed with then.'

'No, sir.' The boy's smirk grew.

Gerald stepped forward. 'And what would Nell have me hear?'

'You are the leader then, sir?'

'I am the one with the larger candlewick.'

The boy smiled openly, his teeth unexpectedly white. 'Miss Nell says there be an opportunity for you, sir. The Bishop of Meath's men are causing trouble not far from here.'

'Nell's in trouble?'

'Not Nell, sir. Another woman. A street woman.'

'Well lead on, lad.' Gerald threw his arms forward. The boy stood still. Gerald understood his protest. 'The quicker you take us, the more coin you will be rewarded.'

At that, the boy's feet took flight and Gerald and Tom followed.

'Here we go again.' Conn Mor followed too.

Harry turned to Jarlath and Manus. 'Yoo might say it takes only a toy t'appease some young'uns. Whelps an' their mischief. Hah!' With that he headed along the laneway following the others.

'He's a Scotsman now?' said Jarlath.

'Come on,' said Manus. 'I suspect you could do with a

fight or four.'

After a meandering run eastward on the heels of the willowy youngster, the men stopped at the dim entrance to a laneway. A glover's shop to the left and a baker's shop to the right, both closed at this late hour. The boy pointed into the shadows and scampered off. But not before catching a coin flung his way from the hands of Conn Mor.

'You will call that a debt, I do suppose,' said Gerald.

'Not if you grant me the lead. If we must play another idiotic game, I want it on my terms.'

'Granted.'

Threads of light stretched from a row of four unshuttered windows on the north side of the laneway. The cobbled pavement danced quietly as puddles caught the flickering glow. Where the light could not reach, the laneway sheltered a murky grey – and trouble.

With quiet footfall, Conn Mor moved closer to the trouble. He counted eight men. Three large of build, five scrawny, all circling one woman. Two poked at the woman's arms menacingly whilst their companions laughed. Eight men against one woman? Not fair. He looked back to Gerald and to Tom. Then to Harry. And then to Jarlath and Manus. His numeracy skills suggested six against eight. No problem.

'God love Nell.' Gerald almost sang his words.

'Tom does,' teased Manus.

'Don't be daft,' argued Tom. 'You don't love whores.'

'The good ones you do, and all for the right reasons,' said Gerald.

'Leave me be!' the woman yelled along the alleyway. Her voice held no fear, but her body spoke a different language. 'You're animals, every one of ya.' She inched backwards, slow step by slow step, attempting to fend off the men with caustic words. She would have done no better if she wielded a feather. Her eyes darted to each of the advancing assailants but for the most part settled on the large bulk closest to her, the one doing all the talking. It didn't take long to comprehend the reason for the quarrel. It seemed this street whore insisted she had the right to specify the number of clients she was prepared to entertain at the one time. These perspective clients begged to differ.

The woman backed herself into the corner. She rose on her toes, a futile attempt to appear more daunting, more able.

Stifled whimpering from his left caught Conn Mor's attention, sounds resembling mewing kittens. Little disturbed Conn Mor. He could kill a man with his bare hands, no balking, no disgust, no regret, but to see terrified cowering youngsters was a bane beyond most. Two small children, with dark hair so knotted they looked like dirty mops, crouched low at the base of the opposite wall, their movements mimicking forest animals burrowing to escape harm, but the cobblestones at their feet would not give way. He guessed this was not the first time these children witnessed the depravities of how their stomachs were filled. They were not much older than Conn Mor's own three little ones: Art Og, Sean and Johanna. The faces of his children flashed before his eyes and his blood boiled.

He looked back to the Bishop's men. His lips twitched. Trouble was about to be dealt a lesson, and he would be sure to enjoy this game. 'It seems your mothers neglected to teach you gentlemen manners when addressing a lady.'

The eight men turned to his voice, and to the end of the laneway, and to the wall of six pretend mercenaries.

'Sod off. This ain't no lady and this business is none of yours,' said one of the scrawny men. The shadows could not hide the man's deformity. A scar running from forehead to chin closed the man's left eye, and his right worked like a beacon.

Conn Mor knew the man counted six and believed that number to be surmountable. But Conn Mor also knew the man to be flagrantly wrong.

Gerald issued a flurry of tuts and shook his head. 'Oh, but you, sirs, are dreadfully mistaken. The sight of a woman under attack from four, five, no,' he paused, 'eight, yes eight men, says to me those men are baseless piss-ants. I can assure you my upbringing taught me such piss-ants are destined for harsh lessons, consequences of sorts.'

The largest soldier sauntered closer, hands on hips. His wide mouth displayed a row of chipped and blackened teeth, an image of a shallow pool full of slime-ridden stones. 'And is you lot to deal such a lesson?' The large man finished his words with a hoarse cackle. His companions joined the laughter like wine-fuelled spinsters at a carnival.

'Do you doubt it?' Conn Mor replied ever so calmly.

The English soldiers readied themselves. Yet before any man could raise a hand, the soldier with the putrid-shallow-pool for a mouth took another step forward, his narrowed eyes moulding to a quizzical frown.

'I know you,' he said to Gerald. 'You and your honey-tongued mouth. You're—'

Before the soldier could announce to all that he was

looking at the son of the 7th Earl of Kildare, Harry stepped forward and with one mighty swing of his fist, the soldier's eyes rolled back into his head. The man was unconscious before he hit the ground.

'So much for me taking the lead,' Conn Mor complained.

'It was past time this man close his mouth,' Harry stated matter-of-factly.

And with that, chaos flooded every inch of that laneway. Fists flew, knees fell, teeth shattered, and bodies flipped in a topsy-turvy fashion. It took no more than a few seconds before the odds were evened. Six against six.

Gerald held a bleeding soldier in a headlock. 'You're too old for this fighting, Jarlath,' he said looking to the rest of the melee. 'Leave this to the young and virile.'

'Hah,' yelled Jarlath, throwing one of the smaller men into the stone wall. He took one step forward and punched a fist into the man's ribs. He heard a telling crack and a sharp moan. The man crumpled to the ground. 'Manus and I have this. Why don't you young ones head to the tavern and order our drinks? We won't be long.'

'And miss this?' Gerald held tighter at the soldier's throat. The man went limp. 'Never.'

Tom offered a wry smile to the scar-faced one-eyed soldier. 'Come on, Cyclops. Show me what you've got.'

The soldier's own menacing grin pulled his scarred eye down into a bawdy wink. With legs bent, the two men circled. Tom caught flickering light on a blade.

'Ah, not fair, my good man,' Tom said casually. 'You don't bring a blade to a street fight. Someone might get hurt.' In four quick moves Tom had that arm bent mercilessly behind the would-be attacker's shoulder and pushed harder until he heard the snap. The man screamed and folded to the ground. Tom kicked away the fallen knife, put his heel onto the broken arm. Manus pocketed the blade before it could be used by another.

'Sorry, Jarlath,' said Tom. 'I know you and Manus wanted this fun to yourselves, but the blade in the hand is an insult.'

'Apology accepted,' said Jarlath. 'There's only four of them left. Let Manus and I show you how it's done.'

A loud thud echoed along the laneway. A soldier laid face down, blood pooling beneath his nose.

'Oh, Conn,' Manus complained. 'Now it's only three.'

'Sorry, Manus. Couldn't help myself.'

The three remaining soldiers stood side by side. One large and two slight of build.

'Who are you men?' the large man asked.

'Your demise,' said Manus with a smile, and jumped, aiming a kick at the middle of the too-wide stance. The soldier uttered a sound similar to *orf,* closed his eyes and knelt. He was not praying.

The last two men took a step backward, and then another. Jarlath and Manus countered their moves. Conn Mor noted the measured paces were taking the fight closer to the huddling children. And closer again. He moved quickly, swept the two children from the ground and shuffled them over one shoulder. With his free arm, he grabbed at the crying mother and led them all from harm's way.

The woman checked her own tears as best she could

then took the children from Conn Mor's grasp.

'Thank you,' she said, her tone tight.

The fighting forgotten for a moment, Conn Mor stared at the woman's fair face. Despite the warning in the tilted chin not to offer pity, he saw utter wretchedness. Her gaze quickly lowered to the ground and he knew they hid a heavy dose of self-loathing.

'Thank you,' she said again, then looked toward Gerald. Gerald stood back as Manus and Jarlath finished off the last man.

'Who are you?' she asked.

'Men of Kildare,' Conn Mor answered simply.

She paused, blinked over and again, watching the last seconds of the brawl. 'Bless the Earl.' Her words were soft.

Conn Mor reached to the purse caught at the inside of his shirt. It was empty. He had given his last coin to the young boy who led them to the alleyway. He wanted to offer something, something to ensure the children stay off the street, if for this night only. He touched at the ring on his finger, a ring bearing the O'Neill arms, the symbol of an open hand. But a niggling feeling told him to keep it for another occasion. He remembered the pendant at his neck, a silver piece etched with one horizontal line and vertical lines sitting above or hanging below. It was ogham script, the old Irish written language, and the pendant held the word *luck*.

'Here.' He tugged at the chain and pulled the pendant free. 'Take your young ones home. Find them a warm hearth and fill their bellies.'

With another softly whispered word of thanks she ushered her children away as quickly as their small legs would allow. Conn Mor returned his attention to the laneway. The fighting had finished. Jarlath wiped at his bloodied nose.

'They got one in?' Conn Mor asked.

'Only one.'

Jarlath studied the handle of the knife Manus pocketed in the laneway. It bore the inscription, Conlan Abu, a tribute to the O'More Clan of Leix. The piece was either stolen, or it indicated members of the O'More Clan lurked in the city, keen to support Bishop Sherwood and see to the demise of the Fitzgeralds. Both were possible, but the latter was fast earning credibility. Those men earlier, they must have been John and William as he first suspected. No surprise really.

Affection was not shared between the O'More's and the Fitzgeralds. Had not been for too many years. And the current political situation presented an occasion for the O'Mores to join the anti-Geraldine hordes.

Jarlath was content to suffer the small indignity of a bloodied nose, for the alternative was that they would be brawling back at their current stables, confronting John and William O'More. John and William O'More, the eldest sons of Dorothea O'More of Leix, and, Thomas Fitzgerald, the 7th Earl of Kildare.

Chapter Ten

Priory of Kilmainham – Dublin

January and February brought the usual seasonal changes. A cold winter faded to a temperate spring, fledgling hawks abandoned their hilltop nests for the endless sky, and two of Thomas' children celebrated their birthdays – Gerald now twenty-one, and Eleanor now thirteen. In addition to the usual, Tom married the daughter of Robert Preston the Viscount of Gormanston, and Eleanor pestered Thomas at every turn to announce a date for her wedding – although the latter could rightly be labelled as usual, rather than not.

Thomas laughed to himself. His eldest daughter was certainly growing and it came about with the blink of an eye. The times he looked to Eleanor he still saw his little girl. Her fourth year shone in her cheeks, her sixth year flit over her smile, her seventh echoed in her lively gait, and her tenth sparkled in those never resting eyes. But she was no longer that little girl. As for marriage, Eleanor would have to wait til she was older. Thomas would have it no other way.

Dwelling on those thoughts caused Thomas to feel more than his fifty-six years. His stride was no longer spritely or agile and his hair had yellowed, the red long-faded. Where did the time go?

He looked up to the heights of the Priory of Kilmainham's grey walls. The spires stretched to the evening sky and caught at the wayward clouds. The sounds of distant flat-bottomed riverboats, winding their way along the Liffey River with the inward tide, drifted over the tenements and echoed against the stones in the courtyard.

Yes, there had been many changes, but not enough. On the far side of that wall, whilst riverboats sounded their arduous task, whilst spring blossomed and hawks hunted, and whilst many a birthday was celebrated, the Bishop of Meath still held power over Ireland, and held Thomas' mind in a state of siege, for his patience grew thin. Yes, his patience grew thin, as thin as Eleanor's.

Thomas met with the Priory's training field. Helmeted men struck and parried, attacked and retreated, each manoeuvre conducted with slowness and precision. One man barked orders, his voice as thunderous as it was eloquent. The Prior of Kilmainham was a man accustomed to obedience.

'You have your men training with little light,' said Thomas, raising his own voice to be heard.

'Keep your feet,' yelled the Prior, then turned to greet his guest. 'If one must battle at dusk, one should train at dusk.'

'Always the shrewd man.'

James Keating, Prior of Kilmainham, dressed in a red surcoat with the white cross of the Hospitallers of St John of Jerusalem, gave a curt nod and a wry smile. Prior of Kilmainham for more than fourteen years, he had been a loyal supporter of the Fitzgeralds for longer. He removed his gloves. 'Good to see you, Thomas.'

'And you, your lordship.'

'I take it your rooms are adequate?'

Thomas knew the question to be nothing more than an

129

instrument of self-adulation, for every room in the magnificent building was befitting the stay of a king. Artworks on every wall, gold-edged vases on every bench, caches of the best wines from Gascony, and an abundance of oranges, limes and red-rich tomatoes piled high on large silver platters, too many to be consumed. The Templar Knight's vow of poverty was nowhere to be seen and Thomas suspected abstinence and obedience were no more in residence, but kept that thought to himself for he genuinely liked the man. 'They will suffice.'

The Prior slapped Thomas on the shoulder. 'So what do you think of my men, eh?' He turned to the fifty men throwing and blocking hefty blows with swords. 'Do they not wield a mighty sword just as the Angel Gabriel?'

'Indeed,' said Thomas, suspecting every man on that field possessed the cunning and the courage of the Prior. James Keating would not stand for less.

'You're welcome to use the apartments for as long as you need.'

'The repairs to my townhouse should be completed by week's end.'

'As I say, for as long as you need. Who stays with you?'

'Joan and my daughters.'

'Not your sons?'

Thomas shook his head. 'James fosters with the Fitzgibbons.'

'The White Knight? A good man there. He has daughters, no?'

'He does.'

'A good marriage to be made then, the Fitzgeralds and the Fitzgibbons. But I suspect you are ahead of my thoughts,

Thomas.'

Thomas simply smiled his answer. 'And Gerald and Tom are out there.' Thomas slanted a look to the high walls.

'Doing?'

'Making the Bishop's stay uncomfortable.' Thomas patted at the folded letter in his coat pocket. 'I have just received word from Gerald.'

'I always knew that eldest son of yours had a penchant for mischief.'

'It will take more than a joking jester to rule Ireland.'

'You think being a scholar is the only thing required to make a good leader? To my way of thinking there are two types of intelligence. The first is scholarly, and the second,' the Prior tapped a finger to his temple, 'is smarts. And I'd prefer a man with the latter.'

'You suggest Gerald has smarts?'

The Prior smiled. 'Come, I'll walk with you to your rooms. I must be gone by the early morn and I'd like to greet your wife before I take my leave.'

The men walked side by side, leaving the sounds of the training field to their backs. The Prior stood a full foot above Thomas, and his stride equated that of a large yet nimble man.

'So, the Bishop of Meath still troubles you?'

'You state the obvious,' said Thomas.

'And since when does a Fitzgerald allow another to best him?'

'I have not been bested. Not yet.'

'It has been six months.' The Prior cast an oblique look towards Thomas.

Thomas nodded with a solitary grumble as they turned

131

beneath an archway, then took the wide stairs two at a time.

'I too, have my own problems, Thomas.'

'As worrisome as mine?'

'I believe so,' the Prior said with a smile, and then raised his voice to float with a patronising quality. 'It seems a Prior cannot govern his Priory as he sees fit. Lomley charges me with being careless of our accounts, and Octavian del Palatio sides with him. I think they fear I will pawn the remnant of Our Saviour's Cross.'

'And will you?' Thomas suspected this man would part with his own ears to ensure his home be on the ridiculous side of ornate.

'Of course not,' said the Prior with little emotion. 'Speak to Octavian for me, Thomas.' It was more an order than a request.

'I'll see what I can do.'

'You have had my loyalty and friendship for many years.'

'As I said, your lordship, I will see what I can do.'

'Good.'

The men marched along the upstairs corridor toward the guest apartments, their boots beating the heavy rhythm of drums. To their left, torch lights flared. To their right, elaborate window etchings stretched high to the ceiling. St John The Baptist's red robe, the Virgin Mother's blue shift, and the red tunics of the Knights, all fell grey with the evening sky.

At the end of the corridor the Prior stood aside, allowing Thomas to walk before him into the guest antechamber. A sombre quiet curtained the room, whilst ink-stained fingers of three scribes moved to no end atop a cluster of desks. Candles burned low. Melted wax fell like a forest of icicles. In the hearth, a fire-worn log cracked. Sparks spat into the air and disappeared, eaten by the quiet.

'The word is mightier than the sword, eh, Thomas?' said the Prior. 'Personally I believe there to be nothing more persuasive than a newly cut throat to have a man—' The Prior ceased his opinion midway. 'Madam, I apologise.'

Thomas turned to see Joan walking through the door. She offered the Prior the expected obeisance in a short curtsey.

'My Lord,' she said. 'Not the words I expected from a man of your position.'

The prior held out his hands. 'Ah, but we are all sinners. Some more than others.'

Joan took the proffered bejewelled hands. 'It is good to see you, James.'

'You have my home for as long as needs be.' The Prior looked over Joan's shoulder at the two girls watching on intently. 'My, my. Your daughters grow more beautiful every year.'

Eleanor curtsied to the Prior and Anne mimicked her sister, her effort a little clumsy.

'Is it true about the fires, Papa?' asked Anne.

Eleanor sent her sister a warning frown, one that none in the room missed.

'So you have heard. Do not worry yourself, Anne,' said Thomas.

'But if Dublin burns so will we.'

'The people raise their voice to the Bishop. That is all. And we are not in harm's way here.'

'Let him burn in the fires,' said Eleanor with the

politeness of an angel.

Joan swung around to face her daughter. 'Eleanor!'

'It is past time, Mama, that man was gone.'

'Can your daughter wield a sword?' the Prior asked light-heartedly.

'I do not doubt,' Thomas answered with the same tone.

'With a little more training, then.' The two men conversed as if no one else was present.

'An admirable soldier, I think,' said Thomas.

'Thomas,' Joan warned.

Thomas shifted his stance wide. 'I would like to hear our daughter's opinion on these matters.'

'Really?' Eleanor smoothed the folds of her gown and adopted a manner of command.

'Begin,' said Thomas.

'Well, to be rid of the Bishop I suggest we inform the King of your greatness.'

The Prior gave a superfluous flick of his wrist to the air. 'An easy task.'

'And in that,' Eleanor continued, her eyes on the Prior's many glittering gems, 'perhaps we should use the example of my betrothal to the Prince of Ulster. No other noble could achieve such a union.'

'A good point.' Thomas nodded.

'Yes, a good point,' agreed the Prior.

'And of course add other examples of your greatness, Papa.'

'And?' Thomas prompted. 'We shall need further.'

'And then,' she added hesitantly, 'and then inform the King the betrothal has become tenuous.'

'Tenuous, you say?' Thomas said.

'She did,' said the Prior.

'Yes, tenuous. It is not the truth but we need to be devious.'

'Devious?'

'She said devious,' said the Prior.

'Yes, devious. Inform the King the betrothal is now tenuous. Tell him the Prince of Ulster will have nothing to do with the nobles if the Bishop of Meath continues to hold power here on our lands. No, say his lands,' she corrected quickly.

'Wise indeed, Eleanor.'

'Thank you, Papa.'

'I concur, lass,' said the Prior. 'A fine mind.'

'Thank you, my lord.'

'Is that all?' inquired Thomas.

'Is more needed?'

Thomas fought hard not to laugh. He gave a quick thought to whether Conn Mor O'Neill knew what lay ahead, marrying this spirited and determined girl. She possessed fortitude and resolve to no end, and the honesty of a well-polished mirror. 'I am sure that will suffice.' He half turned to the scribes and sent an impatient yet harmless gesture their way.

One of the scribes understood the meaning. 'My Lord,' he said, with a slight nod, before his head dipped purposefully as if setting to work to pen Eleanor's words.

'Papa, I may only be eight, but I too, have an idea,' said Anne in a low voice.

The Prior coughed and kept his eyes to his boots. His balled fist concealed his grin. 'Two female warriors,' he whispered.

'By all means, Anne, speak up,' said Thomas, clasping his hands at the small of his back. 'The more ideas we have the better.'

'Tell the King that the Bishop is a churl.'

'Anne!' both Thomas and Joan said in unison.

'By all that is Holy,' the Prior sang, 'these girls have the tact of their father.'

'But James said before he left—' Of a sudden Anne's lips tightened and she dropped her eyes.

'Your brother?' said Joan. 'Your brother should mind what he says within the hearing of ladies. And speaking of brothers,' she turned to Thomas, 'have we received news from Gerald and Tom?'

'We have.' Thomas pulled the letter from his coat pocket. He was keen to share the news with Joan, but not in the hearing of Eleanor and Anne. The word churl would not better the story of Arland Ussher's fright in the alleyway. He turned back to his daughters. 'Perhaps you may like to ask the Prior to show you the remnant of Our Saviour's Cross … whilst it still remains in his possession.'

The Prior laughed. 'Like I said, Thomas. Tact!'

Chapter Eleven

Walking from the doors of Christ Church Cathedral, the Bishop of Meath looked resplendent. From not sixty paces away Gerald caught the sparkle in the man's ornate silk chasuble, his large white mitre, and the purple cope with its thick threads of gold embroidery and lines of precious stones. Gerald suspected the rigid stance of the Bishop was more an inescapable pose than a mere physical achievement, for surely that garment could not bend nor fold. The Bishop was a large man with a girth incapable of concealing his fondness for rich foods. He possessed an impressive height not common to men of the cloth, and with that, Gerald was convinced any sermon from the man's mouth would be as if coming from the Lord himself, delivered from the great heights of the Heavens.

The Bishop had just celebrated Mass and strode purposefully across the circular-patterned pavement followed by secretaries and lackeys and the ever-present men-at-arms.

'The celebrated Bishop of Meath, the righteous William Sherwood?' said Harry.

'In the flesh.' Gerald noted his friend's narrowed eyes and brooding stare.

'I believe the Lord has seen fit to make today a marvellous day indeed,' Harry said through gritted teeth, then spat at the ground.

'What are you up to, Harry?'

'I have manners. I greet people.' He marched directly into the path of the Bishop, his gait remarkably similar to that of his target, only to be thwarted by men-at-arms, men quick to point swords.

'I would have a word with you, Bishop,' Harry said caustically, giving no attention to the sharp blades aimed at his heart.

'And you are?' The Bishop's voice hinted only an inkling of interest.

'The son of someone I believe you once knew well.'

Gerald expected the Bishop to flick a hand to his men and have Harry dealt with as they chose, but Harry added quickly, 'Maebh of Breifne. You knew her?'

The Bishop frowned somewhat falsely, as if searching for a memory, all the while his shrewd eyes studied Harry from head to toe. 'Give distance,' said the Bishop, and his men stepped back.

Harry folded his arms across his wide chest. The Bishop met him stare for stare. Mouths moved, neither in a kindly manner. Gerald could hear naught. Their communication was inordinately short. Harry turned abruptly, leaving in his wake an angry prelate.

For a long moment Gerald watched the man. He seemed to breathe fire. Gerald often cursed at how prelates, who believed themselves closest to the Grace of the Lord, could not be more distant. And it was in the Bishop's side glance as Harry walked away, the shrewd eyes that seemed to stab at Harry's back, that Gerald knew he was looking at one such creature; an evil. Sherwood said quiet words to one of his captains and a small group of men moved from the rest. The Bishop and his remaining men departed with little affair.

Gerald found Harry. He was seated at the steps of a nondescript vacant shop. In the dirtied window sat a toppled line of dust-covered jars and a small set of rusty scales; perhaps once an apothecary's store. Harry held his whetstone in one hand and his dagger in the other. His fingers troubled at the dirty cord wound around the handle. His thoughts, no doubt, were elsewhere.

'You are solitary of a sudden, Harry.' Gerald received no reply. He was not deterred. 'What is the Bishop to you?'

Harry stopped twirling the knife, ran the blade across the stone. The blade hissed. 'Just a righteous swine of the cloth.'

Harry checked the latch on the barn doors and returned to his place of rest. Replete and content, he pulled a ragged blanket up to his shoulders. It was not a night to be billeted with his companions. He was in need of privacy, and had found a suitable place in a ramshackle building behind the dam mills outside the city walls.

As during any other night, his attempts to sleep were eternally disturbed, waking to sounds and perceived movements. Mice rustled through the straw, his horse shifted, a distant voice called from the heights of Dam's Gate. Those sounds he ignored whilst sorting the innocuous from the dangerous.

His thoughts wandered. The day had presented a number of most unexpected events. Never had he thought to converse with the man he believed to be his true father, William

Sherwood. It was not expected, nor wanted, but like a tongue playing at a cut lip, Harry could not prevent himself from forcing an introduction. A few sharp words tossed at the bushy-browed Bishop, eliciting steam from the man's nostrils, made for a well-pleasing end, and Harry congratulated himself on the calculated achievement, for short of his testing desire to slice the man's throat from ear to ear, he had achieved what he perceived to be an acceptable compromise. Stinging anger.

One horse snorted again, and then came another sound. Its simplicity rang very much like the snort of the horse, or perhaps the snuffling of a pig, but was somewhat genteel. He turned his head. His beautiful Gretel lay curled into his side, mouth agape and snoring. Gretel was this day's other unexpected event. Taller than most, with hair the colour of fire, and skin as fair as snow, to Harry, Gretel appeared the vision of Venus herself. Gretel declared she enjoyed his quirky humour, had called him comely, a description Harry never thought to attribute to any part of his being, and had won him over with her full smile. Harry felt her warm breath on his chest and swiped at the fan of hair tickling his neck. The daughter of an English pot-maker lying peacefully at his heart made for a lovely picture. He closed his eyes and beckoned sleep. His own breath fell in time with Gretel's. Sleep came close. Ever so close. Then his ears pricked to yet another sound.

Soft footfall on bracken moved along the outside of the building. An owl called, the harbinger of death, and such a portent brought his eyes fully open. He allowed his sight to adjust to the dark shadows whilst his fingers felt at his side for the corded handle of his dagger. If the owl saw the coming of a death this night, Harry vowed it would not be his nor that of his

Gretel.

He became more alarmed as muffled yells and grunts and bone shattering thuds came to his ears. His eyes followed the path of the sounds. Outside the locked door, then to the eastern wall, then quickly to the rear of the building. Harry was on his feet in seconds, legs spread, dagger in hand – a beast, crouched and ready to pounce.

Gretel stirred. 'Simon?'

'Get to the corner, my love,' ordered Harry, and Gretel obeyed.

The door swung open, the latch no measure for the powerful boot put to its centre.

Gretel screamed, 'Simon,' and pulled the blanket up to cover her naked body. The moonlight gave Harry's eyes only a silhouette, but he could make out the heavily padded tunic. He steeled for an onslaught of violence.

'Your name is Simon?' came the familiar voice from the silhouette.

'Your name is not Simon?' said Gretel.

'Give me a minute, my love.' Harry lowered his knife. 'What idiotic, hare shit trouble are you causing now, Fitzgerald?'

'None caused by me, and I'm sure it was not fatherly love being shared. I believe Abraham was about to sacrifice Isaac … or Simon.'

'Your name is not Simon?' complained Gretel, again.

Harry held up a halting hand. 'Give me a minute, my turtledove.' And then to Gerald, 'So, you now know what the Bishop is to me?'

'Seems so.'

141

'And you are the Lord's Angel come to save me?'

'I have never been accused of being an angel, but feel free to be the first.' Gerald moved further inside. His eyes moved to the woman huddled at the far wall. Harry followed. Gretel's worried eyes were as round as plums and her big toes poked out from beneath the thick wool blanket.

'But it appears you have *your* angel,' said Gerald.

'Eyes away,' Harry warned. 'I don't take kindly to people fondling what is mine. It arouses an urge to cut out their brains through their nostrils.'

Gerald laughed. 'Tell me what you said to the Bishop today. It seems your tongue put him in an unsightly mood, enough to order you killed this night.'

Harry ran his fingers across his chin. Then a cruel smile curled at his lips. He remembered every word, every accusatory and foul sigh. But Harry simply shrugged at his saviour. 'Hello dearest Father, was all.'

'Ah, filial love is a wondrous thing.'

'Why did you not warn me? I could have handled the situation myself.'

'No doubt, but …' Gerald inclined his head toward Gretel and arched an eyebrow.

Harry knew that to be only a slice of the answer and not the whole apple. Perhaps he should be grateful for Gerald's menial measure of thoughtfulness. 'And how did you know of his plans?'

'The Bishop's demeanour curdled when you spoke.'

'Curdled?'

'Like soured cream. And I did not wish for my good friend to become acquainted with a noose for murdering one of

142

God's servants.'

Harry nodded, the full apple explained. 'You used your rancid turnip-brains then?'

'I did. But you must now excuse me, Harry … I mean Simon, and mademoiselle.' Gerald bowed graciously to the quiet Gretel. She had eyes only for Harry. 'Perhaps on the morrow we'll raise a mug to the coming demise of the righteous swine of the cloth.'

'Your name is not Simon?' the woman asked again, this time with a laugh.

'I have been given a mission, a special mission, and need a disguise. Forgive me?'

Gretel lifted the blanket. She licked her lips. 'Then come and be covert with me … Simon.'

Gerald left.

Chapter Twelve

Gerald and Harry rode beneath Castle Maynooth's gatehouse tower, the structure mountain-like in size, and ornate in grandeur. The monkey atop the Fitzgerald crest never ceased to draw Harry's quizzical frown and a sarcastic laugh and rude jests generally followed. But not on this occasion. The two men dismounted in the busy courtyard, handing reins to servants.

'I will ask you one last time, Fitzgerald, why does the Earl summon me?' Harry was more impatient than expectant.

Gerald flicked his hand casually to the air. 'I'll introduce you to my daughter when we are done.'

'I hope the wee thing has her mother's looks or she'll be a frightfully ugly lass.'

'She has, Harry. She has.'

'So you'll not tell me why we are here?' The sounds underfoot altered from crunching stones to booted footfall as they entered the great hall.

'Papa.' Gerald threw the loud greeting toward the hearth and with a wry smile offered Harry a quiet light-hearted, 'No.'

The men marched through the crowded room. Powdered faces nodded Gerald's way in polite welcome and some added congratulations on the birth of his infant child

Margaret. Gerald felt elated, if not a little tired, for he had spent many a late hour alone this past week simply watching the babe in her sleep. In the quiet of the night, her tiny pink lips made the sounds of a babbling brook, and her balled fists wound their way to her mouth. She was a beautiful cherub indeed, with a crop of thick dark hair, just like her mother's, and folds in her arms and chin. An ample healthy weight. The nurses playfully scolded Gerald for his nonsense, suggesting it would be time better spent if he sought his own sleep. His child was oblivious to anyone's presence, they would say over and again. Gerald knew otherwise and simply ignored their jibes. He would sit and watch his child if it was his want. Some yawns and heavy eyes were not too much a cost for such a treasured event.

His father, the new grandfather, looked up from his chair at their approach. 'Ah, good. You are here. You look tired, Gerald. And you look worried, Harry.'

'If annoyance can be construed as worry, then you are correct, my lord.'

'My son has not informed you of the reason for your presence?'

'No, my lord. He has not.'

Thomas gestured to a circle of seats. 'Here, sit.'

Gerald was the first to obey and lounged back, interlocking fingers behind his head. One at a time his booted feet climbed onto a padded green footstool setting its beaded tassels into an ungainly dance. Harry seemed to hesitate. With dawdling movements he wandered noncommittally, back and forth before the hearth, then finally made to claim a vacant seat, and stopped mid-movement. The chairs were not generous in size. He seemed to think for a moment then sat onto the more austere choice, the one lacking frills and dainty additions, the one with heavy thick legs. The wood creaked its objection. Harry pursed his lips and sidled forward perching uncomfortably on the edge.

'Comfortable, Harry?' asked Thomas.

'Comfortable enough,' Harry lied.

'Well first, I have news to share with you,' said Thomas. 'The Bishop of Meath has set sail for England.'

'So the righteous swine flees,' said Harry with vigour.

'Perhaps.' Thomas nodded diplomatically. 'The Bishop has left instructions that I attend the duties of Justiciar in his absence.'

'Then your problems are solved, my lord.'

'For the time being,' inserted Gerald. He raised a finger to a servant, a request for drinks. 'The reason the Bishop gives for his sudden departure is that he seeks an audience with the King. For the relief and succour of the inhabitants of Ireland, were his words. And coincidence or not, the King has withdrawn his army from France, albeit with seventy-five-thousand crowns and a dubious promise of peace.'

'There is no such thing as coincidence,' said Thomas.

Gerald took a proffered cup from a servant.

'I expect patents attesting to my reappointment to arrive at our shores in good time, perhaps in the first week of April.'

Harry rubbed at his chin. 'That is good news indeed, my lord, but I am still puzzled as to my presence here, unless you have orders for me to follow the Bishop and hunt him down. My morality is negotiable. It's in my blood.'

'That will not be necessary, but it's reassuring such

loyalty exists within my son's inner circle.' Thomas glanced at Gerald then returned his regard to Harry. 'It has been suggested I owe you a great debt.'

'There is no debt owed, my lord.' The chair gave another protest, or perhaps a sigh, as Harry stood.

'No? The Bishop leaves Ireland after a few short words with you, and I owe you no thanks?'

'None can say it was my words that sent the pious bag of bile running. But it's nice to think it.'

Thomas laughed. 'Let me make myself clear, Harry. Is there something you want? Name it and it shall be yours.'

'Your news is reward enough, my lord.'

'What about a wife?' Gerald added to the conversation.

'And I cannot find one for myself?'

'Is Gretel an aspirant spouse?' asked Gerald.

'Gretel?'

'The woman in the barn, the girl with the big feet.'

'Her true name is Grace. She revealed the falsehood in the throes of momentous pleasure.'

Gerald spat his wine. 'An image to destroy my day.'

'It be none of your business in any event. Is your son always like this, my lord?'

'Perhaps a squire?' suggested Gerald. 'A good wash, new garments and a trim of your horsetail hair … Simon.'

'Simon?' queried Thomas.

'Gretel is Grace. Simon is Harry. It's like a Latin tragedy,' explained Gerald.

'A Greek tragedy,' Thomas corrected.

'Latin, Greek or English. A tragedy all the same.'

'Harry, I had something totally different in mind,'

147

announced Thomas. 'I would make you one of my captains.'

Harry was not often stuck for words, but there was no verbal utterance given in reply.

'I would expect you to continue your current duties and keep close with my son, keep him from trouble. But I see in you something else, and a loyal friend is a masterpiece crafted by our Lord's hands.'

'A masterpiece you call me?'

'Interpret as you will. And, Harry, I need not remind you of the extra coin which would accompany such a position, if you accept my offer.'

'Flattery and riches. And from whose purse would that extra coin be sourced, my lord?'

Thomas seemed to follow Harry's meaning. 'My son's, of course.'

'I accept, my lord, and of course am honoured. May I be so bold as to ask for an advance on that payment?'

'Your hilarity pains me,' said Gerald.

Thomas stood, his steps taking him closer to Gerald. 'Whatever the reason the Bishop runs, you and your men did well in Dublin, son.' He slapped Gerald firmly on the back, and then again. 'Whatever it was, well done, Gerald.'

Gerald doused a growing frown. Had he just received earnest praise from his father, or was mockery layered beneath that single compliment? Gerald chose to believe a negative connotation was not intended, for his father seemed to look at him with new eyes, and he wondered at the sentiment such menial approval stirred.

'Thank you, Papa,' he replied simply, and then felt the squeeze of his father's hand upon his shoulder. It remained for an inordinate time. In Thomas' quick glance, Gerald spied what he believed to be … worry? The ensuing silence peppered the air with a sense of dread, yet no words accompanied the slightly pitiful look. Just as swiftly Thomas seemed to muster a candid grin, and he turned his focus back to Harry. Gerald dismissed his private concern as absurd.

'And I hear Arland Ussher no longer ventures out after dark,' said Thomas.

'You hear correctly, my lord.' Harry replied with a lyrical tone, his eyes wide like goblet rims, and finished with his usual burst of thunder. 'Hah!'

Gerald was keen to visit the nursery, and moved to quit the room with Harry following behind. But not before stealing another quick glance at his father. The worry had returned.

Thomas returned to his seat and watched the retreating backs until both were swallowed by the crowd. Two fingers tapped rhythmically at the carved oak. His throat worked hard and he coughed deeply, a dog-like growl. He couldn't decide whether he suffered the beginnings of an affliction or whether he choked on the words that needed to spew forth to Gerald, and soon. Ailments of the mouth seemed to plague him incessantly. Another tooth was giving trouble and his throat felt raw. Could the good Lord not see to gifting him one day void of trials? He looked to one of the tapestries on the wall, the slaves—not angels—caught in storm clouds. Right at that moment he felt as if caught in his own downpour.

A hand touched at his arm with the weight of a snowflake.

'You did not speak to him?' asked Joan.

'Now is not the time.'

'If not now, when?'

In the stead of a reply, Thomas pursed his lips.

'Gerald almost met with John and William in Dublin. And I hear Dorothea is in Meath.'

'That woman's name is not to be mentioned in my home.' Thomas spoke low and fast, yet his tone lacked not of ferocity.

'Do you wish for your son to discover the truth from another?'

'No,' Thomas said tersely. 'You think me a fool?'

Joan sighed. 'No, my love. I do not.' She splayed her fingers through his hair. 'But what I find saddest is that you credit your son to be one.'

Thomas flinched, not sure if his scratchy throat or Joan's words dealt that last pain. He wiped at his forehead. Beads of sweat wet his palm. A cup of hot wine with honey was called for. He moved to apologise for his boorish outburst, but Joan had vanished as effortlessly as she had appeared.

Chapter Thirteen

Eleanor's dreams stole her away to a time nine years now gone, a time when shouts had snatched the four-year-old Eleanor from blissful sleep. A time when news of Ainnir's late-night riding accident travelled up and down the castle's corridors. That was the week before Ainnir married Donal.

The shouts flew on a constant dreary drone, like the toiling within a beehive. The four-year-old Eleanor climbed from her bed, a well-worn blue coverlet trailing her every move across the stone floor. She opened the door, saw servants racing, her mother and father speaking in hushed tones about a dead horse. Donal, her father's cousin, listened intently, his face full of worry.

'Eleanor?' Anne spoke her name but was nowhere to be seen. Of a sudden darkness devoured the corridor. She stepped out into the dark. And then ...

Eleanor woke with a start, blinked and blinked again. It was all just a dream. She was not four. Donal was not in the corridor. He was long dead. And in that languid time between slumber and wakefulness, she rolled and snuggled back under the coverlet.

Again her name sounded. *Eleanor.*

'Eleanor?' Anne stirred at her side. 'Is it morning?'

The shouts droned on again. This was certainly no longer a dream.

'No.' Eleanor sat bolt upright. Chatting moved with haste past the chamber door. It was not merriment. It was not frivolity. As her toes touched the cold floor, the bedchamber door opened and a servant bustled in.

'What is it, Agnes?' Eleanor asked of the girls' nursemaid.

Her hair askew and apron untied, Agnes circled once then twice, keeping eyes to the floor. 'You girls are to dress at once.'

'Why?'

Agnes stilled her spherical wanderings and snatched one riding cloak, then another and then another from the wooden pegs hammered into the wall. Three cloaks. With manic movements she bounded to the largest of the oak coffers and pulled out a green skirt, one that no longer fit Anne nor Eleanor. Then stockings, one pair. A moss-green shawl, a red one, and another green, lighter in shade. Boots—five—and no two made a pair.

'Why?' Anne echoed Eleanor's words.

A rattled Agnes dumped the nonsensical array of garments at the foot of the bed. Her hands flew to her face and she sobbed uncontrollably.

Anne wiggled closer to Eleanor and held tight to her arm.

Joan marched into the room. 'This is no time for questions, girls. Out,' she ordered Agnes, and gave the maidservant no more of her attention. 'You must dress, and quickly.'

'Mama, what is wrong?' asked Eleanor, a quiver in the last of her words.

'It is nothing to concern yourself about. Your father's fever has worsened during the night and his physician believes

152

it best that you take up other accommodation.'

'Mama, is Papa very sick?' Anne fretted.

'No … yes.' Joan's tone held little emotion. She lifted the garments from the bed one at a time giving no more than a second to study the pieces.

Eleanor sensed her mother's control contrived. 'You will be coming too?'

'No. I will stay with your father.'

'Then I will stay.'

'Eleanor. I need you to look after your sister.'

'But—'

'I have spoken. Now dress in something warm, then get yourselves down to the courtyard. A carriage awaits.'

Eleanor looked to the open door. Flickering light from the sconces made the walls tremble. Alice and Gerald hurried past carrying their infant child.

Joan choked back a white-hot lump of fear. Fits of prolonged coughing seized Thomas yet again. The clusters of swelling around his neck had enlarged, and the physician's examination found further swelling to the armpits and groin. Edward Burnell's round face could not hide his grim thoughts.

'Madame,' Burnell began, taking a deep breath and deferring its release with a lengthy pause. He was a man not keen to pass on his diagnosis. 'I can only hope I am incorrect.'

Those few words did naught to lessen Joan's fear. They tossed and speared, wrenched and whipped. The room seemed to spin and rock at unimaginable angles. Nothing felt real. Joan clutched at a chair to remain upright.

The physician tried again. 'My reluctance to confirm the worst is that a true outbreak of the plague has not been reported for more than eighty years, but I must confess, there have been reports of persons exhibiting these same symptoms in England of recent times. You have removed your children from the castle?'

And there it was. The word. Plague. It swam through her mind, splashing and kicking.

'Madame, have you heard my words?'

'Yes. Yes, I have,' she answered, tears blurring her vision. 'My husband may or may not have the plague. I believe that is what you are telling me.'

'Madame, take comfort in the absence of a rash on his body, for the lack of any is a good sign, one that suggests we need not fear the worst. Your children have left?' he asked again.

'To our lands in Meath.'

'Good. I encourage you to keep hope.'

'Hope? I have never seen him so pale,' Joan whispered. 'His skin turns the linen to yellow.'

'Perhaps you too, should leave. Have the servants tend the Earl.'

'No.'

The doors to the chamber flew open.

Joan turned. 'Why are you still here? The carriages have left.'

'You did not think I would leave?' Gerald's eyes rested with none but his father. 'My God, what is wrong with him?'

Joan turned away, unable to hide her fear.

'Tell me.'

154

No one gave an answer.

'Tell me,' Gerald repeated with more urgency.

'Perhaps a simple fever,' Joan began, then turned back to face her eldest child. 'But your father shows the first symptoms of pestilence.'

'No! You are wrong. It was only a racking cough yesterday.'

'This is why you must leave.'

'I leave when you leave.' Gerald's tone lacked forbearance.

Burnell stepped closer to the bed. 'As I have explained to your lady mother, there are certain symptoms which have not shown themselves, and with this I can only pray that my first fear is dreadfully wrong.'

'Mama?'

Joan turned to the hushed voice at the door. 'Has obedience suddenly acquired a bitter taste amongst my children? Gerald, I ordered you to—'

'Do not blame, Gerald,' Eleanor began defiantly, yet an intruding softness betrayed her vulnerability. 'He could have tied me to that carriage and I still would have escaped.'

Eleanor inched closer to the bed, her eyes set on her father's unconscious body. Her fingers absently reached for Joan's hand, perhaps clawing for buoyancy for her flailing courage, reassurance to cheat her fear.

'I am staying with you, Mama. I am staying with you and Gerald and Papa.'

Joan turned to the physician. 'Tell us what needs to be done.'

155

What little strength remained with the Earl plunged swiftly, too swiftly, shredded and beaten by a relentless storm of quivers and fitting, coughing and retching, chills and profuse sweating. By the third day fortitude and grit were bygone words, figments of a fevered imagination. It seemed little Joan did brought any measure of relief to Thomas' suffering, but nevertheless she tended him as an anxious mother does an ailing child; privately fearful, wordlessly fretting, outwardly stoic.

Terrified servants avoided the stuffy sickroom, and it was only after Joan unleashed a torrent of threats that necessary supplies were gathered and delivered, but carried only as far as the bedchamber door. She understood the panic, and in collecting the pile of cloths, candles, herbs of calendula and thyme, and fresh water, Joan took a moment, rested on her knees thankful for the small triumph.

None other than Thomas suffered the sickness, and any form of rash failed to appear. That should have been enough to nurture optimism, but Thomas grew weaker by the hour. With hope as frail as a water reed, Joan bathed Thomas' body and changed soiled sheets, laid cool cloths at his forehead, and dabbed oil at his cracked lips. The times Thomas woke, she gently tipped water and honey to his mouth and encouraged him to drink. And when in pain, his face contorting to that of a gargoyle, Joan stroked his cheeks tenderly.

Stone-faced, Gerald and Eleanor sat quietly, watching, waiting, praying through the endless hours, and protested when sent away to rest.

'It will do your father no good to have us all exhausted,' Joan argued.

Her words succeeded. Her children ventured to their chambers to find scarce moments of sleep. And in that private time when only the walls and the hearth's fire had ears to listen, she spoke to an often-sleeping Thomas of happier times. Joan trusted Thomas heard her every word.

She spoke of one of Anne and Eleanor's many explorations in the castle's kitchen garden three years afore, and how their daughters mischievously appropriated one of the family's more valuable trinkets, a Spanish chalice with silver and gold detail, edged with red and yellow jasper stones, and then used it to hold pilfered sweetmeats, sharing them ever so carefully with Thomas' hounds amongst the rosemary bushes. And how, when confronted with their expensive adventure, Eleanor stated matter-of-factly that Anne was too young to be punished, and that she alone should bear the brunt of their consequences.

She spoke of James' secret adventure, spying on Matthew O'Bithechan, the Abbot of Monasterevin, after castle gossip had fallen to his ears suggesting the Abbot possessed a fondness for one of the nuns of the Order of St Brigid in Kildare town. James reported back to Thomas with his findings, his observations written in detail, and Thomas discussed not the content, but his son's excellent penmanship. James was convinced the rumours held truth, and offered further reconnaissance services if Thomas so required. Thomas declined the offer and sent James on another adventure; to spy and report back on the castle's armoury keeper. It was suggested for no particular purpose other than for the annoyance of the man, for such an awkwardly dry and short-tempered man Thomas had never met.

She spoke of Tom and his placement of frogs in Christopher and John Plunkett's beds, in retribution for having his feet tied together with leather strips as he slept the previous night. Unbeknown to Tom, the beds were set aside for guests from England, not for Tom's childhood friends, and the wife of the chancellor, who suffered a nervous disposition, was none too impressed.

And Maurice, their sweet departed son, and his peaceful existence, his happiness in the companionship of his siblings, of his love of riding with Donal and only Donal. Of his smile, that when came, lit the room no less than a noon summer sun, and in those particular moments, how they believed their son's distant mind understood their deep love for him.

And now, in that eerie time between night and morning, when night animals silence their calls and the birds are yet to sing the coming of day, she spoke of Gerald.

'Do you remember, Thomas, the day you first permitted Gerald to ride at your side to do battle?' She looked to Thomas' face, strangely hopeful to witness a nod. None came. It did not matter. She moved to the hearth and placed another log onto the dithering flames. Sparks spat through the air like fireflies. 'It was the time when you and Donal headed out to fight the O'Byrne and the O'Toole,' she continued. 'Our son feared I would not allow him to join you and promised with every blessing he could muster to remain safe, said he feared my wrath more than his own death if he did not return.'

She returned to the bedside and sat. 'He was fifteen, Thomas. Irascible and mulish and looked to you with bountiful awe. He still does, you know? Together you put a stop to the raids along our borders, but we lost Donal. And—'

'And that was when I was in England, fighting alongside the King's brother, Richard of Gloucester.'

Joan turned to the voice at the door. Jarlath's hair hung limp, a wispy beard darkened his chin, and mud caked his knee-high boots. And despite the eloquent ease of his tone, Joan heard his distress.

'You rode through the night?'

'I departed as soon as your news arrived.'

'Do none of you listen to orders?'

Jarlath's fixed stance belied his hesitance to cross the room, as if the distance between he and Thomas' bed were a pitching sea. Then just as quickly he strode across the floor, and in that summoning of courage Joan felt a sense of inexplicable relief, her burden now shared.

'Did you truly think I would stay away?' Jarlath took Thomas' hand in his own whilst Joan held the other. His eyes wandered up and down the unconscious body and Joan knew Jarlath's mind pained to make an inventory of the deterioration in his uncle's appearance.

'No. I did not,' she said with a tired smile.

Jarlath returned his own. 'On that night they rode to the fight that killed Donal.'

'Yes, the occasion that still burdens my son greatly.'

'Gerald is not to blame.'

'No one is. And blame changes naught. If blame exists, forgiveness is craved and becomes a festering obsession.'

'You speak too, of Maurice's death?'

'No.' Joan's release of breath was audible. 'Not really. There is something you do not know. Gerald forbade me to speak to Thomas or to anyone for that matter, of the truth. It

159

was not he that Maurice wandered from. It was his brothers. Gerald chose to protect Tom and James from Thomas' unforgiving wrath. And for that he has worn too many layers of his father's disappointment, and for too long.'

'I never knew.'

'And that is how Gerald wanted it, still wants it.'

'There is something I must ask.'

'Ask.'

'Has Thomas told Gerald of John and William?'

'No.'

Both sets of eyes fell to Thomas. Grey lips were lined with weeping cracks, eyes weighted by dark circles, cheeks hollowed and taut. Muscles vanished and bones seemed to be the only thing to shape the body's skin.

Outside, a sparrow began the treetop morning chorus. Joan once found the trill a beautiful song, but now it was simply a hideous ode marking the marching hours. 'Stay with me, Jarlath. Let us speak to Thomas of happy memories.'

The sun rose. The bedchamber's shadows grew limbs of grey and blue. Outside, dark-beaked jays joined the sparrows mimicking their cry, spreading high-pitched birdsong along Maynooth's busy courtyard and outlying fields. In a room already bereft of freshness, a rancid smell assaulted the air like a cloud of smoking dung. Joan and Jarlath made no move to react. The blood oozing from Thomas' ankle looked like fatty black oil with splotches of a murky green. Edward Burnell finished the bloodletting and moved to lance buboes at Thomas' groin.

Standing at the physician's side, Joan readied a warm poultice of garlic, onion and butter and gently applied the linen pouch when Burnell stepped away from the bed.

'I shall bleed him again this evening. Keep him from sleep as best you can.'

Joan ran her fingers across Thomas' forehead. 'He fights me. Too often he slips back into sleep as he does now.'

'Look,' said Jarlath.

Thomas' eyelids fluttered but did not open. His bottom lip dropped, a thread of clear spittle stretched and snapped. 'Only a foolish man disobeys his wife.' Thomas' words came as gritty croaks.

'You have the right of that, Thomas,' said Jarlath, his voice soft.

'Thomas, love, you must stay awake.' Joan caught the slight movement at Thomas' mouth. It sufficed for a smile. One eye opened, then the other.

'For a time,' Thomas murmured.

'No, stay with me. You must not sleep.'

Jarlath marched to the antechamber and shouted orders to the servants to rouse Eleanor and Gerald.

Thomas' eyes closed then opened again. The circles beneath seemed to darken and grow to the size of oranges. He looked up, a movement which obviously brought pain, and his once-hazel eyes now stared awash with grey. 'I fear I am called elsewhere.'

Joan's breath caught in her throat, trapped in her bosom. It seared and severed and stung, then escaped on a strangled cry. 'Oh, my love.' She raised his heated hand to her cheek, kissed at his palm.

Joan felt Jarlath at her side and heard the receding footfall of Burnell, leaving the chamber and what cherished time remained to the family.

'Have I confessed?' asked Thomas.

Joan sniffed back her pain and opened her mouth to answer. Not a sound came forth.

'Yes,' Jarlath answered. 'You have made your peace with God and masses are being said.'

Joan found her strength. 'Across County Kildare, in every lane and field. All Ireland prays for you, Thomas.'

'I always tried to be a good husband, Joan.'

'Yes, my love,' Joan cried. 'You were a good husband. A wonderful husband and a wonderful father to our children.'

'And to me, Uncle.'

Thomas' next breath came on a gurgle, and a time passed before he again spoke. 'My grave once teetered far into the future. It seemed an eternity away. But time, time is a soulless thief. It has pilfered the miles I once had.'

'I have prayed for you day and night, my love.'

'Mama? Papa is awake?' Eleanor stood at the doorway, her blue night robe tied at the waist, her hair loose and unkempt.

'Yes, Eleanor. Come.' Joan held out her hand in invitation, and ingratiated her daughter with what she trusted to be a hopeful smile.

'Papa.' Eleanor walked nearer to the bed, her steps dubious yet ardent.

Tall though she now may have been, on Eleanor's fair face, lovely on a slender long neck, real fear brought a vulnerability Joan had not seen for a time.

'Eleanor,' Thomas rasped.

'Papa,' she said again, her doe-like eyes brimming with tears. 'I read to you last night, while you slept. Do you remember? I read the Divine Comedy from your Alighieri collection, and then our story of the Pooka Fairy. Do you remember how I loved that book when I was a child?' A sob caught in her throat. 'Do you?'

Joan saw the slow rise of Thomas' chest and knew he struggled for breath. She placed Thomas' hand into Eleanor's.

'Oh, do not go, Papa. I could not bear it. First Maurice. Now you. Coldness coils in the pit of my belly, and I do not think I could breathe if you too, were to die.'

Thomas looked to Joan with heavy eyes. She had no reply for his unasked question. How does a dying father console his fretting child? She feared that she too, would fold under the burden. Time was aiming to pilfer more than Thomas' hours.

Thomas' eyes returned to his daughter. 'I remember,' he said weakly. 'My favourite.'

'Our favourite, Papa. Our favourite.'

'Perhaps I will tell Maurice the same story.'

Eleanor's sobs could no longer be tethered and burst like cart wheels rolling across a cobbled street.

'Papa?' Gerald rushed into the room. With eyes on his father he placed a welcoming hand to Jarlath's shoulder. 'How long have you been here?'

'Only a few hours,' Jarlath answered.

'Papa will be glad you have come.'

'It seems you still hold command in this family, Thomas,' said Joan with a melodious tenderness. 'You speak and your children come running.'

163

'Son,' Thomas began. 'There are things we need to speak of.'

Fitful sobs again escaped Eleanor's lips and she turned from the bed, threw herself into Jarlath's arms, hiding her face from the inevitable.

Gerald leant in closer to his father. 'Wait til your strength returns, Papa.'

'We should speak now.'

'Yes,' said Gerald, swatting at his eyes, catching an errant tear.

'A college,' said Thomas. 'Build me a grand college here in Maynooth. I want knowledge and learning to be my legacy to our people.'

Gerald nodded. 'Of course. It will be so magnificent all of Christendom will speak of its walls.'

'And lead Ireland well, son.'

Gerald nodded again. 'As you have, Papa.'

'No, lad. Lead as you will. I trust in your courage.'

Joan almost melted at that small yet precious slice of validation dealt from father to son, given as casually as if teaching offspring the game of cards. Such a gift was as needed as it was belated, and for a time she had feared Thomas' moments of lucidity were all but gone. But he did not fail her, did not fail their son, and Joan sent a silent prayer of thanks to the Blessed Virgin Mother. She waited for Maurice's name to be uttered. Perhaps forgiveness would be granted, an unnecessary forgiveness, but one that would be a momentous gesture. And she waited some more, wondering whether she should break her promise of silence, tell Thomas that Gerald was not at fault that day.

'And you must take tubs to the Abbey of Achad-finglass in Idrone. Large tubs,' whispered Thomas.

'Tubs?'

'A debt seven years overdue. Jarlath will explain.'

'I will,' said Jarlath.

Jarlath and Joan shared a wry grin, a miracle in a room flooded with such sorrow and tearful anticipation. They both knew of what Thomas spoke. Thomas had often sought rest and sustenance at the Abbey when riding south of County Kildare and into Carlow, and the bathing tubs provided by the affable Abbess were of a size to fit only a small woman, not a man as big as Thomas. Once, as Thomas bathed, Donal suggested he resembled a pair of tavern whore's breasts in a too-small gown, and with that endearment Thomas promised to rectify what he saw to be an unfortunate injustice in the humble home of such a devout order. But the occasion never seemed to present itself. Life became busy. Life always became busy.

'Anything, Papa. Just ask and it will be done.'

Thomas' eyes remained with Gerald whilst he addressed the room. 'I would speak with my son alone.'

Joan leant in close. 'Are you sure, my love?'

'Yes.' Thomas closed his eyes.

Exhaustion showed itself in the antechamber. Joan had convinced Eleanor to fetch food to break her fast whilst Gerald and Thomas spoke privately, and now, side by side, seated on the quilted window bench, Jarlath held Joan's hands in his own.

'We are about to lose him.'

'Yes.' Jarlath could say no more for he knew the

165

inevitable was not long in coming.

Joan sniffed back her tears, and turned to the window, looking out to the early-spring garden below. 'I cannot remember a time without Thomas.'

Jarlath followed Joan's line of sight. A drizzling rain distorted the scene. Pathways of loose stone wound through the blankets of green and seemed to lead to nowhere. The wind played at glistening leaves. 'Nor I,' he said.

'He loved you like a son, did he not?'

'I never felt less,' Jarlath granted.

'Even when you burnt down the stables.'

Jarlath smiled. 'Yes, even when I burnt down the stables.'

Joan's eyes lifted to the closed bedchamber door. 'You know what Thomas speaks of now?' she asked, her question more a statement.

'Of Dorothea, I suspect, and John and William.'

Joan had no opportunity to respond. Wind hammered at the window just as the bedchamber door flew open. Jarlath and Joan stood to meet a manic face.

'Gerald.' Sympathy coated Joan's one utterance.

'Why did you not tell me sooner?' Gerald circled, boots striking the floor. 'I should have known my father would have bastard children all over Ireland.'

Joan's hands flew to her heart. She took a quick step forward. 'That is not the way—'

'Is it not? Is it not, Mama?' Gerald smiled a smile of disgust. 'No. You are right. They are not his bastard children. They are his legitimate children.'

'Gerald, you are wrong,' said Jarlath. 'The annulment

papers saw to that.'

Gerald's sudden frown looked painful. 'You knew too? And those men in Dublin, the group you prevented me chasing down. Were my brothers amongst them?'

Jarlath lowered his face. 'Yes.'

'Yes. John and William O'More of Leix.' Gerald threw his hands in the air. 'My brothers.'

'It matters not, Gerald. We ensured no recourse could be made,' said Joan. 'You are your father's heir.'

'Yes. I am my father's heir!' he spat with the heat of a raging sun. 'And no one …'

Gerald fell mute. The anger seemed to melt, lugging him to a place of supreme loneliness. His eyes studied the walls. He blinked over and again. 'Papa is about to die,' he whispered. 'Can it be so? And he forgave me for Maurice's death. He gave me his forgiveness, said I was to forget.' Gerald's next breath caught on one high-pitched sob.

'Oh Gerald, we should have told your father the truth from the beginning.' Joan took another step forward, rested her hand on his arm, but he recoiled.

'And have Tom and James suffer his eternal ire? I think not.' He lifted his chin, altered his stance. His grief gone, anger returned. 'No one,' he began again, 'whether of my father's blood or not, will take what is mine.' With that he headed for the door and before turning into the darkened corridor, shouted to the air, 'Get me those annulment papers. I wish to see for myself that my inheritance cannot be bargained for.'

Jarlath moved in pursuit.

'No, Jarlath. Leave him. Let my son's anger run its course. It will wane.' And Joan returned to the bedchamber, to a sleeping Thomas, and to the distressing wait.

On the 25th of March in Our Lord's year of 1477, and at the age of fifty-six, Thomas Fitzgerald the 7th Earl of Kildare, passed from this world and into the realm of Heaven's Peace. Earl Thomas was buried beside his father, John Fitzgerald the 6th Earl of Kildare, in the Monastery of All Hallows just outside Dublin.

Ireland's Council, a seven-man assembly comprised of deeply loyal Geraldines, confirmed Gerald Fitzgerald, the 8th Earl of Kildare, to the position of Justiciar to rule the green lands west of England's shores.

The new Justiciar ordered scholars and doctors of law to study the annulment records pertaining to his dead father and his first wife, Dorothea O'More of Leix. Their assessment suggested Gerald sleep soundly, but the 8th Earl of Kildare refused to entrust the might of the Fitzgeralds to the opinions of mere academics and the buttered hands of chance. Certainty was more appealing.

Part Two

18 months later

Chapter Fourteen

Parliament was to meet at Dublin Castle. The duties of Justiciar often took Gerald from his family and Maynooth, but on this occasion his wife and daughters were comfortably housed in the family's townhouse in Dublin's Thomas Court.

Growling like a lion, Gerald crawled around the nursery floor. His two eldest daughters, Margaret and Ellie, giggled with delight at their father's antics whilst his infant daughter, Elizabeth, slept soundly in her cradle.

'You will ruin your new velvet tunic, my love.' Alice sat by the open window enjoying the late spring air.

'Then I will order another. No, I will order eight. And of eight different shades.'

'I must admit, I am enamoured with your new-found attention to dress. It is a pleasant change from the riding garb you once insisted on sporting morning, noon and night. You look positively regal.'

'A splendid opinion, Alice.'

'And I have an opinion about the furry caterpillar that encroaches upon your top lip.'

'You like it?'

'No,' Alice laughed.

'I am the Justiciar. It is only fitting that I present well.' Gerald rolled onto his back and lifted a chubby Margaret high above his head. It seemed she grew heavier by the day. Her plump legs and arms kicked and thrashed. 'It is fashionable.'

'I'm a bird, Papa.'

'More an overfed turtle, my girl.'

Ellie gurgled a string of unintelligible words and clambered up onto Gerald's chest. With a quick hand the little child grabbed at Gerald's encroaching caterpillar and tugged hard.

'Ahhhh,' Gerald complained good-naturedly, an empty sound with only one functional lip.

Alice moved to rescue her husband. 'Ellie, dearest, you will hurt your father.'

'She does no harm, Alice. Our daughter's nails need tending, 'tis all.'

'No less than your moustache. But they are girls, Gerald, and should be shown the proper ways of courtly ladies.'

Alice plonked a wriggling Ellie onto her bottom on the floor. The determined child rolled quickly to her hands and knees, crawling back to the play.

Gerald threw Margaret into the air, her dark hair and petticoats flapping with her arms, and deftly caught the giggling child. 'If my daughters wish to climb the beech and the yew of our lands, play in games of hurling, or dig for worms with their pearl and shell hair combs, they have my blessing.'

'Then it is past time I gave you a son.' Alice patted her belly. 'Perhaps this child will be a boy.'

Gerald sat upright, depositing Margaret onto the floor beside her pushy sister. He sent Alice a questioning tweak of his brow. 'Again?'

Alice nodded with a girlish smile. 'Yes. I am sure of it.'

Gerald laughed loudly and rolled back to continue his task as a conquerable mountain, whilst his daughters played clumsy mountaineers. 'Would you like a brother to play with,

Margaret?'

'I don't like boys,' the child replied, stepping onto her father's stomach with little care.

'Not yet, but you will one day. And you, dearest Ellie? Would you like a brother?'

Ellie mumbled her reply, neither adult comprehending her opinion at the prospect of a male sibling, if indeed she possessed one at all.

Jarlath appeared at the open door.

'Jarf!' Margaret jumped from the mountain top, scrambled from her father's reach and ran to her cousin.

'Welcome, Jarlath,' said Alice.

Of a sudden Margaret stopped short. Her small slippered-feet crept slowly backward to the safety of her mother's lap, all the while her eyes remained fixed upon the enormous frame standing behind Jarlath.

'Ah, my escort.' Gerald pulled himself up brushing dust from his knees and picking unnecessarily at his blue tunic. 'I agree with my daughter, Harry. You can be a frightening sight.'

Harry took one step into the room and shrugged. 'I'm not too fond of little ones myself. They can be dangerous at both ends.'

'Hello, Harry,' said Alice, then spoke softly at Margaret's ear. 'It is only your father's friend, dear Margaret.'

'We're ready,' announced Jarlath.

'And that means I must be too.' Gerald moved to the side of the cradle and gently brushed at the cheeks of the sleeping Elizabeth. 'And Manus?'

'Is late,' explained Jarlath. 'We cannot wait further.'

'Is Ainnir here, Jarlath?' asked Alice. 'She journeyed

173

with you?'

'She and the children will be up shortly. Conor demanded a visit to the kitchen be their first stop.'

'Oh,' said little Margaret on an inward breath, caused by the mention of playmates or the kitchen, none could be sure.

'And you, dear Margaret, have spent ample time in that place this week,' said Alice. 'You will become the turtle your father spoke of.'

Jarlath stood at Alice's side and petted Margaret on the head. 'I wish to speak to you again, Gerald, of your decision to—'

'Pointless,' Gerald interrupted. 'I have decided.'

Jarlath protested. 'Some of our supporters already question the granting of—'

'No,' Gerald said more firmly and turned from the cradle. 'I am Ireland's Justiciar, am I not?'

'You are.'

'Then I decide to whom the coins of these lands are paid.'

'As you wish,' Jarlath allowed diplomatically.

'Good. My wife gives me great news, Jarlath.'

'News?'

'I am again with child,' Alice explained.

'My congratulations,' Jarlath offered graciously, with a slight bow of his head.

'If we are sharing good news, I will speak of mine,' said Jarlath. 'Ainnir is also with child.'

Alice squealed her excitement, and with Margaret on her hip, she stood from her seat and placed a kiss at Jarlath's cheek. 'Oh, that is wonderful. And she is well?'

174

'In the mornings she suffers a little, but otherwise fine.'

'I never suffered such a thing with my children, but I hear watered wine with lemon is good for that malady. Oh,' she said turning to Gerald, 'we must send Ainnir home with a supply of lemons, and have more delivered to Kildea.'

'A wonderful idea. I shall leave you to the arrangements.' Gerald grabbed his cap from the sideboard and fussed with two large peacock feathers stitched at the band. Their colours complemented the blue of his tunic. His sleeve made light work of buffing the row of ruby-red jewels at the cap's hem, before he positioned the headwear on his head.

Both Jarlath and Harry stared unapologetically.

'It is the latest fashion from Rome,' Gerald detailed unnecessarily.

'Then the Romans have queer habits,' said Harry. 'Why does a man wear his daughter's bonnet?'

Jarlath laughed and turned to begin the men's departure. The girls said their farewells, not before Margaret elicited a promise from her father to return to the townhouse early enough to retell a story at bedtime.

Gerald and Harry walked side by side down the stairs, a distance behind Jarlath, their boots thudding a fast gait on the steps.

'You know, Harry, you could do with a little attention to your own dress? Perhaps that is why my daughter fears you.'

'I will place a frilly bonnet on my head the day you listen to wise counsel.'

'You speak of Jarlath's protests?'

'I speak of Jarlath's acumen.'

'Acumen?'

175

'Do you not understand? Do you need me to translate?'

'It's English.'

'Then you understand.'

'When did you become my political advisor?'

'The moment you put that dead bird on your head.'

King's Hall in Dublin Castle did not possess the grandeur of Maynooth's great hall, yet the dark table and ornate seats at the dais boasted a stately ambience of their own. Dark carvings of small animals pawing and lurching and pouncing, decorated the high backs of the chairs, and intricate lettering, wisdom from scripture, rambled across the headrests. With peacock feathers bobbing at his head, Gerald took his seat, vanishing two hungry lions and *Deo juvante* – With God's Help.

Beneath a row of life-sized portraits of England's past Kings, James Keating sat to Gerald's left and Roland Eustace to Gerald's right. Jarlath seated himself in the audience at a distance, selecting a position along the sidewall gaining an excellent view of the entire hall and its occupants. He marvelled how James Keating presented a figure similar to his dead uncle. Tall and large of presence, the Prior clapped Gerald on the shoulder in a paternal gesture.

Scores of men hovered and chattered waiting for the beginning of deliberations. Some quieted as Gerald took his seat. Others, too focused on conversation, remained unaware of the imminent commencement. Robert Baron of Howth spoke animatedly with Robert Dowdal of Louth, bold hand gestures flying through the air like hawks. Brothers Alexander and Edward Plunkett laughed with Richard Bellow. Barnaby

Barnwell of Meath and Lawrence Taaf nodded their welcome to the many faces that passed their way. And the ever-present Harry retreated to the shadows, standing lazily with one shoulder resting on the wall, his eyes never still, suitably playing the role of Gerald's protector.

After ordering an attendant to place the ceremonial sword to the front of the dais, Gerald brought the unaware aware. 'We have many matters to discuss this day, gentlemen. Let us forge our way without further delay.'

Chairs scraped noisily as men found their seats. Gerald waited for murmurs to lower.

'This Parliament meets in Dublin Castle,' Gerald began, his head raised high, his voice racing to the back of the hall, 'in the eighteenth year of the reign of King Edward IV before the Justiciar and the good people of Ireland. Please read for the assembled parliament matters and statutes for declaration this day.'

A scribe stood. Hunched and heavily bearded, the man cleared his throat and read from papers held loosely in his hand. 'The first matter, my lords, relates to unforeseeable absences of our appointed Justiciar. On the occasion Earl Gerald is absent from parliamentary sittings, Sir Roland Eustace, Lord Portlester and Chancellor of Ireland, shall have full power to prorogue, continue or adjourn parliament when necessary.'

Bland agreement stirred from the floor. Gerald nodded, seemingly pleased with the lack of opposition to the first declaration. There were more declarations to come, and Jarlath knew discord would be only a matter of time.

'And so enacted. The next item,' Gerald prompted.

177

The scribe sniffed a lazy nasal sound. 'By royal patents Sir Roland holds the office of Chancellor on the same terms as Sir William Welles once held the position. Sir William, in his term, was granted four score marks yearly from Drogheda. Therefore the mayor and sheriff shall pay Sir Roland the same amount from farm fees gathered from its people.'

And so it began.

Rumbling from the floor, a hum of discontent, sounded louder than the previous stir of agreement, but no challenges were expressed directly.

Gerald nodded in the same confident manner. 'So enacted. Next item.'

The scribe again cleared his throat. 'In addition to the four score marks, the said mayor and sheriff are also to pay to Sir Roland the fifty-two marks which the King gave by letters patent for the making of a bridge which they have thus far failed to construct.'

The discontent grew to a heavy drone. Men leant close to their neighbours, whispering opinions. Some exchanged quizzical looks with others across the floor.

Gerald flicked a gesture to hurry to the scribe.

The scribe obliged. 'If the said mayor and sheriff refuse, they shall forfeit to Sir Roland for each offence, one-hundred pounds.'

Men turned in their seats.

'You rob Drogheda of coin for its people,' came the first decipherable objection, more a blithe announcement than condemnation. 'Pay for the bridge yourself, Portlester.'

'That coin is for the people of Drogheda,' came the second, a balled fist punching the air.

'You err. 'Tis not right.'

''Tis fair,' argued one voice against the antagonists.

'Agreed,' responded another.

Gerald raised his hand for silence. 'Let it be known the forfeited coin will be paid to the King's coffers, not those of Kildare.'

'And not Sir Roland's?' came another voice. Men close to the voice laughed aloud.

'Continue,' Gerald ordered the scribe.

Manus Eustace slid onto the bench beside Jarlath. 'Just in time for the dramatics?' he said in a low voice.

'Your presence was needed earlier.'

'Our journey took longer than expected. I've just left Meg at Thomas Court with the womenfolk.'

'Ah, then you have filled Ainnir's day.'

'I have?'

'My wife's plan to save you and Meg from a life of dullness and misery is foremost in her mind.'

'Still? I admit to receiving an unexpected salutation of 'enjoy your day' as I left the townhouse. Perhaps Ainnir succeeds somewhat.'

'Progress?'

'It did not hiss like a cat. Call it what you may.'

'Well, even if you had arrived on time and supported my pleas, I doubt Gerald would have listened.'

'So the Earl still plans to bestow more riches upon the rich?'

'He does,' replied Jarlath.

'And the less rich complain?'

'They have, and they do.'

179

More voices of discontent raced.

James Keating bellowed his own disgruntlement at the opposition from the floor. 'Fair, I say. And only the foolish would think otherwise.'

'Your view is wise, Prior Keating,' acknowledged Gerald.

'The King's money is not intended for birds for your hats, my lord,' yelled a voice to the front of the room, bringing echoing laughter to replace debate.

'What is Gerald wearing?' Manus asked.

'His daughter's bonnet is Harry's way of telling things.'

James Keating called for order. It came, but not hurriedly.

The scribe raised further matters for discussion by the assembly. The granting of proctors from alien lands to parliament. Pestilence was discussed with a sombre mood, as outbreaks were reported in four counties. Previous grants to the Archbishops of Dublin, Richard Talbot and Michael Tregurry were withdrawn. The design of coinage. The conditions and criteria whereby the Justiciar could adjourn parliament.

Some items were received with loud agreement, many were not. Some were enacted. Some were not. The murmurs ebbed and flowed, writhed and decayed and grew anew, and more than twice, Gerald's cap received further comment.

'Sir Roland shall receive,' the scribe began with the next matter, 'a third part of the lordships of Naas and Ballykeyn in county Kildare, and a third part of the manor of Rathfarnham of Dublin.'

More dissent. Spittle flew. Frowns knitted brows. Chairs scrapped along the floor as irritation shifted men in their seats no less than lice in their codpieces would cause.

Manus whispered to Jarlath, 'Does he plan to bestow the Roman Empire on any man present? Perhaps grant France to the Prior? Scotland to Harry?'

'Or Heaven to Hell.'

'A subsidy is to be paid to Sir Roland,' said the scribe, 'for the walling of Kilcullen and Calfstown, a safeguard against Irish Enemies.'

'Would Sir Roland like my hounds as well?' came an impossibly nasal voice from a gentleman with an impossibly long nose.

'Sir Roland can have my wife,' said another to the enjoyment of the crowd.

'I'll take your wife and your daughter if you're selling,' came another comment, followed by even more laughter.

'The granting is only right,' argued one voice, bringing seriousness back to the debate.

'Agreed,' announced another.

Arland Ussher sat at the far end of a bench. His acerbic grin contorted his already unfavourable face. He stood, the movement being that of an aging man.

'This ought to be interesting,' Jarlath whispered to Manus.

'My lord,' Ussher began with superfluous panache, his bejewelled fingers flicking through the air. 'Does this imply the great Earl of Kildare fails in his attempts to bring our Irish enemies to obedience? Do you fear attack? Should we all fear attack? Does the Baron fear attack?'

'Acquiring peace is a never-ending process,' Gerald replied evenly.

'Yet you advise the King over and again, my lord,' Ussher turned to take in the crowd, 'that the Gaels heed English rule and they yield to our ways flocking like sheep to a shepherd.'

'It is so,' confirmed Gerald, his peacock feathers still.

'And you are the shepherd?'

'We, the representatives of the King are all shepherds.'

'Then why a wall,' Ussher bowed his head, 'my lord?'

With the flurry in the hall at that last comment, Harry's silent steps went unnoticed … by most. Standing beneath a portrait of William the Conqueror, Harry positioned himself in Ussher's line of sight. Above Harry, on the painting, a deep crease in the form of one stroke of a dark brush to the right of the painted King William's nose, lifted his rose-coloured lip into a sneer, and a gold crown concealed a portion of a frowning forehead. Harry raised his hands above his shoulders as if stretching stiff muscles, almost petting the painted King's crotch, then turned a sly smirk upon Ussher, his expression not too dissimilar to the conqueror's sneer, yet was accompanied with an unprepossessing come-hither look.

Ussher caught sight of the stretching Harry, the monstrous man who had once cornered him in a dark Dublin street in search of sinful deeds. The sardonic grin slid from his face, the bejewelled fingers retreated stiffly behind his back, and the now reticent man folded back onto his seat, not another word uttered.

'Harry is definitely mad,' whispered Manus. 'Perhaps irreparably crazy.'

'Only when it suits him … apparently.'

Gerald called for silence. 'The Prince of Ulster is to

marry my sister, the Lady Eleanor, and soon. Is there a man among you who can boast a more affable bond with the Irish natives?'

'Why not have Sir Roland purchase the Gaels' favour with all the coin you award him?'

'He could purchase the loyalty of the Devil with that lot.'

'Why not include your bond with the O'Mores of Leix as an achievement?'

Gerald's head snapped to the left seeking the source of that comment. Feathers waved. His frown informed his audience his search failed. Jarlath expected a rampage of abuse from the dais, for Gerald's hate for the O'Mores bordered on manic.

Yet none came.

Gerald seemed to summon a bounty of patience. His lips thinned and the feathers in his cap stilled like a goose in winter. 'I will accept those comments as a reply in the negative, gentlemen. Continue,' he again ordered the scribe.

'Take what you want, Kildare, if any is left,' said a gentleman waving his walking-cane in the air.

The scribe continued and announced various grants to James Keating, including the position of Constable of Dublin Castle, and the granting of an orchard to Keating's sister and brother-in-law for a period of thirty years at thirteen shillings and four deniers of silver per annum.

The next matter dealt with the disorder of the Ormonds. Piers Butler and other men were ordered to deliver themselves to Dublin Castle, to answer a charge of high treason and open preying and robberies on the King's faithful people.

Gerald's excessive bounties continued in the form of rights bestowed to James Keating over the parish church of St. Bride in Meath.

A messenger came as a saving grace, interrupting the shouts. Haste-filled steps carried the man toward the dais. With one hand Harry stopped the fellow midstride, relieved him of his missive and delivered the message himself to the dais. Gerald seemed to study the seal before passing the unopened letter to Roland.

Roland patiently broke the seal and took a few moments to read its contents. 'News from England,' he finally announced to the hall. Silence came. 'Prince George, the Duke of Clarence, the King's brother, has been put to death.'

'Why?'

'When?'

'The details, my lord?'

'At the order of the King?'

'At the order of his own brother?'

Only two questions could be answered. 'At the order of His Grace the King, on the fourteenth day of February.'

Roland spoke quiet words to Gerald and the Prior. Gerald's eyes remained low.

Jarlath suspected there to be more to the letter, and none of it good.

James Keating stood from his chair, fingers splayed on the table. 'Parliament is adjourned, gentlemen,' he announced with his usual strident delivery. 'We will meet again in Connell after the Feast of the Nativity of the Blessed Virgin.'

Chasing Roland's exit, Jarlath and Manus moved through the crowd.

'There's more?' Jarlath asked of Roland in a low voice.

Roland's face altered little. 'The King sends Lord Henry Grey to be his new Justiciar.'

It was inevitable, Jarlath thought to say, but held his tongue.

'We will resist.' Applying his usual illegible scrawl Gerald signed the last of the documents presented to him by the scribe, then slouched in his high-backed chair and crossed legs atop the solar's table.

'How?' Jarlath stood at the opposite end of the table, his fist wrapped tightly around the King's missive.

'It does not matter how. It matters that we do.'

Jarlath pained to conceal his impatience. 'The King appoints Grey three-hundred men-at-arms and archers and a list of commissioners, and you think a nondescript *resist* will resolve all? I tell you we will not see this man from our shores without a decisive plan.'

'Grey is a man, not God.'

'He is the infamous Lord Grey of—'

'Yes, yes, we have all heard,' Gerald interrupted blithely. 'The great Lord of Condor.'

The sound of the closing latch marked the departure of one scribe.

'Codnor,' Jarlath corrected. 'The Lord of Codnor. A brutal soldier who fought alongside King Edward at Barnet and at Tewkesbury. A man who also fought against Edward at St. Albans. His horde of scruples is less than minimal, no mere apparition to wipe from your mind.'

'Condor or Codnor, it matters not. It is I who keeps the King from our shores, and Lord Grey will be less of a bother. I rule this land.'

Silence. A tense silence.

Jarlath knew the other men in the room—Manus, Roland and James Keating—held their collective breath at Gerald's declaration, words that if heard outside those walls would invite a charge of treason and the fatal wrath of the Crown.

'Out,' Jarlath ordered the one remaining servant. 'And close the door behind you.' He waited. 'Best your opinion never be repeated, Gerald, around prying ears. The royal axeman takes pleasure in dulling his blade on impudent necks.' What was wrong with this man? Was it his arrogance or stupidity? His ignorance or idiocy? Or the lot?

Gerald shifted uncomfortably in his seat, refusing to meet Jarlath's glare. 'Commissioners,' he muttered, diverting the debate. 'The King names John Butler as one.'

'A point I did not miss.' Jarlath flung the pages across the desk. 'I warned you of your largesse, Gerald.'

'It is not your place to warn me of anything. I am Ireland's leader. Not you.'

'Your father listened to all counsel. He would not have made such errors.'

'My father?' Gerald's feet dropped to the floor. He stood from his chair. 'I am not my father.'

'And all the more reason for us to be troubled. Now how do you plan to heave us from this mess?' Jarlath gave Gerald his back, a deliberate move to leave Gerald with the question and use what little wisdom God gifted him rather than

186

concoct a meaningless retort.

All other eyes remained with Gerald, and Jarlath read the men's expressions.

Manus expected the spitting of further insults.

Roland expected belittling chastisement.

James Keating expected a trade of punches.

Incorrect in their assumptions, Gerald straightened his jacket, removed his feather-laden cap and adopted a rare manner of control.

Moments passed before another word was uttered.

'Roland, you will refuse to surrender the Great Seal,' Gerald ordered. 'Such an act will hinder public business under Grey's hand.'

'It can be done,' said Roland in his usual patient manner.

'And, my lord Prior, you will refuse Grey entry to Dublin Castle.'

'It will be an honour,' said James Keating.

'And?' Jarlath demanded more.

'And what, Jarlath?' Gerald said with contrived restraint, then, with a balance between acceptance and sarcasm, 'What would my father do?'

Jarlath stalked to the windows and looked east, out to the busy streets. ''Tis not enough,' he said, more to the outside world than to his companions, and then to himself, silently – what would Thomas do?

In the distance, the grey tower of St. Audeon's Church peaked high above the city buildings. Jarlath knew beneath the church roof rested Portlester Chapel, a chapel funded by Roland, dedicated to the Blessed Virgin Mary. Three fine arches, gilt bowls, carved monuments, marble flooring and more, all furnished by Roland and his monies; Ireland's monies. Monies needlessly handed to perhaps the wealthiest parish in all of Ireland. Oh, Jarlath knew Thomas too, had been a generous benefactor of the church. But Thomas had possessed shrewdness in excess, where Gerald lacked it in enormity. Gerald, the 8th Earl of Kildare, a man who foolishly believed himself Ari of Ireland, could have ensured Roland's generosity continued without encouraging public hostility. Gerald, a man who over and again acted in a self-seeking manner, had single-handedly piqued the ire of King Edward himself, and with that, brought uncertainty to the continued power of the Fitzgeralds.

It was not the first occasion His Grace had sent an envoy across the sea to alter the balance of Ireland's political holdings, and if history indicated correctly, it would not be the last. But Jarlath doubted not, that Lord Grey of Codnor was sent to control Gerald, not Ireland.

Was it all too late? Could things be rectified? What would Thomas do, he asked himself again. How would Thomas see them from these troubles?

Jarlath's breath steamed on the window pane. St. Audoen's tower disappeared. 'Lord Grey has been appointed by King Edward's Privy Seal, has he not?'

'Your point?' asked Gerald.

Jarlath turned to face the men. 'Law dictates Ireland's Justiciar is to be elected by Irish Council.'

Manus smiled. 'Grey's appointment is therefore invalid.'

'Exactly,' said Jarlath.

'So we simply ignore the man.'

'Simply? It may not be simple, but we can certainly try. Seventeen years ago parliament enacted that England be afforded no say in the election of our Justiciar.'

'Is that true, Roland?' Gerald asked of his father-in-law.

Roland nodded, one slow methodical movement. 'Your cousin is correct. A law championed by your father.'

'Good,' said Gerald. 'So, as I am the legally elected Justiciar, we continue to hold Parliament and make laws for this land.'

'With a less generous hand,' Jarlath added hastily.

Before debate of blame could again erupt, the solar doors flew open and in marched a gaggle of women and children.

First Alice with a sleeping Elizabeth in her arms.

Then little Ellie close behind, wobbling and holding precariously to her mother's skirts.

A chubby Margaret and a lithe Siobhan skipped hand-in-hand. Siobhan's movement was the more eloquent.

Then came Ainnir.

Then Meg.

And in their wake, a trail of savoury scents; apple blossoms and spices, possibly cloves, and something tart. Lemon?

'You are home,' observed Alice. 'So early?'

'Women and more women,' Gerald said with laughter, the mood of the previous conversation left to the past. 'Is a man to have no peace?'

Margaret and Ellie clambered up onto their father's lap. Alice dropped their infant daughter into his arms.

'I am forever surrounded by skirts and hair combs,'

Gerald complained.

Conor was the last to enter the room, so too, the smell of freshly-baked almond cake. The young boy darted around Meg's skirts enjoying a game of chase-goose; Conor being both goose and hunter. Meg raised her hands to avoid contact with the sticky fingers.

'At last, another man,' exclaimed Gerald. 'Come here, young Conor. You must save me from this terrible arrangement.'

Conor was too busy to abide. With a mouthful of crumbs he circled Meg, watching her twist and turn and twist again to keep him at a distance. The more she turned, the more Conor tried, and the more she became complicit in the flying of yet more soggy crumbs from his lips. Her swaying sky-blue gown brushed his cheeks and ruffled his mop of dark curls. She was now the goose. A crumb covered goose.

'Oh dear,' she complained, receiving no sympathy, nor acknowledgement.

'Dour faces on our men,' noted Alice. 'Parliament not to your suiting, Gerald?'

'Always to my suiting. I would have it no other way.'

'That is why I love you so.'

'Come here, Conor, before those blue folds devour you, boy,' Gerald encouraged again. 'I need a man to help me control these girls.'

'I am coming.' Conor hoisted himself onto the table, first rolling onto his stomach and then sitting up straight.

'Now stand, my boy,' said Gerald. 'Raise your head to the clouds.'

Conor did as asked. 'Like this?'

'Exactly. There. Now you appear a King. We can all be Kings, can we not?'

Gerald's eyes remained on the young boy, but Jarlath did not miss the intentional slight.

'Lift me up,' Siobhan said to Meg.

'I think not,' answered Meg.

''Tis fine, Meg,' said Gerald. 'All Fitzgeralds should stand tall and proud.

'But she is a little lady and should not—'

'She is a child.' Manus completed the task Meg would not, and Siobhan stood tall by her brother's side. Within moments the other children also stood on the table, all except the baby, Elizabeth.

'Now dance.' Gerald clapped a bright rhythm, as he jiggled Elizabeth across his shoulder.

Booted and slippered feet banged noisily. Giggles flew through the air. The children appeared butterflies hopping from flower to flower. Noisy butterflies on noisy flowers. The room drowned happily in the sounds of roistering. Even Roland and the Prior took up the rhythm. Ainnir and Alice grabbed the hands of the younger children, ensuring they did not fall, and they themselves tapped their feet to the beat.

'Join us, Meg.' Ainnir raised her voice to be heard.

'No, thank you.'

'Aunt Meg.' Siobhan held out a free hand.

'You are being summoned, Aunt Meg,' said Manus.

Meg did not move.

Manus did.

Where Meg should have been the one to bring a little enjoyment to the young girl, in her stead Manus grabbed

Siobhan beneath her arms, swung her high in the air, circled and returned her to the hip-high dance floor.

'Smile and join the play,' Manus said to his wife, more a futile order than an ask.

'I do not wish to,' Meg protested. 'And do not attempt to embarrass me.'

'You do not need my help for that.' Manus turned from Meg and took Ainnir's hand, twirled her around, then repeated the same move with Siobhan. Ainnir curtsied low, so too did Siobhan, clumsily, and Manus rescued the young girl from a high stumble.

Manus smiled generously, took Ainnir's hand again. He seemed to be enjoying himself.

A white-hot stab of jealousy speared Meg's heart. Her husband flagrantly treasured his time, his touch with this woman. It was as though he saw Ainnir in full colour and all else in mottled greys, and she, paling woefully to transparent. Meg's loathing gave speed to her virulent tongue. She would put an end to his fun. She would paint Ainnir a lesser picture in greyscale and cease Manus' joy. Her mind raced, then...

'You look blissfully happy with your family, Ainnir.' Meg paused before she delivered her first sharp blow. 'Just as you did when your brother visited your home. Bradan, was it not? Or was it your elder brother? No. It was Bradan. I am sure.'

Manus' smile lost its sincerity.

Jarlath's eyes grew dark.

Ainnir's feet stilled.

Oblivious to the surging tempest the butterflies continued to clip and clop and slap.

192

'Has Bradan since visited?' Meg continued her malice. 'Oh, but your maidservant dearly loves him, so surely he has. Marared is her name, no?'

'What does Meg speak of, Ainnir?' Jarlath's tone matched his eyes.

'Of ...' Ainnir began, but no further words came forth.

'Of what?'

Meg decided the situation required more spite. 'Bradan came to Kildea when I spent time at your home. It was not his first visit, I'm sure.' Meg blinked over and again, the flutter of her eyelids slow and deliberate. 'Have I said something I should not?'

'That is enough,' ordered Manus.

'Enough?' queried Meg.

'Yes, enough.'

'Your brother visits your home, Ainnir?' Gerald returned his infant daughter to Alice and moved to Jarlath's side. Meg watched those Fitzgerald eyes, those owl eyes. They penetrated. They flared hate. 'Your brother has been in my lands?'

'Why yes, he has,' Meg answered for Ainnir, a little too quickly. 'I saw him myself when—'

'Meg,' Manus seethed.

Ainnir raised her chin. 'My brother has visited, yes.'

'And when were you to inform me of this?' demanded Jarlath.

'I knew you would react this way. I thought it unnecessary to burden you.'

'Burden me?'

'The O'Toole and the O'Byrne?' demanded Gerald. 'Do

they too, walk Kildare?'

Ainnir shook her head, her chin now lowered. 'Just Bradan.'

Gerald stormed from the room.

With her one free hand Alice carefully lifted the dancing butterflies to the floor, herded them through the doorway promising treats for all. Margaret's exit was the loudest for her applause. James Keating and Roland bowed their heads low and also vanished.

Now there were four.

Jarlath ran a hand through his hair. 'Do you realise what fuel you have just dealt Gerald?'

'I am sorry, Jarlath.'

'Sorry? Sorry will not repair the damage.'

'But it was not my intent.'

'Nonetheless, it is done.'

'Perhaps I should speak to Gerald myself?' Ainnir made to move to the door, but was halted by a tight grip.

'He would not entertain your presence.'

'Have I committed mortal sin?'

'To Gerald's thinking, you have.'

'Bradan is my brother.'

'And Gerald's enemy.'

'Are Bradan and I the only two who wish this feuding to cease? Is there not another soul who longs to live in peace?'

Jarlath turned on his heel.

Now there were three.

Ainnir stared at Meg, disbelief pooling the corner of her eyes. The sad face then turned to Manus, her eyes now filled with – was it sympathy? Pity?

With nothing further said, Ainnir too, left the room.

Now there were two.

Manus studied Meg intently, his glare eagle and craven, not at all like the Fitzgerald owl.

'What?' she asked, feigning innocence.

'The miserable are at their most contentedness when grey clouds thunder upon all.'

'You speak nonsense, Manus.'

'Do I?'

'It is not my habit to interfere. I simply attempted to converse of family matters. The children were having such fun. You were having such fun.'

Manus' features twitched. He looked like the malevolent grey clouds he spoke of. 'You rain, no, you pour misery upon yourself and others, Meg. Life never needed to be this way.'

'This way?'

'Yes, this way.' He opened his palms, gestured back and forth between the two remaining in the room. 'Do you think I speak of the deliriously happy Gerald and Alice, or the eternally love-struck Jarlath and Ainnir? They know nothing but happiness. But you—'

'I am none too pleased, Manus, with all your—'

'And surprise, surprise,' he laughed sardonically. 'Up to this point you appeared so tickled.'

His mockery drew more rage than Meg could control. She raised a hand and slapped his face, fast and hard, the sound as sharp and as cold as her spite.

Manus did not move, yet an unmistakable look of hate materialised.

That same culpable hand flew to Meg's neck. 'Oh Dear Lord … Manus I … I am … whatever came over me … I do not know what to say.'

'Then make no sound.' Manus quit the room.

Now there was one. A lonely, soulless one.

Something tore at Meg. Something inexplicable. Something alien. Something wretched. It pained like a rusted blade to the thigh, a blade slicing incessantly and brutally engraving nothing of praise nor flattery nor victory.

And there it appeared in her mind, a mirror, a self-image. A human vessel full of a burrowing, gnawing disease labelled odium and malevolence, a malady in severe want of remedy. Hate for her mother. Hate for her dead father. Hate for her life. Hate for everything in her world. She felt the full weight of her ailment, and it brought her to her knees. Never had she felt so ashamed.

Once the decision was made to remain in Dublin, the men set to work to ensure Lord Grey's stay be less than jovial. Their first point of order was to send the women and children home. Alice was thrilled to return to Castle Maynooth before the onset of the hot summer. Ainnir was dismayed that peace had not yet been achieved with her husband. And Meg slunk away, obsequious in her departure, steps quiet, head low, eyes avoiding. An altogether estranged countenance for one so magnanimously endowed with cocksureness and brawn-reeked opinions.

By the following morning, the Fitzgerald townhouse in Thomas Court was void of little ones and females, save for one rotund cook and two dark-haired young servants who nattered incessantly of dreams and young men who paid them little attention.

Not days after the arrival of Lord Grey to Ireland's shores, and contravening the King's orders, Gerald summoned another sitting of parliament. On this occasion the portraits hanging from the walls of Dublin Castle's hall almost outnumbered the men in attendance. It seemed the anti-Geraldine of Ireland were keen to abide by King Edward's edict to look to Lord Grey as their new Justiciar. Others, with a mixture of flaccid allegiance to the Fitzgeralds and a view neither resolute nor committal, chose to abstain. It was only Gerald's steadfast allies who attended with hearty voices and elated humours.

Gerald sat at his place at the dais. His fingers absently stroked his stringy moustache, then moved nimbly to adjust his day's chosen headwear, a purple creation with ostrich feathers from the Holy Land. James Keating and Roland sat to either side of Gerald. The Prior, with his head held high, studied every man in the room. Roland, his head lowered, listened intently to the scribe's monotones announcing the procurement of lands in Wexford, fines imposed upon the Butlers in Ormond for a myriad of offences, and penalties to be issued against the O'Mores of Leix for injurious deeds done against the people of The Pale. Applause met with each announcement. A conflicting scene to the last sitting.

Lord Henry Grey was given no mention.

Jarlath and Manus sat to the back of the room. Late to arrive, brothers Tom and James slid across the long bench seat to join Jarlath's side. Gerald nodded a welcome to his siblings.

The ostrich feathers waved their own greeting.

'I thought you busy at Laccagh?' Manus asked of Tom.

'And miss the fun?' Tom answered. 'I've left Katherine's well-being with Mama and Eleanor and Anne. They fuss, and Katherine enjoys the fuss.'

'Is something amiss?' asked Manus.

'Not amiss. My daughter was born two days gone.'

'Congratulations,' the two older men whispered.

'And you, James?' asked Manus with devilry in his voice. 'How many children do you have?'

'None have made claim to be mine, and my mother no doubt is joyous. But give me time. I am to be married to Eleanor Fitzgibbon next month.'

The scribe's voice rose. 'And land adjacent to Castle Maynooth is set aside for the future creation of a college, built to the memory of our beloved 7th Earl of Kildare. The land is bequeathed by the 8th Earl, our Lord Gerald.'

More cheers from the floor sounded the room's agreement. A flurry at the door interrupted the merry shouts.

'My lords!' A young man with a mop of curly, straw-coloured hair stepped forward eagerly, only to be halted by one of Harry's huge arms. The young man looked up to Harry's face, his eyes wide as hurling balls. 'My lords,' he repeated hesitantly, still insistent on being heard.

'Speak, Francis,' ordered the Prior.

Harry's arm rose like a portcullis and the young Francis stepped forward, stopping beneath the portrait of the sneering William the Conqueror.

'My lords,' repeated Francis. 'Lord Henry Grey an' his army approach the castle.'

The Prior stood. 'The gate?'

'Locked, my lord.'

'And the oil?'

'As you ordered, my lord.'

A grin peeled across the Prior's lightly-bearded face. 'Then let us greet our guest.'

From the battlements, Gerald and his men gazed outside the castle walls and across Dublin City's rooftops and angled streets, and far north to the city's eastern tower, Isolde's Tower, some one-hundred-and-fifty paces away. Grey's men came. Battle axes, war hammers, fluttering blue and white banners, and standards with Lord Grey's chosen talisman, the badger, all pointed to the sky. The hoofs of one-hundred horses pounded an irregular beat, and two-hundred archers marched behind. Chains rattled, swords clanked, horses snorted. Curious townsfolk gathered along the streets to watch the procession of chainmail and yew bows.

'Seems Lord Grey means to do business,' observed Gerald.

'And we shall not disappoint the man.' James Keating stood with hands on hips, his feet wide.

The pounding lessened, and lessened more as Grey and his men pulled in rein at the far side of the dry moat. Lord Grey looked up high and squinted, the noon sun breaking through the clouds. His grey hair glistened white.

'In the name of His Grace, King Edward, I demand entry to the castle.' Lord Grey's pompous tone soared to the battlements.

'And who are you, sir, to demand such entry,' James Keating bellowed back.

Coarse laughter lifted from Lord Grey's lips. 'You know who I am, and I presume I speak with the Prior of Kilmainham.'

'Prior of Kilmainham, and, Constable of Dublin Castle,' the Prior added with a finely tuned sense of delivery.

'Constable you say?' replied Lord Grey, no less comically. 'Well now, my Lord Prior. His Grace our King has granted the castle to the keeping of Thomas Danyell, knight and Lord of Rathwyne, and Edward Danyell his son.' Grey looked to his men with a smirk. They chuckled in unison. 'That would suggest the title you claim, to be false.'

'Granted by what seal?' asked the Prior.

'Why, by the King's seal, of course.'

'Then such a grant is null and void,' shouted the Prior, 'for the Irish are subject only to laws made under the Great Privy Seal.'

Grey spat on the ground. 'And if the Baron of Portlester would give over the Privy Seal, all will be set to rights.'

'I cannot do that, Lord Grey.' Came Roland's voice.

More coarse laughter. 'And I am now speaking to the Baron?'

'You are.' Roland stepped forward to the embrasures to show himself. 'Baron, and, Lord Chancellor of Ireland.'

'So, Lord Eustace, you cannot …' A brown rat scurried along the ground. Lord Grey whipped a knife from beneath his cloak, and in one fluid movement flung the blade at his target spearing the rodent through its fat stomach, '… or will not give over the seal?'

'Will not, my lord.'

The merriment fell from Grey's squinting face. 'Damn you, Keating. Let me in.'

James Keating raised a gloved hand.

A lone arrow was loosed from the gatehouse and flew through the air landing close to the feet of Lord Grey's mount. The horse shifted. Its ears pressed back. The dead rodent now sported a blade and an arrow head.

'You dare to threaten the King's envoy?' yelled Lord Grey.

'If my intention was to cause injury, that arrow would not be sprouting whiskers from that rat,' said the Prior with an even tone.

'Let this be your last warning, Prior. We have come prepared, will rip your doors apart to gain entry if need be, then demolish your bridge to keep you out. Now open the gate.'

'You would demolish my bridge?'

'You heard correctly.'

'Then if you insist.' The Prior nodded graciously.

'If he insists?' Gerald frowned heavily. 'Is that all the resistance you plan to offer?'

The Prior's gaze remained squarely on Lord Henry Grey, and in a low voice he said, 'If anyone is to damage my bridge, it will be me.' He lifted another gloved hand.

The screech and rattle of chains sounded from the gatehouse. Cogs turned, men yelled orders. The portcullis began to rise, inch by slow inch.

It seemed Harry comprehended the Prior's intention. 'The man makes pure Irish sense. You cannot threaten a man's bridge. 'Tis wrong.'

The Prior turned to the new voice and looked over Harry, head to toe. 'And your name again?'

'Harry, my lord.'

'But they call you something else, no?'

'Harry, my lord.'

'Harry or Harry,' the Prior said with his own grin, turning his attention back to the men outside the castle walls. 'Then Harry it is.'

'Your plan, my lord?' queried Gerald, a little worry to his voice.

James Keating swung his arms out wide, gesturing to the people of Dublin mutely looking on. 'Entertain the crowd.'

Lord Grey steered his horse toward the bridge, his only means of passage over the deep banks of the moat. Some of his men followed.

Gerald spied two familiar faces amongst the crowd below. 'Butlers!'

'Good. More unwelcome guests, ready for a warm welcome,' the Prior scoffed and again raised a hand. From the heights of the gatehouse another arrow, this one flaming, flew through the air and with a thud struck the bridge.

And then another.

And then another.

And three more.

Slick black oil, brushed on the upside of the beams, caught quickly. Fire spread. Flames stretched high. Some of the gathered townsfolk screamed.

'Have you lost your wits?' said Gerald. 'Setting fire inside the town walls?'

'Do you really want Grey inside?' asked the Prior patiently. 'Or Butlers from Ormond for that matter?'

Lord Grey and his men backed away from the building flames. Horses screamed their panic. One large ball of flame spewed from timber rails along the bridge. Black smoke spiralled high.

'You have not heard the last of me,' Lord Grey yelled to the air as he pulled on the reins and galloped away. His men and their weapons followed, moving like a quivering forest of leafless trees with badgers scurrying amongst the branches. The doubly-speared rat was trampled to the thickness of parchment.

Gerald laughed and laughed, and laughed some more. 'I would not have believed it if I had not seen with my own eyes.'

The bridge was fully alight. James Keating waited for a long, worrying moment, allowing the structure to burn further, then again raised a hand. Servants armed with wet blankets rushed from the gatehouse and slapped at the blackened bridge. Steam hissed. Pails of water followed. Smoke rolled and leapt toward Isolde's tower.

'Surely, my lord Earl, you did not doubt my resourcefulness?' asked the Prior.

'Seems I did,' Gerald announced, his eyes flashing across Dublin City. 'But your bridge?'

'It was I who ordered the damage. It is my bridge to do so.'

'And Grey did not remain to do battle,' said Jarlath, a query more than a statement. 'Why?'

Harry turned to Gerald and looked pointedly at his head. 'Fearful of the ostrich feathers would be my guess.'

The Prior threw back his head, roared his laughter. So too, did Tom and James.

Chapter Fifteen

Summer burned to autumn; leaves reddened. Then autumn iced to winter; birds sought cover. James married Eleanor Fitzgibbon; the Fitzgeralds celebrated. Eleanor received a new set of shimmering gowns to accommodate her emerging curves; Anne envied. One of the Butlers of Ormond suffered two broken legs in a brawl with men loyal to Gerald; County Kildare laughed. Tom's first child died in the cradle; Tom mourned. And the wrestle for control of Ireland remained a bubbling cauldron.

With Dublin Castle securely in the hands of Prior Keating, Lord Grey was forced to conduct his parliament sittings at Trim and Drogheda. Gerald held his in Naas, Connell and the Prior's Dublin. Each sitting enacted laws to void the other's.

In Maynooth's upstairs solar, little Margaret swatted at Gerald's leg impatiently, doing her best to interrupt business.

'Come here to Grandmamma,' called Joan, her arms outstretched.

Conceding defeat, the plump child clambered up into Joan's lap. Joan uttered a polite and almost hidden groan beneath the exertion of assisting the climb. The child sported folds of flesh on her neck and wrists.

'I must speak to the cook of locking lids on the cake

jars.'

'Speak to her mother,' Gerald suggested with a smile, reclining lazily into his high-backed chair.

'Alice is confined to her bed. She cannot be blamed.'

'She will soon give birth to my son, and then Margaret will once again be given what she demands.' Gerald picked at a piece of spiced currant cake.

'Papa,' whined Margaret demanding her own share. She was not denied.

Dark crumbs fell to Joan's lap. 'Do you yourself not comprehend the benefit of the word *no*?'

Amusement flickered across her son's face as he looked to his male companions, Jarlath, Manus and Roland. He licked at his fingers.

Joan refused to indulge her son's monumental if not bizarre pride. If Thomas was still alive, she lamented, and not for the first time, objections and chastisement would be voiced in liberal quantities, and none too composed. Oh, she knew Gerald's methods as Justiciar and head of the Fitzgerald family were as like his father's as a rabbit is like a bundle of straw, and that such disparities should not be judged in the negative. But she worried. Nothing seemed certain, nothing ever settled. Everything was constantly in turmoil, shifting restlessly like steam keen to escape a boiler. This trouble, this quandary would not exist if Thomas still lived, and there seemed no reprieve from concern. She had buried one child, a husband, one grandchild, and now watched as the English schemed and plotted to wrench Ireland from her family's grasp. She felt as weight-burdened as her lap.

Joan loved all her children equally, yet there existed a

206

heightened intensity in her bond with Gerald. Being her first born perhaps made certain the inexplicable distinction. Or perhaps it was her sympathy to Gerald's plight whilst growing up in his father's mighty shadow. Perhaps it was simply his cheekiness. Perhaps all three.

She looked to Jarlath, a man she loved like a true son. For weeks now Jarlath carried an ill mood, entrenched in his stubbornness, refusing to forgive Ainnir for her minor deceit. His wife-with-child had been sent home with few fond words, and he had not replied to her letters. To Joan's mind, the only sin committed by Ainnir was a conspiracy to encourage love. Did Jarlath truly forget his own young love so quickly, those years ago when a union with Ainnir seemed impossible? Oh, how Joan remembered well, witnessing the pain that denied-love inflicted. And all these weeks, it did not help that Gerald mentioned Ainnir's infraction at every opportunity. Mulish men, every one of them.

Eleanor strolled through the open door, her chin tilted high, her footfall light. The gown of turquoise and silver suited her well. Her red hair glistened as it swung with each stride. Joan gave a rueful smile, one that none witnessed. Her eldest daughter fought her own internal struggle; that of a girl blossoming into a woman. No longer did Eleanor's giggles and jumps and bumps echo along Maynooth's corridors. No longer did the girl hang upside down from branches of the yew and beech. No longer did she join with the cook's thin grandson in fierce sword battles in the kitchen garden, wielding harmless branches from the poplar tree. No longer did she hide hens in guests' bedrooms, or lame birds in bread baskets.

A sliver of Eleanor's eternal gaiety was lost with the

death of Maurice, then more with the passing of Thomas. But time was the Lord's healer, and now and again, with the coming maturity altering her daughter, those ever-alert eyes widened in undisguisable delight. Joan trusted more would return. She prayed to the Blessed Virgin Mother that Eleanor never lose that enchanted look of pure bliss. Life intermittently deserved a piece of unspoilt fancy.

Eleanor nodded to those present before demurely sitting beside Joan and Margaret, and received returned greetings and a brilliant crumb-filled smile from Margaret.

'Continue,' Gerald ordered the elderly scribe.

News of Lord Grey's latest parliament had arrived earlier in the day. The family and men had gathered to hear of Grey's most recent edicts.

The strings of the scribe's dark cap swayed at his neck as he lowered eyes to the letter held in a set of gnarled hands. 'The Earl now pretending himself to be Justiciar of Ireland, is commanded to cease from imposing any subsidy, tax or tallage upon the King's subjects. Demands made by the previous parliaments, held by the pretender are null and void, and of no effect or force in law, and no citizen is to be debited.'

'Our Lord Grey includes such an order in all his sittings,' said Gerald. 'Does he not know he wastes his breath? Perhaps he grows fickle with age. Continue.'

'Judges of the King's Courts of Records, having them beholden to enforce rules made by the pretender, shall cancel such rules and ordinances, otherwise be removed from their position and suffer one-thousand pounds to the King.'

'Does that present a problem?' Gerald asked his companions.

'To not expect swings of loyalty in such times would be unwise,' answered Jarlath.

'Then make them steadfast in their loyalty,' Gerald said, as if such an accomplishment was as easy as pulling on one's boots. 'Continue.'

The scribe obeyed. 'Elections of the Justiciar are not to be left solely to a select seven. Instead, the Justiciar will be elected by the whole King's Council, along with the Archbishops of Armagh and Dublin, the Bishops of Meath and Kildare, the Mayors of Dublin and Drogheda and all the spiritual and temporal lords of parliament of the four counties.'

Gerald shifted uneasily in his seat.

So too did Joan, with great difficulty, all for a different reason. Eleanor blinked, and remained mute, ignoring Margaret's whining pleas to play.

'They are our enemies,' Gerald announced unnecessarily, 'every one of them.' He flicked a hand through the air and raised his spirits. 'We simply ignore the ruling. Continue.'

'The Great Seal in the possession of Sir Roland Eustace is annulled, and the Master of all the King's mints in Ireland is ordered to make a new Great Seal, much like the annulled version, with the difference of a rose in every part.'

'Again,' announced Gerald, 'we simply ignore the hasty eel-brained Lord Grey.'

Harry appeared at the door. 'You have a visitor.'

'A visitor?'

'Lord eel-brained Henry the badger Grey.'

Gerald stood from his seat. 'Lord Grey? Here?'

'Do I speak in a foreign tongue to you?'

Jarlath looked out the window. 'I see no men-at-arms.'

'The badger is accompanied by two men on horses, and no more,' explained Harry. 'He's either courageous or lost.'

Joan held a breath, waiting for her son to decide his move. With mouth pursed, his eyes darted to every point in the room. Gerald frowned, as if deep in thought. She waited some more. It seemed so too, did all in the room. The men trained their eyes expectantly on her son; Jarlath as still as a marble statue, Manus, rocking on his heels, Roland, a dour look marring his usual inertness. Joan noticed an enchanted look of mischief threaten to break fully upon Eleanor's face, and just as quickly, the young woman adopted a sombre, quelling air.

'Seems our hasty eel-brained enemy wishes to discuss terms, dear brother.'

Joan's chortle joined the men's, hers joyous and placating. She should have known. Eleanor's adventurous cheek had not vanished.

Then she turned back to Gerald and steeled for what was to come.

The solar emptied, leaving the two men alone. An ashen light fell through the high arched windows in long luminous bars. Rows of candles provided a cheer of yellowed white. Logs in the hearth flickered orange. A worn log split and tumbled, the flying sparks golden. In the corner, an aging black hound stood, stretched, then gently shook his coat before performing circles on his shaky legs and returning to his slumber.

From across the chessboard, Gerald thought Lord Henry Grey appeared a slowing man, not the formidable foe his reputation proffered. A barrel-chested man, his wispy hair reflected his name aptly. A raised mark on his cheekbone, sat above a scar that raged red to the top of his ear. Hair sprouted like icicles from his ears and nostrils. The whites of his eyes glowed pink, much like his bulbous nose.

Grey moved his bishop, captured a pawn then nestled back into his chair. The semblance of an ominous smile seemed to alter the man's lines on his forehead. 'As much as I am enjoying Ireland's hospitality, I find your rudeness at the inauguration of my parliament to be less than gracious, Kildare.'

Gerald moved a knight. 'You expected less?'

'I hoped for more.' Lord Grey scratched at his chin. 'And now, now this place tires me.'

'Tires you?'

'I would prefer to be home in bed with my third wife, or riding the steeped banks of the River Trent.'

'I am yet on my first wife.'

'Give it time, lad. They fatten quickly and lose their youth. A change due to the death of one's wife is not always a bad circumstance.'

'Would you say that in the hearing of your wife?'

Lord Grey gave one determined shake of his head and looked down to his codpiece. 'I value my ballocks too much.'

Gerald thought this man before him an intriguing enigma. Buttery with humour. Little eye contact. Cryptically withholding any sign of tension, discomfort, anticipation or intention.

'You come to Ireland to bid the King's wishes, yet you fought against His Grace at St. Albans.'

211

'I also fought against him at Towton,' Grey quickly reminded Gerald. 'You see, it is important a man recognises from where his wealth is likely to appear.'

'But you were captured at Towton.'

'And released.'

'For a promise?'

'Indeed.'

'A promise to alter your loyalties?'

Lord Grey's hand hovered above the chess pieces. His jewelled fingers splayed wide as if the man was indecisive, each finger short and chubby like pork sausages, nails bitten down to the quick. Two sausages, with the help of a thumb, moved a pawn to cut off Gerald's attack on Grey's queen. 'Some have unwisely charged me with possessing dissolute habits. But I did what a man must do. All great men do, do they not?'

The black hound gave a sound, something between a yawn and a growl. The dog shifted and his paw tapped a repetitive rhythm on the floor as he scratched at fleas.

'So, you are here to alter loyalties?'

'I am loyal to the Yorkist King Edward,' Lord Grey announced haughtily, then lowered his tone. 'But as I said, I wish to be home. I wish to be privy to the King's self-pitying angst following the execution of his brother, and watch his conceited queen rage over His Grace's dearly-loved whore, Jane Shore. Hah!'

'Jane Shore? She is beautiful?'

'Enough to visit the King's bed often and keep his attention. But I am here to discuss terms not nipples and earlobes.'

'Terms?'

'Are you deaf, lad?'

Gerald grinned and looked down to the board. 'No, not deaf.'

'I offer peace.'

'Should I piss on your peace?'

'In truth, I don't give a vixen's arse who controls this land. I am here begrudgingly albeit by the King's order, and with no will to do battle until one of us is dead and the other crowned Ari, or whatever damned word your people use to speak of Kings in this land.'

'It is Ari.' Gerald moved his queen, taking Lord Grey's bishop. 'So your proposal?'

'King Edward has expectations. I have a reputation.'

'You want your reputation intact, and all to assume expectations have been achieved.'

'A bright lad. As bright as your father.'

'You speak as though you knew my father?'

'That should not surprise you.' Those pork sausages snatched a piece of spiced currant cake from the low table next to Lord Grey's chair. 'Six years ago. I remember you too.'

'Me?'

'Chasing buxom breasts you were, at Fair Green outside Dublin's walls.'

'We are lurking perilously close to the subject of nipples.'

'Forgive me. I am simply taken aback that you do not recall my time here.'

Gerald served Lord Grey a quizzical look, despite his memory being as clear as a running creek. An image of an arrogant man, one with a contemptuous frown and less cheer than a dead cat, pushing his way through the merrymaking crowds, ran through his mind. It may have been six years ago, but the man seemed to have aged sixteen. And Thomas, his father, had disliked the man, distrusted him, thought him a vulgar viper feeding on diseased rats. Gerald's opinion, so far, married that of his father.

'Best you rectify that lapse in your recall, lad. A great leader forgets naught.'

'I agree, my lord,' Gerald permitted. 'And what was my father like?'

Lord Grey's regard flicked to Gerald with what the 8th Earl suspected was surprise. Grey did not answer immediately, instead, took his time making momentous work of another mouthful of cake. His spindly eyebrows arched revealing a small scar at the peak of one, a light-coloured scar so small it disappeared as the eyebrows fell back into place.

'You do not know of your father's merits?'

'I know of them. I am interested to know another man's opinion.'

Gerald spotted that small scar again. Lord Grey's lips quirked and puckered and stretched, his tongue running over his yellowed teeth cleansing his mouth of all remaining crumbs.

'Your father,' he said pointedly, 'was a man who knew himself. Never swayed from his beliefs.'

'My father held no dissolute habits?'

'He for certes was not bold like his son,' said Lord Grey with an unconvincing laugh. 'If you want my advice, Kildare—'

'And if I don't?'

'I shall still give it,' Lord Grey returned equably. 'Your father took good counsel and refused weak counsel. But first and foremost, he knew his own counsel to be the wisest. Be rid of your naysayers, Kildare, your advisors who do not see as you do. I saw in their faces they did not condone my request for this private talk. Trust no one. Trust only your instincts.'

Gerald gestured to the board, prompting Lord Grey to continue the game. 'Like my father, I will decide whether yours is good or weak.'

'Like I said, trust your instincts.' After silent study, Grey looked up from the board. 'We have a stalemate. This game has come to an end.'

'Then no loser.'

'Nor a winner.'

'So where from here, my Lord Grey?'

'Do you like the sea? I suggest an audience with the King. If you follow my lead at his court we'll both appear loyal champions and both be rewarded admirably. I will have returned to my home and the fun I am missing, and Ireland will be returned to you. You can once again play Ari.'

The men regarded each other for a long quiet moment, like wolves over a freshly-killed stag. There was something alluring about Lord Grey. Perhaps the man's audacity, his impudence, his narcissistic boldness; traits both men shared. For certes it was not those hairs hanging from the wide nostrils that stirred with every inward breath. Did Gerald applaud their likeness of character? Was it their commonality that fed his curiosity? Possibly, but it made naught difference, for Gerald could play at the same game, and play it better.

Gerald knew this man held little deference for the Earl of Kildare. Like everyone else, this Englishman seemed to believe him to be a distracted imbecile. They all did and it stung no less than a sharp blade between the toes. Gerald had not failed to notice the concern on his mother's face when Lord Henry requested a private audience. His father had believed him reckless. Jarlath thought him unscholarly and lacking in language. Even Harry, his hired man; take note of Jarlath's acumen, he had said. Did none have faith in his aptitude, his shrewdness, his sense, his wit?

He would prove them all wrong. He would wager his place in Heaven they would all come to see the wisdom of the new power in Ireland. And with that pledge, he remembered a long ago correction to his mispronunciation of Wyrd biþ ful āræd—fate remains wholly inexorable! Was there really such a thing as fate? Could paths be altered? Of course! Nothing was impossible. Fate remains wholly inexorable? Not in Gerald's world!

Gerald broke the silence. 'And what did your last parliament sitting decide for the Prior? Your arrival this day interrupted the telling of the news.'

'The blusterer, James Keating?'

Gerald nodded.

Lord Grey spat a currant seed onto the floor. 'Removal of the man. Appoint a keeper for Kilmainham pending a replacement nominated by the Grand Master of Rhodes. And, of course, have the Prior pay for a new bridge for Dublin Castle.'

Gerald made no reply. The quiet returned.

'So how did you go?' It was Lord Grey's turn to break the hush.

'Go?' queried Gerald.

'Chasing buxom breasts at Fair Green.'

'Exceeded expectations,' he replied with a smile.

'One more bit of advice,' said Lord Grey, his sausage fingers reaching for a chess piece.

Gerald predicted what was coming. He knew all along the game not to be a stalemate. He knew only one more move need be made and he would have been the one to declare checkmate. But he allowed Lord Grey to assume the son of Thomas Fitzgerald an underling Lord, inexperienced, too trusting.

Lord Grey grabbed at Gerald's knight, moved it to the centre of the board, trapping the Englishman's king.

'No stalemate,' Gerald allowed pragmatically.

'Trust no one.' Grey's nostril hairs danced.

Gerald relaxed back into his chair, and turned his hands, palms up. 'So tell me of our audience with the King.'

Chapter Sixteen

News of the death of Arland Ussher reached Maynooth. Alice gave birth to another daughter. And Lord Grey departed Ireland. The King granted a patent of safe conduct for Gerald and his men to travel to England.

In Maynooth Castle's stone courtyard, the clank and jangle of reins and bridles sounded the impending departure.

'Gerald.' Eleanor followed on the heels of her brother. The hem of her gown concertinaed as she skipped down each step.

'Sister?'

'I hear my betrothed is to travel with you to England.'

'I have summoned Conn, so indeed. He is to meet with me at the ports of Dublin,' Gerald replied pulling on his gloves.

'Would you see that he receives this letter, and, that he reads it? It is written in French, English and Gael, so I trust language cannot be called upon as an excuse to ignore me.'

'An excuse?'

'To not reply. Conn never replies.'

Gerald took the sealed missive and raised the pages to his nose. Scents invaded the air. Floral, perhaps roses, yellow roses, and citrus. 'Hell fire, you play unfair, young woman.'

'And play I will until that man takes me as his wife, or at least until he reads one of my letters.'

Gerald arched a conspiratorial eyebrow. 'The Prince of Ulster has not seen you for a time, has he?'

'Not for eighteen months. I could tell you the number of hours there are in eighteen months if you wish.'

Gerald laughed out loud. Eleanor was growing into a beautiful woman. Conn Mor would be impressed, very impressed. And it pleased Gerald that his sister would find pleasure in this match. He loved Eleanor. 'Then I look forward to the day he does, for he will notice you, sister. I can promise you that.'

Joan and Jarlath followed quickly down the steps.

'You will shadow my son, Jarlath, on this journey?' she said quietly, with a hand on his arm.

He squeezed her hand. 'I will try.'

Jarlath climbed into the saddle. His horse danced sideways.

'Keep safe, son,' Joan called to Gerald.

Gerald offered his mother a bountiful grin. He loved his mother too. 'And keep Ireland, Mama?'

London - Westminster

The barge carried the men along the Thames River through the muck of the stench-ridden waters about London's port to the landings at Westminster Palace. It may have been a comparatively eventless journey, but Manus's face still possessed the strange green hue he acquired during the crossing of the Irish Sea, and a few days of sleep and a change of clothing did little to return a healthy appearance.

'A flagon or seven before our next sea voyage, nephew,'

suggested Roland. 'I fear unconsciousness may be your only pre-emptive tonic.'

'Sea water is the devil's making, Uncle. It and I will never be affable acquaintances.'

Ahead, the royal barge was moored at the largest of the landings. Curtains of purple silk and green brocade created a shelter to one end of the barge. Gold cords and tassels dangled from its supports, a colour palette not unlike the garb adorning Gerald; purple tunic over a dark green shirt, with gold trim at the wrists.

Their barge pulled up alongside and men moved quickly with grappling hooks, securing ropes.

A plump young servant bowed low to Gerald and his companions. 'This way, my lords. His Grace has asked that I show you to his rooms.'

With no headwear this day, Gerald whispered to Jarlath, 'The King wishes to see me immediately. An encouraging portent.'

'You seem confident. I wish I shared your view.'

'You should. You see, fate does not remain wholly inexorable, Jarlath.'

The fast-stepped servant with his wide gait—a performance which shunned the customary heel-toe strike and instead enacted a comical toe-only dance—led the men through a maze of crowded corridors and rooms. Boots clopped noisily on stone floors. Pointed archways led their trek from one room to another, and then another. Candelabras held dozens of candles, perhaps hundreds. Lengths of red velvet, draping from the height of the ceilings, created smaller recessed rooms. Baubles decorated earlobes, and necks glistened and shimmered. Beards and moustaches failed to mask mouths ripe with intrigue. Rush lights dotted the narrower corridors like quiet sentinels. Intricately carved pillars framed white statues of mournful Saints with lifeless eyes. People loitered. People whispered. People studied the Irishmen with undisguised boldness. This was a place where influence was peddled, alliances and promises made for ill or for good, and it mattered more who talked to whom than what was spoken.

'I have heard much of this place,' announced Harry, with no concern for the curious ears close by. 'Double dealing and plotting, everywhere to be found. By day it is sleight of hand and sleight of tongue. In the evening, 'tis in the indulgence of rich foods and mind-wilting wines. And then at night, in the dark shadows, they celebrate wanton debauchery.'

'I think your schedule of wickedness is a little askew,' said Manus. 'Did you not see that dalliance in the half-curtained window seat we just passed? 'Twas a fair leg I saw, held unnaturally high, and a white-as-white merkin hiding the lass's … imperfections. I'm beginning to feel better.'

The men were led up a set of wide stairs lit by the many windows. Men in shining armour stood straight and focused, guarding the way at equal intervals.

On the second floor, a sergeant in mail coat made noisy work of opening a door. The chamber they entered was all but flooded in darkness. A solitary side window to the far end of the room allowed a miniscule of sunlight to illuminate one wall and no more. Two candles aided little. The walls were drab, a grey stone. An occupied chair sat at the blurred line where the candlelight was lost to darkness. Men in fine clothing mingled. Serious and sombre frowns hinted at a staid conversation.

'Your Grace.' The toe-dancing servant announced their intrusion.

'Fitzgerald!' said His Grace standing from the chair, his green coat opening with the movement.

Gerald stepped forward.

'Your Grace,' both Gerald and Jarlath said in unison, their heads bowed.

Gerald stole a sideways glance at his cousin, startled at Jarlath's move to offer greeting to the King. Jarlath's face wore a hint of a smirk. Gerald looked back to His Grace.

It was not the King. It was the King's brother, Prince Richard, Duke of Gloucester. The Prince moved into the relative darkness, passed Gerald, and greeted Jarlath. He was a man of thirty-plus years, dark hair, clean-shaven, formidable in a comfortable fashion with a domineering yet genial poise.

'It has been …'

'Eight years, Your Grace,' Jarlath provided.

'Yes, eight years. The battle at Barnet was it not?'

'Indeed, Your Grace.'

Prince Richard flicked a hand gesture to the air. Shuffling sounded and within moments rush lights lit the entire room. A canopied bed appeared, so too, a side table and a posse of servants.

'And you, yes you,' the Prince said to Manus. 'The Baron's nephew. No?'

'Your Grace.' Manus offered a deep bow.

'A fine win that day. And you must be the Earl of Kildare.'

'Your Grace,' said Gerald, again offering his obeisance.

'I must tell you, I recently acquired three goshawks,

imported from Ireland. Impressive birds.'

'Impressive, Your Grace, yes,' replied Gerald. 'And now rare in Ireland.'

'How rare?'

'Extremely.'

'I am disappointed, for I would have been pleased to add more such excellent creatures to my collection.'

'It seems our merchants have taken advantage of England's demand for these birds. The falcon and the tercel too. Our skies are now void of preying flight.'

The Prince quirked an eyebrow. 'Try export duty and taxes. Solves a multitude of problems and more. But you have not been summoned to my rooms to speak of birds. I heard of your planned presence here. You have come to speak to my brother the King?'

'We have, Your Grace,' answered Gerald, a little intrigued at the interest shown by the Prince.

'Pleading for?'

'For Ireland, my lord.'

'For Ireland?'

'The King recently sent an envoy to see to—'

'Yes. Yes. Lord Grey of Codnor.'

'Yes, Your Grace. Lord Grey was sent to replace me as Justiciar of Ireland, and I am now here to persuade … to present to His Grace the King, reasons why the running of Ireland is better left in my hands.'

'Lord Codnor is one of many who finds it difficult to adhere to promised loyalties.' The Prince snapped his fingers. Servants hastened from the chamber. 'My brother is in a mood. Edward wallows morbidly over the execution of our brother, the Duke of Clarence. And so he should.' The Prince uttered the last words with syrupy venom. 'You may need a tithe of assistance in your persuasion, or was it presentation?' The Prince smiled. 'I do not forget kindnesses. Your father was ever loyal to my family, my dear Earl, and two of your men here I do recognise as my comrades in battle. And of course, my mother taught me the advantages of repaying a benevolence.' Prince Richard moved toward the door. 'And I also enjoy salting the fresh wounds of my brother. Let me accompany you to the hall.'

'Your Grace,' Gerald bowed low, lower than before, extremely pleased at the powerful ally this unexpected deviation brought.

As rats are drawn to grain, the great hall of Westminster brimmed with sycophants; the hopeful wheeling and dealing for the King's favour. The crowds parted at the approach of Prince Richard, and the Irish contingent followed in his wake. Men bowed their heads, women curtsied. The murmur of high-pitched voices to the end of the hall illustrated the fervour in which audience members presented their asks to the King, and a fractious grunt suggested the last ask was denied. The arched timber frames of the hall's roof marched innumerably from one end of the room to the other. The vision reminded Gerald of the hull of a mighty ship, an enormous upside-down ship. Sunlight fell from the high windows and painted squares of white across the heads of the crowd. As the men progressed forward the small image of the King atop the steps grew in size, the window behind him dousing him in a sparkling halo.

King Edward sat in a resplendent red-cushioned chair.

For a man only a little older than Prince Richard, he seemed fifteen years his elder. His face bloomed red like his cushion, his cheeks were swollen, his belly distended, his look unfocused, disinterested, irritated. That did not dissuade Gerald. He had mulled over his scheme for the past week. None but he and Conn Mor knew of the surprise to come, and he trusted the King's interest would be piqued, and very soon.

'And so my brother graces my presence,' announced the King, his voice without welcome. 'What cause brings me the pleasure?'

'Is an official occasion needed to publically display our brotherly love, Your Grace?'

'Of late it seems so.'

Richard nodded to his brother, a minute movement that offered little respect. He gestured with an open hand. 'The Justiciar of Ireland seeks an audience.'

Those in line for the King's ear were forced back. Their turn would have to wait.

'And you are here to ensure he receives my ear, brother?'

'Always perceptive.'

Lord Henry Grey stepped forward from the side walls. ''Tis indeed the Earl of Kildare, Your Grace.'

Gerald nodded a curt greeting to Grey, a brusqueness which hinted a prologue to the events about to unfold. Grey's sudden unease suggested the message was received, and remembering their game of chess at Maynooth, Gerald returned his focus to the King, moved one pace forward like a pawn. There would be no pretence of a stalemate, not this day. 'Your Grace.'

225

'Ah. Our kind and good Lord of Kildare. No man comes to my court without a desperate wish, and your journey was indeed overly long. What is yours, then?'

'Your Grace, it is my understanding Lord Henry Grey arranged for this audience. Although it gifts me with no greater honour to be in your presence, I come at his bidding.'

Lord Grey threw his chin to the air and hands to his hips, and the King's interest seemed to awaken at the sensed tension.

'Lord Codnor's bidding?' the King laughed.

Prince Richard climbed the steps and whispered words to his brother.

The King sniffed irreverently. 'And so he did, I am now reminded. Who comes with you, Lord Kildare?'

'The Baron of Portlester and the Prior of Kilmainham, and—'

Prince Richard whispered more words.

'I am just now reminded of the loyalty of your men who did fight alongside my armies at Barnet.'

'Indeed, Your Grace. And we remain equally loyal to this day and the days that follow.'

A woman glided into a high-backed chair not far from the King's. Her beauty beyond words, Gerald suspected the lady to be the Queen consort, Elizabeth Woodville. Why would a man have need of a mistress, Gerald wondered, when able to bed such a bright jewel, both day and night? A white ball of fluff in the form of a cat, sat on the Queen's lap, its pugnacious eyes glared then blinked heavily at every stroke to its head. The Queen wore a black gown with gold brocaded collar and cuffs, her hair hidden beneath a tubular cap of the same brocade, and a veil as sheer as air fell to her bosom. From beneath overly plucked eyebrows, the queen sent a delicate smile winging its way to Lord Grey, then turned to Gerald with a look no less truculent than the ball of fluff at her lap.

Gerald knew Elizabeth Woodville held no love for the Fitzgeralds. The woman was partly responsible for the beheading of his father's cousin, and also tried to see his father kneel within the same axeman's reach. And that's why the King does what he does, Gerald advised himself. Beauty can often contain ugliness.

'It is to the political leadership of Ireland that we wish to speak, Your Grace,' explained Grey, his words full of humour, a suggestion the subject be of little importance and little bother.

'It was to Ireland I sent you, Lord Grey, to repair the financial state of my lands.'

'It is true, Your Grace, and—'

'And you returned to inform me I need to spend coin to repair a bridge.' The King turned an eye to the Prior.

The Prior smiled boldly.

Lord Grey inclined his head respectfully and his fat fingers gripped tightly to the belt at his tunic, but he gave no retort.

'And so, Kildare, why should I trust Ireland to your hands?' asked the King.

Gerald knew Lord Grey expected the King would hear praises of his diligence during his time in Ireland, his keen eye and fair hand, and his urging to ensure Gerald mend his obverted ways. And in return Lord Grey would sing of his trust in the conviction and reliance of the new ways of the Earl of

Kildare – just as they had planned.

But he would not. Gerald would not have it that way. He would show the world he was not a man to be toyed with.

'As already stated, Your Grace, the Fitzgeralds have ever been loyal to the Yorkist cause and not once betrayed your trust nor given succour or support to your enemies. Unlike some.' The laughter behind Gerald intimated many followed his not-so-subtle poke at Lord Grey. 'And it is only we, the Fitzgeralds, who seem able to keep peace with the Gaels, Your Grace.'

'I hear reports of battles not peace,' complained the King.

'Ah, but there seems more battles on your Irish shores when Your Grace sends envoys to alter my duties.' Gerald knew himself to be impudent with that last, and his eyes audaciously did not waver from the King's, and then just as lightly he added, 'No land can be free of squabbles, Your Grace, not even the most blessed of marriages.'

The King laughed loudly at that. The Queen did not react, but the stroking and the cat's blinking ceased.

'May I introduce to Your Grace's presence, Conn Mor O'Neill the Prince of Ulster?'

Conn Mor stepped forward and lowered his head, kept it hanging for an inordinate time.

'The Prince is the son of Henry O'Neill, the native King of Ulster, and is also betrothed to my sister, the Lady Eleanor.'

'Good for you that my laws no longer forbid the marriage of Gaels to nobles. But tell me, Kildare, is this betrothal for a purpose?'

'Are not all, Your Grace?'

'Not all.'

'Not all?' Gerald knew the King's marriage was made for a selfish want, not a selfless pact.

'No. And perhaps that is why some suffer the squabbles you speak of.'

'Your Grace,' Gerald allowed, not permitting his eyes to wander to the Queen.

'Continue.'

'The Gaels of the north are now keen to abide by your laws.'

'Keen?'

'Yes, keen.'

'How keen?' the King shifted in his large chair.

At that small and ostensibly trivial movement Gerald knew his plan was all but complete. It seemed Prince Richard suspected the same, for the Duke of Gloucester sharpened the tilt of his chin.

'Very, Your Grace. The O'Neills of Ulster are prepared to submit to Your Grace.'

Murmurings moved like a tidal wave through the hall. Gerald caught the surprise in Jarlath's eye, and felt cleverly pleased knowing these men would revise their opinions of him by the end of the day, for submission by the strongest of the Gaels heralded the beginnings of a move to allow the King of England to also claim to be King of Ireland, and therefore ensure the Fitzgeralds of the King's favour and gratitude.

'Submit?'

'Perhaps the Earl of Tyrone be an apt title awaiting my future brother-in-law.'

'This is true?' The King looked to Conn Mor.

'Sincerely true, Your Grace.'

'Welcome to my court, O'Neill.'

'Your Grace,' said Conn Mor, again lowering his head.

'And you could not encourage this accord, Lord Grey?' The King turned to the Lord of Codnor.

Lord Grey held his hands open. 'Your Grace, it has—'

'Has been achieved by Kildare, and not you.'

'Your Grace,' Lord Grey allowed sheepishly.

But Gerald made no room for pause. 'May I also report to Your Grace, that many of your subjects are now lacking coin, debts not paid at the behest of Lord Grey. Much hospitality was shown him in his short yet pleasurable stay, but none was intended to be free of charge.'

'Your prevarication is unwelcome at the King's Court,' warned Grey.

Gerald held no notion to the meaning of prevarication but wasn't about to confess. 'So too, your acrimony,' he parried, using another word no less alien to his vocabulary, but hoped it fitted well.

'Nor is the celerity of your tongue.'

Gerald was lost, and it seemed so too was the King.

'Will you men speak your King's English?' ordered the King in a lazy fashion as he fiddled with buttons at his wrist. The room obediently erupted with laughter at the King's comedic attempt. It seemed to gather speed and travelled the length of the hall.

'Of course, Your Grace,' allowed Gerald. 'Forgive my insolent attitude, or should I say aptitude?' Those words, he knew.

The King smiled.

'Your Grace, if I may, it will not impede the eagerness of relations between your faithful people and the Gaels, if our Lordly King was to visit the shores of his Ireland. Is it a possibility, Your Grace? Castle Maynooth would indeed be honoured.'

'No,' replied the King on an upward note as if he intended to give the matter some thought. 'Not in the interim in any event.' He paused then grinned. 'You are mettlesome, Kildare. Note I say mettlesome, not meddlesome.'

'Better than muddlesome.'

Laughter erupted again. Prince Richard whispered further words to the King then pitched a droll smirk to Gerald.

'It would please us greatly,' said the King, 'if you would gift me with a dozen tercels of good breeding. You will arrange that on your return home?'

'I shall ensure the impossible is possible, Your Grace,' Gerald replied, bowing his head to the Prince more so than to the King in a gesture of humble defeat.

Conversations continued and new ones were created, more being relevant to the possibility of the submission of the Gaels, but nonetheless all ran to the favour of Gerald. The King questioned the men of their lodgings and Gerald explained the Prior had arranged billeting in London, compliments of his Brothers on these shores. They spoke of the Guild of Saint George, Gerald's father, Irish trade and merchants, and the King's wish that Ireland be returned to Gerald's trustworthy and capable hands.

When dismissed, Gerald bowed graciously to King Edward and then Prince Richard. Then with even more diplomacy, Gerald offered the Queen a bow which lasted overly long. As he turned to leave, he threw to Lord Grey, 'Checkmate, my lord.'

Some of the men settled into The Fighting Cocks Inn to enjoy a short celebration before heading back to their lodgings. One hour became two. Two became three. Three became many more. The men were drunk. Their tongues and limbs flopped and flapped like banners in an unforgiving wind.

Gerald rubbed his brow then looked to the lap of a snoring and dribbling Harry sitting beside him, his friend obliterated by far too much ale. 'The man's pissed himself.'

To the other side of the trestle, Jarlath's eyes were heavy, his shoulders slouched, and he spotted the upturned mug at the edge of the table. 'He's not pissed himself. He's spilt his drink.'

Gerald blinked a slow, inebriated blink. 'Wasteful.'

'Unlike this journey, cousin.' Jarlath smiled lazily then lent forward. 'Would it be condescending if I suggest your father would be overly proud of what you did today?'

'Yes it would,' Gerald said with all seriousness, then lightened his tone. 'But you may.'

'Then, he would be proud.'

'Would he?'

A sliver of sarcasm tainted that simple question, but Jarlath also detected a sad hopefulness, and perhaps a faraway regret. It surprised him, for much of Gerald's celebrations to this point bubbled at an excessively raucous level, full of buoyant conceit and ill-sung tunes.

Jarlath squinted heavily, cautious and unhurried in the

planning of his reply. 'Thomas was not easily persuaded to another man's way.' Ale sloshed from his cup with his first words. He wiped at his wet sleeve. 'Donal and I were content to obey without question. But you, you were ever one to force the issue. You act from instinct not from thought. It was not your father's way.'

'And that made my way wrong?'

'In your father's mind? Perhaps. But if so, this day you proved him wrong.'

The men shared a moment of silence, before Gerald's face turned dark.

'I miss Donal. Miss him very much.'

'And so do I.' Jarlath tapped a pointed finger on the table then looked around studying the contents of the inn.

Women with low cut gowns settled their curvy bottoms on the knees of rowdy and amorous patrons. Smoke from the hearth created a slow-moving cloud at one end of the room. Serving wenches wandered with heavy jugs, keen to lighten their load. Above, two cart wheels, each laden with spluttering candles, hung from the ceiling by thick chain. The candles were tallow wax, the stench offensive.

'But you are not to blame for his death,' said Jarlath.

'Who says I blame myself?'

'Your face. Your hatred for the Wicklow Gaels. Your caustic—'

Gerald shrugged. 'Am I not to blame?'

'No.'

'Donal took that arrow for me.'

'And that does not lay culpability at your feet.'

'Then nor are you to blame.' Gerald smiled his parry.

'Your absence did not bring his death.'

Jarlath drank wantonly from his mug. 'Seems our opinions will always hold opposing views, for we both know things would be different had I not left for England.'

Gerald tossed a hand gesture to the Heavens. 'Only the Lord knows that. Maybe it's time we both rid ourselves of self-blame.'

'Maybe you are right. You know, your mother told me the truth of Maurice's death?'

'And she should not have.'

'But glad I am that she did.' Jarlath frowned, and after a hiccup that ventured with a loud burp. 'Why did you allow Thomas to believe you at fault?'

'In truth I was, partially. Maurice was my responsibility and the injury to my shoulder should not have stolen my focus. But I knew Tom and James were destined to ever wear a heavy regret. I thought it best they not also be burdened with my father's unforgiving nature.'

'A martyr?'

'Hah! None have ever accused me of being Saintly. Although Harry did once ask if I was an angel.'

'Then let me be the first. Saint Gerald. Saint Gerald the … the …'

'The capable,' Gerald finished.

'Saint Gerald the Capable,' Jarlath allowed. 'And tell me, Saint Gerald, will Conn truly submit to English rule?'

'One day, I suppose he will. If not Conn, then his children. They will be my kin.'

'Yet you told the King—'

'I told the King what was necessary to keep his favour,

'nothing more, nothing less.'

'And Conn's true thoughts?'

'He too, knows how to act upon the royal stage.'

'Like I said, your father would be proud.'

'Now it is my turn to ask a question.'

'Ask.'

'Why did you remain silent when my father arranged the betrothal of Ainnir and Donal? You loved her even then.'

Even with his mind foggy, at that question Jarlath's grip tightened on his mug. There were numerous retorts he could offer, and none would explain all. If he had not remained silent all those years ago, yes, much may have been altered; different routes taken, deaths avoided, love lost, love won. But his grip lightened just as quickly. The tonic of years brought the relinquish of regret.

'I suppose I loved Donal and Ainnir equally, and your father of course. I respected his wishes enough to remain mute.'

'Liar.'

Jarlath laughed. ''Tis true, partially,' he said, mimicking Gerald's earlier reply. 'But further to that, I did not know not how to make my own opinions or wants known.'

'Oh and how things have changed.'

'Well, I no longer flee to the safety of my yew tree.'

'Your yew tree?'

'A tale for another day. But to another point. Your plans for the O'Mores of Leix?'

Gerald absently flicked at his moustache then picked at a morsel of mutton wedged between two teeth. 'All in good time. I need to find plausible reason to bring them pain.'

'And the O'Byrne and the O'Toole?'

'We will raid,' he answered without pause.

Jarlath nodded slowly.

Gerald shifted unsteadily, lifted a leg and straddled the bench seat. 'I will not order you to accompany me on that march, Jarlath.'

'You cannot make that promise now.'

'I can and I do.'

'I must join you. I am a Fitzgerald and ever loyal.'

'That I do not doubt. But you are also like a brother, and your wife is daughter to the O'Byrne. So I repeat, I will not give that order.'

'We will see when the time comes.'

'Perhaps. But what of your wife?'

'What of Ainnir?'

'Good to see you remember her name.'

'What do you mean?'

'Have you made your peace?'

'You suggest I should forgive her, forgive her for allowing enemies to the Fitzgeralds into my home?'

Gerald shook his head. 'No, I do not say that at all. You know my hate for the O'Byrne and his sons. It burns almost as brightly as my hate for the O'Toole. But do you wish to live the remainder of your married life like Meg and Manus?'

'Like Meg and Manus?'

'No sex. An ignored cock.'

Jarlath spluttered on his drink. 'God keep me from such agony. No. I suppose I do not.'

'Wyrd bið ful āræd,' said Gerald with a grin. 'I believe there is such a thing as fate, but, we also have choices.'

'Your pronunciation has improved.'

'Seems much in me has improved.'

Jarlath had delayed contemplating ways to end the war between he and Ainnir, but now with Gerald's words, he began to wonder. His hot-headedness had seen them estranged for a period, and he missed her madly, missed Siobhan and Conor too. He would be home soon, perhaps in three or four days. Things could be mended. Yes, things should be mended. We have choices.

And it seemed other things were being mended and choices made, for this was the first occasion Gerald had spoken openly, calmly, so plainly.

'Are you offering a truce?'

Gerald swung his leg back over the bench seat. 'Jarlath, I am learning that many elements of one's mulish mettle need to vanish, and it is only ourselves who can allow such excesses to melt.'

'Very poetic.'

Gerald laughed. 'And somewhat true.'

'Yet some elements remain too intractable to melt?'

'Intractable? Me? Intractable is a little harsh. Try coyly stubborn.'

'Saint Gerald the Coyly Stubborn.' Jarlath spied two familiar faces heading his way; perhaps four, for he was seeing double. 'Oh, how I will suffer in the morning. I am drunk, Gerald. Drunk I tell you.'

Conn Mor and Manus slid onto the bench seat.

'Ah, my future brother-in-law,' Gerald slurred, no less at the mercy of a lip impediment than Jarlath, and for perhaps the fourth time waved Eleanor's scented letter before the Prince of Ulster, his wrist not so governed in its motion this occasion.

'How many messages of love has my sister sent you to date, Conn, or should I say Earl of Tyrone? Five, fifty or is the count closer to five-hundred?'

'Keep going and I'll slash you another hole in that hindmost place of yours, Fitzgerald.'

Gerald pounced, took Conn Mor into a headlock. Conn Mor found himself bent over the table and grinned at his assailant's attempts to drag him around the room. Gerald was by no means a small man, but a mere shadow when placed next to Conn Mor. The Ulster Prince could have shaken free with little effort, but instead, released an almighty blast of wind from a place similar to where he threatened to slash Gerald a second hole.

The tallow wax candles were no competition to Conn Mor's effluence, and the function achieved the desired result. Gerald backed away. 'Damn you, Conn. That one came from the sewers of Hell.'

Jarlath waved a hand before his nose and frowned. 'That stench is acrimonious, even prevaricated, and … what was the other word you and Lord Grey used, Gerald?'

'More to the point, what do they mean?' added Manus.

'Celerity,' laughed Gerald in response to Jarlath's question. 'And I have no idea as to its meaning, nor the other words. We could have been speaking Spanish and I would have been none the wiser.'

A wayward elbow clocked Harry on the head. One bloodshot eye opened. 'Is celerity something I can eat?' he croaked. 'I'm mighty hungry. Oh shit. Have I pissed myself?'

'Yes,' Gerald lied. 'And best you clean yourself up. Time to head back to our apartments. The King has arranged a surprise to be delivered to our rooms.'

Manus' interest piqued at that news. 'A surprise from the King?'

Harry farted, like a trumpet at a coronation. The complaints began anew.

Trays crashing to the floor in the corridor produced a noise to rouse the dead, and Jarlath indeed suspected he may have been deceased, perhaps decaying even. His first thought was to squint his already-closed eyes to the morning sun streaming through the unshuttered chamber windows, but that movement pained his head, his neck, his toes, his everything. His tongue ventured a flicker and felt as rough as parched earth. An involuntary groan muffled in his throat.

A similar sound came from his right, one less gravelly.

And again.

Jarlath rolled gingerly, risked opening one eye. It proved a difficult task—even eyelashes protested his waking, preferring to be tightly knitted—but not impossible.

Long strands of honey-coloured hair fanned across the sheets. A bare shoulder, white as snow, performed a minute shrug, a blithe twitch, then with another gentle groan the body curled, snuggling further into the warmth of the coverlet.

Ainnir? Why was she here? Where was he? Home in Kildea?

Then it dawned. The King's surprise!

Before curses of regret found rhythm to topple from his mouth, the chamber door burst open.

'Good morning, my friend.' Manus' cheerfulness

pained Jarlath as much as his own movements.

'Damn the King for his Gascony wines.'

'It was not wines the King did gift you.'

The woman stirred, stretched with the grace of a cat, her luscious sigh almost a purr then returned to sleep.

'Ah,' sang Manus in a whisper, 'the blissful sound of gratitude.'

She had none of Ainnir's beauty. Plump cheeks, a freckled nose, and two overly large lips.

'Don't,' Jarlath uttered with grating seriousness.

'Don't?'

'Enough, Manus.'

Gerald entered the room. 'A pleasant night, cousin?'

'Don't you start either, lest you wish to risk our truce. We did make a truce did we not, or did I dream it all?'

Gerald laughed. 'We did indeed.'

'Gerald,' said Manus, 'I think we should summon a confessor?'

'A confessor?' said Gerald.

'Indeed. A confessor. Jarlath wishes to repent. He suffers guilt. And I too, am in need of absolution, for last night I lay my devil-ridden hands on a woman's bottom and kneaded each cheek like dough, then allowed it to rise, and rise again.'

'Then I too, am in need,' added Gerald with no less humour, 'for I wickedly enjoyed the company of two breasts, one larger than the other, both with nipples as pink as my lips. And as I look back upon that lustful, sinful moment, I again stir.'

'Enough,' growled Jarlath.

'You don't mean to tell us you did not find enjoyment

in your night?' asked Gerald.

'I do not remember the night.' Jarlath held a hand to his pounding forehead.

Gerald nodded to Jarlath's ephemeral bedmate. 'Well there lies a prompt. Quite delicious. Does she have a name?'

The woman came fully awake. Brown eyes fluttered above the smudge of freckles, and finding three men staring her way, she lifted a sheet to retain what little privacy remained.

Jarlath swung his feet to the ground. 'Leave.'

'My lord?' The woman's eyes flew wide. 'Now? In this state?'

'Now.' Jarlath spoke more forcefully.

'You suffer needlessly, Jarlath. We men were built to accommodate foibles.' Gerald's eyes trailed the small jiggling breasts, and the lissom white legs scampering to the corner of the room.

Jarlath's mind ventured a different path. In his youth he was not averse to escapades with as many women as life generously offered. He remembered parting with his virginity during a moment with a dark-haired whore in a bawdy house, a woman with tight curls and a tight tongue, one who didn't giggle at his maladroit enthusiasm nor drown him in false endearments of love and crooning. After that first frolic, he believed himself a man of experience and sought his sport where business transactions were unnecessary. And as nephew to the Earl of Kildare, women ran to him with no less eagerness than cows with full udders run to farmers.

Jarlath had stopped counting his conquests after forty and guessed his tally to now be tenfold that number, or more. But on marrying Ainnir, he made a solemn promise, a promise he viewed with more regard than any Christian vow. He would never forget the pain of being apart from Ainnir, and often thanked the Lord for the time he granted, with a promise of eternal fidelity.

But this night …

Now …

What had he done?

He stood from the bed, naked as the moment of his birth. 'Get me home.'

Chapter Seventeen

Manor Kildea

Three kneeling bodies set a nonfigurative circle on the floor.

'It's too hard,' complained Conor.

'No it's not,' argued Siobhan.

'It is, I tell you.'

'Practise and more practise is all that is needed, Conor. It's your turn, Siobhan.' Ainnir rubbed at an ache in her back, then patted her expanding girth. It had been four months since her heated exchange with Jarlath in Dublin. Four months. Their babe grew, and kicked and kicked, showing his, or her strength and impatience to join the family. She too, longed for the joining of her family. She missed Jarlath dreadfully.

Little word had been received, and none from Jarlath.

Alice had sent crates of lemons, twice, and both deliveries were accompanied by letters from Joan. The first arrived as a short note to indicate the men had arrived safely in England. The second, a little more wordy, informed Ainnir of three matters: that Anne had grown a full inch; that she pass on a peculiar request to Patrick, Kildea's gardener, to consider striking a copse of tercel-egg trees, a request for which she begged pardon for her dry humour; and that the men were expected home within two weeks. It had been one month since that last message. Jarlath had not returned.

Siobhan picked up the small stone with her right hand

and closed her fist. Her tongue poked from between pressed teeth, a sign of pure concentration. She looked at the five knucklebones waiting to be captured. She had succeeded before—two knucklebones being her best—and there was no reason why she couldn't do it again. The stone flew high into the air. Her eyes moved to the floor, to the knucklebones. A mistake. Her left hand grabbed at the floor, captured one piece. Her eyes moved back to follow the downward flight of the stone, but were too late. The stone hit her upturned palm, bounced to her chest, then hit the ground.

'See, it is too hard, and you can't use both hands,' said Conor.

'It's not too hard, and yes I can.'

'No you can't.

'Yes I can.'

'Mama?'

'What rules did we set?'

'One hand,' said Conor.

'You didn't say one hand,' argued Siobhan.

'Did so.'

'I can't do it with one hand.'

'See. I told you. It's too hard.'

'Not if you use two hands.' Siobhan took up the stone again. The tongue reappeared. The stone flew high. Her eyes never left the stone. No mistake this turn. The left hand slapped at the floor in the general direction of the knucklebones, and scooped up two. The stone dropped into the centre of her right palm.

'I did it.'

'You did,' said Ainnir.

244

'With two hands. Let me try,' demanded Conor.

'One or two hands? Set the rules,' said Ainnir.

'Two,' both children replied.

Conor tried once. He tried a second time. And a third. Conor had not yet learnt to keep his eyes on the stone.

'Maybe when you're bigger,' said Siobhan, an effort at a pity of sorts.

'I am big.'

'No you're not.'

'Yes I am.'

Outside, an axle squealed like an excited lass, interrupting their squabble.

'Is it Papa?' asked Siobhan.

The three lifted their ears, listened intently, hopefully.

Patrick's voice.

Mrs. Mulhearn.

Some laughter.

The squeal of the axle again, and the squawk of caged ducks.

'No.'

'I miss Papa.'

'Me too,' said Conor. The children agreed on some things.

'And I also,' added Ainnir, looking dolefully to the door. A small frown appeared at her brow. Her top lip hid her bottom lip.

Siobhan stood and placed her arms about her mother's shoulders. 'He will be home soon.'

Ainnir patted her daughter's hands. 'You are very right. So we must practise more if we are to beat your papa at this game.' She grabbed at the stone. 'One hand.'

'One hand,' the children agreed.

Ainnir threw the stone high, snatched at one knucklebone, and captured the falling stone. She threw the stone again, snatched at another knucklebone and again caught the stone. She threw the stone again. Snatched again. Three knucklebones captured. Four knucklebones captured. Five.

The children applauded.

'One hand, Mama,' said Siobhan. 'It's because you're bigger than us.'

'No it's not,' argued Conor.

'Yes it is.'

'No it's not.'

'Children. Please try to get along.' Ainnir shifted her balance, and suddenly felt dizzy. An afflicting pain thudded at her temples. She climbed to her feet. 'I am tired, and in need of a rest. You must—' A wooden rapping sounded on the floor. She looked down. The knucklebones had dropped from her hand. The room seemed to spin. She grabbed at a chair, steadied herself. The room came to a standstill, then rushed past her again.

'Mama! Mama!' she heard, before realising she had collapsed to the floor.

'Mama!'

Then nothing.

Bradan O'Byrne took the steps of Manor Kildea with one leap then rushed beneath the Fitzgerald crest and through the doors. His skin boots made little noise. A tearful Marared ran into his arms.

'Where is she?' Bradan masked his worry with a sentiment of gentleness.

'Oh, Bradan. How did you know to come?'

'News was sent to Glendalough.'

'News? But how?'

'Joan Fitzgerald sent a messenger.'

'The Countess? But how did she know? We have sent news to none.'

'Never mind. How is she?' asked Bradan.

'We do not know what more we can do for Ainnir. Your sister grows weaker by the hour. 'Tis frightening.'

'She is truly that ill?'

'Yes.' Marared choked on her breath. 'A fever we cannot control. Coughing spasms. She barely wakes.'

Bradan's mask slipped. His eyes flew wide. 'No,' he whispered.

Mrs. Mulhearn's even steps scuffled along the floor. 'Bradan! Praise the Dear Lord. It is good you have come.' No smile met her lips.

Not far behind, clonks and tinks sounded as Emma dropped a shallow bowl of steaming water. The young servant's eyes were swollen from ceaseless crying. Adding more tears, Emma promptly attended to soaking up the mess with the soiled sheet draped across her shoulder.

'We left as soon we received news,' Bradan explained.

'News from where?' asked Mrs. Mulhearn. 'We sent no news.'

'The Countess Joan.'

'The Countess. But we sent no news to Maynooth. And

who's the we you speak of?' A knot appeared at Mrs. Mulhearn's brow.

Marared sniffed, wiped at her cheeks and stood from Bradan's embrace with the same inquisitive expression. Emma looked up, no less curious.

An elegant woman, wrapped tightly in a long brown cloak and a saffron shawl, entered the home. The woman removed the shawl from her head, revealing honey-hued hair lightened by threads of grey. 'Take me to my daughter.'

Brigid O'Byrne believed she looked upon death. Ainnir's sweat-covered body lay restless, twitching like a prisoner enduring the lash over and again. The drawn, white face turned sheets to the colour of churned butter. The distended belly, full with babe, appeared unnatural, a heavy boulder on a frail autumn twig.

This was Brigid's daughter, her child borne of her own body, given a name to mean one who refuses to abide by rules, one with spirit and laughter to greet her every day. The name now riddled a crude jest. No passion, no fervour, no blissful smile, no cheeky sparkling eyes. Brigid had not seen Ainnir since the day her daughter rode from the walls of Glendalough with Jarlath six years ago. This was not the scene she expected on the day they reunited.

'How long has she been this way?'

'Four days,' answered Mrs. Mulhearn.

'And my grandchildren?'

'The lass took to her bed this morning, but the boy is fine.'

Brigid felt Ainnir's feet, her forehead, her balled fists;

248

hot, hot, cold. 'Does she have lucid moments?'

'Few.'

'And Jarlath is yet to return from England?'

'Yes.'

Brigid tucked her daughter's hands under the covers. 'Now, take me to my granddaughter.'

Brigid stepped into the past, a time twenty years gone. A small girl lay beneath a pile of blankets; her hair honey-gold, her face heart-shaped, so like Ainnir at that age. Pale eyelids fluttered open. The blue was brilliant. Yes, just like Ainnir.

Brigid held a hand to the girl's forehead. The heat was instant.

'Siobhan, this is your grandmother,' explained Mrs. Mulhearn.

'My grandmother?'

Brigid summoned a glorious smile, one to belie her fear. 'Grandmamma, if you'd like.'

Understanding dawned. 'Grandmamma. Your name is Brigid?'

'Why yes. It is.'

'Are you Uncle Bradan's mama?'

'Yes, your uncle Bradan's, your mama's, and also your uncle Eamonn's too.'

'I have not met Eamonn.'

'No. There are many kin you have not yet met, many who love you so much without even knowing you, Siobhan. Bradan is here. See?'

Bradan leant above the child. 'You are still Kildea's

most beautiful fairy. I have missed you.'

'It hurts.'

'What hurts, dear one?' asked Brigid.

Siobhan touched at her head, then her chest then her stomach.

Brigid summoned the courage she knew necessary. 'I know what you need. I shall prepare a special tonic to make the pain vanish, and will make sure to add plenty of sweet honey. Will you drink it for me when it is ready?'

Siobhan offered a weak nod then closed her eyes. Those eyelids, just like Ainnir's, refused to close fully; sentinels declining to relinquish their duty. The child's lips gently touched, and fists balled. For as long as Brigid could remember, Ainnir looked no different in sleep. Yes, just like Ainnir.

Brigid led Mrs. Mulhearn out to the corridor. Bradan and Marared followed. Brigid kept her voice low. 'And the boy? My grandson?'

'Conor is not yet touched with the sickness. We keep him to the other end of the house, away from these rooms.'

Brigid thought for a long moment. 'Bradan, you will take Conor to Glendalough.'

'Oh, but—' Mrs. Mulhearn began.

Brigid ignored the protest. 'Marared, you will return to my home with Bradan and the boy. A child needs familiarity and I trust you love the lad.'

'Oh, yes, yes,' replied Marared.

'I thought as much. My daughter would have nothing less from those in her employ.' Brigid managed a weak smile. 'And I think my son would like you away from these sickrooms too. Leave now. Do not dally.'

'You will stay, Mama?'

'My daughter and granddaughter need me. Now go. Keep my grandson safe.'

Brigid remained busy through the afternoon, sharing her time between the two sickrooms. A brew of blessed thistle, butterbur and mint was prepared. Henbane was added to Ainnir's share, and honey to Siobhan's. Much of Ainnir's tipped from her mouth, the action of swallowing absent, perhaps impossible. At first, Siobhan gulped like one freed from a desert, but the child seemed to worsen quickly, slipped into a permanent dream state, her sleep filled with twitches and sweat.

Mrs. Mulhearn placed a sprig of valerian across Ainnir's pillow. 'This will ward off any plans the Devil may have for our girl. The Lord may dislike my use of pagan beliefs but I refuse to leave anything to chance.'

'The Lord will bless you, not revile you for your care. Have you placed some onto Siobhan's pillow?'

'A whole bush.'

Brigid's hands stilled on Ainnir's stomach. Her eyes blinked in thought. She repositioned her hands and stilled again. 'Movement,' she announced. 'It is slight, but the babe lives.'

Together the women lifted Ainnir's head and shoulders. Brigid tipped some of the tonic into her daughter's mouth, and could only hope a little trickled down Ainnir's throat, for much, again, escaped from those parched lips.

'Are you sure the henbane will not hurt the babe?'

'I am sure of nothing. But this child will want its

251

mother alive.'

'She cannot die. Ainnir cannot die.' Mrs. Mulhearn sniffed after her words.

'We shall do our best.'

'This home was never a home until our mistress arrived. She and the children, they are our family. The master too.'

'My daughter was always one to win hearts.'

'Well she has all of ours and more.'

They lay Ainnir back down.

'Mama?' Ainnir's voice was weak, barely audible.

'Yes, love. Your mama is here.' Brigid leant over her daughter, placed a hand on Ainnir's forehead.

Ainnir's jaw twitched. Minute lines of blood appeared as the skin on her lips cracked with the movement. 'The children?'

'The children are fine. They are fine.'

'Promise?'

'Oh, I promise. They run the fields with Marared chasing puddles and collecting mushrooms for our evening meal.'

'Mama.'

'Yes, my daughter?'

'Tell them my eyes will always be open. I will always see them. They should never fear.'

'What do you mean?'

But no more words came. Oblivion claimed Ainnir once more and the twitching began anew.

Mrs. Mulhearn dabbed a cool cloth at Ainnir's lips. 'I know what she means. Ainnir believes her time has come. She promised the children she would always watch over them, even from Heaven.'

The sounds of a newly arrived guest stirred outside the walls of the sickroom. Hunter barked. Carriage wheels churned stones. Tack and bridles chinked. Servants spoke in lively voices.

'Who could it be at this hour?' Mrs. Mulhearn listened intently to the sounds and the voices, then announced with a frown, 'Pardon my cursing, madame, but the bloomin' Devil's amusing himself with a mighty vicious game. What more misery could he bestow upon us?'

'Not a welcome guest?'

'No. Meg Eustace, wife to Manus Eustace. She's none too fond of the Gaels.'

Brigid sensed a solemn shadow sweep across the air; unseen, unheard, yet persistent and corporeal. Hunter ceased his guttural barks. Bridles no longer chinked. The very stones of Manor Kildea seemed to cease breathing. Her world heralded a harbinger. What was it?

An agonising scream suddenly came from the corridor. Emma rushed into the room. 'The child! Siobhan!'

'What is it?' demanded Mrs. Mulhearn.

'She's dead. Siobhan is dead.'

'No,' Mrs. Mulhearn gasped.

'She's dead I tell you!' Emma then ran into the arms of Mrs. Mulhearn. The two hugged and clung tightly. Wails tore the air.

Brigid spied the stir of the women's skirts, and felt the folds of her own gown play at the touch of a warm breeze. Nothing else in the room was disturbed, not even the candle flame. A corner of a bed sheet fluttered ever so slightly. The valerian no longer rested on the pillow. It had vanished.

The solemn shadow lifted. Breath began again. Hunter howled. Horses neighed and the wind bayed, knocking at loose shutters.

Brigid looked to her daughter grateful for the redundant stupor Ainnir suffered. Those last words were not heard. Ainnir knew not of the passing of her daughter. A small blessing. The twitching abated. Brigid checked Ainnir's breathing. Restful.

Meg burst into the room. 'Dear Lord, no.'

Chapter Eighteen

Gerald kept the men in London for an inordinate time, the spoils of court-life too alluring. But the time to return had arrived. In contrast to their stay, the voyage home aboard the caravel with its three mastheads was unexpectedly speedy. Catching the heavy winds, the white sails slapped and snapped, then bulged like a wet nurse's breast. At this time of the year, all expected the Irish Sea to present a sailor's challenge, but today seemed to naysay any logic in the seafarer's seasonal bible. Moderate waves lapped at the hull's strakes as the ship flew across the sea with little hardship, yet with every forward lurch, Jarlath could have sworn unseen swirls pushed the ship back half their gain. His niggling conscience, a festering itch, made him eager to be back at Manor Kildea. What he would do with that guilt, he did not know. But the thought of returning home brought with it a sense of imminent pardon; a promise that holding his wife and children would wash away all remorse. And, of course, his companions mocked him constantly, for regret was not meant to be a part of a man's make-up.

The men stood swaying on the deck watching the slice of land ahead grow larger. Manus however, lay awkwardly across a coil of thick rope, oblivious to the journey. Manus succumbed to excessive indulgence of ale, an intentional ploy to avoid the expected manic bouts of seasickness. He preferred the sufferance of the day after, to the sufferance promised by a sea voyage.

The ship dropped anchor off the eastern coast of

Ireland. Row boats pulled up alongside to ferry passengers ashore. Harry threw a flaccid Manus across his shoulder, and climbed down the netted rope to the waiting row boats. Manus' head sounded a thump when it hit an unmanned oar, but no reaction came. He had drunk an awful lot.

Jarlath and the Prior were the first to step onto dry land, and wandered through the crowds to organise the remainder of their journey home.

'My lord Prior! My lord Prior!' came a young animated voice.

'Francis? What are you doing here, lad?' bellowed the Prior.

The boy manoeuvred through the crowd with no less ease than the caravel's sea crossing. The boy's fingers worried at a cap in his hands. 'I've been 'ere two days waiting for you, my lord. The old Countess, the Lady Joan sent word to Dublin Castle for one of us to meet you 'ere.'

'And why?'

'Because … because …' Francis' eyes remained low. If his hands pulled harder that cap was sure to rip into two.

'Speak, boy.'

'To deliver urgent news, my lord, sir.'

'Then what is it?' the Prior demanded.

'Not to you, Lord Prior, to the lord here, to the Fitzgerald.' Young apprehensive eyes looked up.

Jarlath stepped forward. 'No more hesitancy, Francis.'

'You are to rush home, my lord. Your lady wife is ill. Very ill.'

'What?' Jarlath's heart knocked. 'How? What has happened?'

'I know no more, sir.'

'No more questions, Jarlath. I will see to Manus' return home and explain your hasty departure to the others. You have a horse readied, Francis?'

'Course, my lord.'

'Good lad.'

Night was coming. His mount fought on. Manor Kildea was in sight. Winds and rain created silver lines, lines that danced and wavered across the pond's surface, bending reeds and ferrying leaves and twigs taken prisoner by the season.

Old Patrick stood to the front of the home. He straightened from his normal stooped posture, his coat hanging from thin shoulders like an empty bag draped across a wooden scarecrow. The greying man removed his hat and lowered his head unperturbed by the rain running the length of his face. He looked a man offering condolences.

No! Jarlath screamed silently. Do not let me be too late.

Up the stairs, through the doors of his bedchamber, his booted feet barely touched the ground. Putrid sickness hit his senses, devouring the reek of his wet and muddied mantle, the tang of the sea, the once-lingering stench of London.

A pallid shell appeared lost amongst a pile of coverlets, its golden-hair darkened and flat. It was the care administered by the woman—a blonde servant with her back to Jarlath—the gentle dabbing of a cool cloth to a fevered forehead, the neck and to the grey cracked lips, that had Jarlath find his breath. Such tenderness, such attention would not be given to the dead. Relief almost felled him to his knees. The servant straightened, rubbed at an aching shoulder, then stretched her neck left then right, catching sight of his presence.

'Jarlath!'

'Meg?'

The tangled blonde hair was swept back in one tie. There was no powder on Meg's face. Dark circles weighted her eyes. She wore a plain smock over a brown kirtle.

'We did not know when you were to return.'

'How is she?' Jarlath strode to the other side of the bed and planted kisses at Ainnir's cheeks and hands. 'She is fine?' he asked with hope, ignoring the heat at his lips.

'She grows no worse, but grows no stronger. There is hope. I have hope. She fights the illness, for both she and the babe.'

Jarlath's hands and eyes moved to the large belly. 'The babe—'

'Is alive.'

'Dear God, thank you. I prayed all the way here. My family … I could not bear … I could not bear …'

Meg turned away.

'Why are you here?' Jarlath's rudeness was unintentional.

She turned back, swiping at a trickling tear. Meg seemed to hesitate, and snatched a deep breath, before offering a gentle smile, one Jarlath had never seen grace Meg's face.

'Ainnir is my kin, Jarlath. I am here to help.'

Jarlath did not believe a word, and Meg seemed to understand. She returned to Ainnir's side and fussed at the pillow.

'I cannot fault your caution. I am not known to be …

selfless. I am not too proud of the Meg that was. Since we last met, there is much I have toiled diligently to change. The Countess sent word of Ainnir's illness, and I—'

'Aunt Joan?'

'Yes. I was equally surprised. Seems both she and Ainnir thought me a plight worthy of salvation. I travelled south immediately.'

'Aunt Joan ensured news awaited me at the docks.'

Meg's regard travelled to the door. 'We are not the only ones she got word to.'

'It is good you are home, Jarlath.'

'Brigid?'

Brigid smiled. 'I am pleased you recognise this aging woman, but you place yourself in danger being close to the sickness.'

'No more than you. No more than Meg.'

'Yes, I suppose not.'

'Tell me. Tell me all.' Jarlath caught sight of Brigid's deep breath and the swallowing action at her throat. 'What is it? Is there something you are afraid to tell me?' He looked to both women, to two weary faces, then to Ainnir's unconscious body. 'The truth. How is she really? And our children? Where are Siobhan and Conor?'

'Ainnir fights, Jarlath. My daughter fights to stay on this earth. I refuse to believe it is her time. And you should too.'

Jarlath clasped Ainnir's hands. 'God forbid. I need her. She cannot leave me. She cannot leave us.' Then added with a different tone, 'Our children? Where are our children?'

'Marared and Bradan took Conor to Glendalough.'

'They what?'

'Away from the sickness. Do not fret. He will be well-cared for. He is my kin too.'

In the hollow pause that followed, recognition dawned.

'Siobhan? And … what of my daughter?' he asked, his voice hoarse.

Brigid stole Jarlath's hands, held them tenderly. 'Come.'

Lengths of white linen covered the small body. Candlelight spiralled, eerily standing vigil at the chamber's corners. The purple of the heliotrope flower was the only bright hue to peep from the green vines placed on the bed around the dead child.

Wrapped against the cold air with shawls as thick as fur rugs, the two women watched Jarlath lift his daughter from the bed. Purple and green rained to the ground, so too did the sheets of white. Tresses of hair stretched downward and bounced, the child's head lolled across her father's arm.

He held the small body tight, sniffed back a lone tear and swayed back and forth as if nursing a child to sleep. The tears grew, multiplying until falling by the hundreds. Painful sobs began. Singular choking sounds at first. Jarlath nestled into a chair and laid Siobhan across his lap. The grieving father crooned and ran fingers along a cold nose and ears and cheeks. Words were said, soft words, words unheard by the women. Kisses covered Siobhan's temples. The sobs grew to a wail and Jarlath pressed the precious child hard to his chest.

The women backed away silently, allowing Jarlath privacy with his sorrow, a black and harsh companion that would walk with him for a time.

An hour later, while tending Ainnir, Meg turned to loud purposeful steps marching along the corridor. She heard the front door fly open. The sounds of rainfall, heavy rainfall shattered the home's quiet. Meg and Brigid left Ainnir's side, moved to the open door.

In the mud, beneath a grey weeping sky, Jarlath rocked on his knees, his mouth contorted, held weirdly agape. The rain turned everything about him dark. Mucus ran from his nose and he pulled erratically at the sides of his hair. A ragged howl came.

A curious Hunter sniffed at his master, and as a second howl burst forth the dog flinched, retreated awkwardly.

Old Patrick stood a discreet distance away, his head lowered, but his eyes intently focused upon Jarlath. He made a small hand gesture and Hunter moved to stand at his side. Both hound and servant waited in the wind and the cold and the pouring rain, and waited some more in the event their master had need of them.

This village, this manor, this family, even the animals, all loved Jarlath and Ainnir dearly. Meg knew none in her life would be so giving, so selfless if she was in need. And since meeting Ainnir, she had come to understand she had only herself to blame for such a void.

She made to move out to the rain and bring comfort to Jarlath.

Brigid laid a halting hand upon her arm. 'Leave him, Meg. Jarlath needs this.'

261

Chapter Nineteen

Three nights passed. Ainnir flitted in and out of consciousness. Assiduously, Jarlath sat by her side leaving the chamber only once, to bury his daughter beneath the glossy leaves and wrinkly bark of the alder trees in the village churchyard. He returned to sentry duties immediately after.

His cheeks and chin grew a thick beard and his eyes bore dark gutters. He spoke continually to Ainnir of joy and happiness; only joy and happiness to encourage her recovery. Not once did he mention Siobhan's passing. Though his heart agonised, he spoke only of joy and happiness and love and fun and friendship.

He retrieved Ainnir's treasured bracelet from her trinket box and placed it upon her wrist. It was made of dried bog rush entwined into a circle, a gift he presented Ainnir when they first met all those years ago in Glendalough, and a gift his wife held more dear than any gold or silver adornment their world could offer.

'Remember this?' he murmured over and again, his thumb rubbing gently at the bracelet. 'This is a memory that brought us back together, so long ago when I asked you to be my wife. Remember now, Ainnir, and return to me. Please, return to me. I need you.'

He prayed often, and sent instructions to the village priest for masses to be said daily. Bells were heard clear across the hills.

Brigid and Meg insisted Jarlath eat, but it was only at

the stern words of Mrs. Mulhearn, which threatened an irksome war of nagging if ignored, that any heeding to nourishment was given. And in that same progress he was ordered from the house to take in some fresh air with the promise the women would continue the vigil.

Jarlath obeyed.

The world was white. A stark change from the dark sick room. Early snow blanketed the fields. Hunter walked to his side, their footprints leading a trail through the garden and toward the front gates and around and back again. The imprints differed in size and regularity, yet the line and distance between the two could not have been more symmetrical. Hunter was remaining at his master's side.

On the high branches of the pines and beech, a pair of red-breasted robins hopped and flustered in their perky way. Tails fanned and twitched, heads bobbed and tilted, then off they scurried to another vantage point studying the intruders.

Jarlath wandered with little thought and found himself atop the familiar rise near the pond's edge. It was a place he and Ainnir often sat and chatted while their children played and rolled and tumbled down the rise, side over side, laughter and giggles splicing the air, grass and leaves tangled in hair and clothes. Too often he was persuaded to join the game, dizzy as he reached the bottom, only to find his wife crashing into his side, skirts askew, hair wild and tussled, and no less grass-covered than he.

He sat down upon the garden seat beneath the wide-reaching branches of the oak. Hunter rested his head on Jarlath's knee.

The sun tried to break through the clouds. Jarlath

suspected it brought a measure of warmth he could not feel, for clumps of snow on the high branches intermittently fell with splats and plops. Hunter's one twitching ear and darting eyes intimated an interest in the first few fallings but curiosity waned as the dog succumbed to the enjoyment of a scratch behind his ear. Of a sudden, alert to further movement, his head flew from Jarlath's knee. Eyes turned looking down toward the manor house.

'It is too cold for you to be out, Meg,' yelled Jarlath.

'Nonsense. 'Tis invigorating.'

Jarlath pointed south, to the steps.

'I know my way,' she announced with a weak grin.

Meg wound around the bottom of the rise to the patchwork of bluestone and climbed one step at a time, her arms outstretched for balance, determined the snow-covered stones would not see her unceremoniously upended.

She sat herself down beside Jarlath, and absently petted Hunter's pushy nose.

'You were ordered out too?'

'No. I thought to keep you company. Brigid and Mrs. Mulhearn sit with Ainnir, although the housekeeper's head flops at times. Did you know the woman snores?'

Jarlath smiled. 'No, I did not.'

'And her tongue makes a lapping movement with every inward snort.'

Jarlath's smile transformed to a muffled laugh, a grunt of sorts deep in his throat.

'There. If nothing else, I have made you forget your troubles for an interim.'

'I do not forget them.'

The world would have remained silent for a moment if not for the two birds above chattering in song.

'Ainnir is strong, Jarlath. If she was to fully succumb to the sickness she would not be with us now.'

'Yet she looks …'

'Her body fights, and is doing a damn good job.'

'A damn good job?' Jarlath tweaked his brow at Meg's cussing.

'I cannot think of a better term to use, and sometimes it is best to come straight to the point of things.'

'Thank you for your help.'

'You are surprised.' It was not a question.

'And again, you are straight to the point of things. I will not lie,' admitted Jarlath.

'And so you should not.'

'You once detested the Gaels, Meg. You once detested Ainnir.'

'I once detested many things.' Meg rubbed her gloved hands together and wrapped her shawl tighter around her shoulders.

'And what changed you?'

'Not what. Who. Your wife.'

'Yes. Ainnir makes a habit of that.'

'Ainnir and your children.'

'My children,' he said on a painful sigh.

Meg touched his hand. 'They have shown me the uncountable wealth of love, and the contentment such a state can bring. I want that.' Meg's regard wandered from Jarlath to the home and down to the pond. 'I want what I see here, what I feel here. And after my appalling behaviour in Dublin I saw the depth of the pain I brought Ainnir by my betrayal, the trouble I brought you and Gerald, and … and I also saw a ferocious loathing in Manus, a hot hatred speared at me. You all walked from that room leaving me to feel things, things that stung mightily. Something snapped that day, Jarlath. I didn't want to be me anymore, and have pondered long and hard ever since.'

Jarlath also looked to the water. No water-bred birds ventured onto the icy pond. A lone row boat sat along the banks.

Meg sniffed heavily. 'Ainnir once said, "Never forget what it is to love, and never underestimate the splendour of being loved". It was here beneath these branches she spoke those words. I did not understand at the time. But I do now. She saw the love I have for Manus, one I barely recognised myself, and saw that I had no idea how to show it. I do love him, Jarlath. I know that now. Ainnir was so right.' She lifted hopeful, questioning eyes.

'It is never too late, Meg.'

'Do you believe that? Truly?'

'Truly.'

'I do not know if Manus will ever forgive me.'

'You can only ask. You have not yet sent word to him that you are here?'

'No.' Meg's skirts began to flutter around her ankles. She looked down. 'Isn't that the strangest of things?'

'That you have not sent word?'

'No. The folds of my gown swayed as if bothered by a breeze, but there is no wind and I felt warmth, not chill, and in this weather. Brigid has spoken of similar occurrences, so too, Mrs. Mulhearn. And Emma.' A large dollop of snow fell heavily onto Meg's head and slid down the side of her face. She laughed. 'Oh dear.'

They both looked up. The two robins bounced about, and from the same branch, another dollop of snow splattered, this time on Jarlath's shoulder. The birds chirped. 'I think the birds laugh too.'

Hunter turned quickly, looking across the kitchen garden to the back of the manor. Jarlath's focus followed.

'The snorer awakes and comes our way,' he announced. 'Do you women not feel the cold?'

'Come in, quickly!' yelled Mrs. Mulhearn, her arms flailing like a damaged windmill. 'Quickly!'

Ainnir drank deeply from a mug Brigid held to her mouth, then settled back onto the pile of plump pillows. Her voice carried low and slow.

'At Glendalough? That is wondrous. Our children will see my mountains, my lakes, my old home.' She stopped for a breath, her chest rising minutely. 'And will meet Papa and Eamonn, and Muirne. Do you remember Muirne, my nursemaid?'

'Of course,' replied Jarlath, his lips smothering the hand he held dearly.

'I am awfully hungry,' she added sleepily.

'Soup,' ordered Brigid, looking to Mrs. Mulhearn and Emma. Emma knuckled at her tears.

'Enough of that nonsense, girl,' said Mrs. Mulhearn, knuckling her own. 'You heard the lady. Soup! Soup!' The two bustled off to complete the errand almost tripping over one another's feet, and rushed past Meg who stood away from the bed, near the door.

Brigid's next move was to pitch Jarlath a look of support, for she could see his strain, the bend in his mettle. His teeth gnawed busily at the inside of his bottom lip. They all troubled to mask their grief, even with this small yet marvellous progress in Ainnir's recovery.

'Muirne married Ferghal our blacksmith, Ainnir,' Brigid announced lightly, 'but of course, you would know that, my dear, would you not?'

'Yes.'

'It seems my brother-in-law has been exceptional at ensuring Glendalough's affairs reach the ears of my wife,' said Jarlath, not unkindly.

'You have forgiven me?' asked Ainnir.

Brigid placed a hand on Jarlath's shoulder. 'A harmless deception, Jarlath. My children were ever close. They could never be parted for long.'

'Everything. As you must forgive me.'

'Forgive you?'

'Yes.'

'I thought Siobhan came to me in this room and removed something from my pillow. A fern perhaps? Was she here?' asked Ainnir.

Meg moved further into the room leaving her sequestered place at the door. Brigid and Meg exchanged looks. Meg's eyes wide and round, Brigid's narrow in warning that Meg quell her astonishment.

'No,' Brigid answered.

'It must have been a dream then,' Ainnir conceded.

'Yes, it must have, for she came with a warm breeze, a summer breeze, and it is winter. I feel the chill.'

Brigid felt Meg's fingers grab at her hand. She adjusted her stance concealing that silent communication in the folds of her gown. 'Shush now. You'll exhaust yourself,' she ordered. 'You need more rest for both you and the babe.'

'Yes. Our babe thrives. A small miracle.' Ainnir's lazy eyes seemed to sweep through Jarlath, then, 'Mama, thank you for being here.'

'You're welcome, my child.'

'And Meg—'

'Save your breath,' said Meg.

The scaly, white skin on Ainnir's lips cracked as a splinter of a smile blossomed. 'There is something I wish you to have.'

'I need nothing.'

Ainnir's smile grew wider, albeit tired and lopsided. She instructed Jarlath to pull a pendant from her trinket box. 'You will need this. 'Tis an Ouroboros. I will speak to you later of its powers.' Ainnir returned to her slumber.

Jarlath moved from the bed and gulped on a sob. 'Oh God. How do I tell her?'

'Jarlath,' said Brigid, 'not yet. Let her regain some strength. Then—'

'And then?' he spat in a whisper. 'Tell her our daughter is dead?'

A long pause ensued.

Noise clopped along the corridor and the two servants returned, one armed with a bowl of cabbage and herb soup, the other with a wooden platter topped with dried bread. They were

269

met with sombreness, a stillness that for all its silence vociferated like a wolf howling in the woods.

'Yes,' said Brigid, then she slowly told him of the strange occurrences at Manor Kildea.

Chapter Twenty

Manor Ballymore's rowdy spaniels were herded out of the room as servants delivered the evening meal to the table. Blanchette escaped the roundup, circled back, nostrils twitching, sniffing at the air, only to be prompted by the blunt end of Manus' persuasive boot. Conceding defeat the dog trailed her three playfellows and retreated along the corridor in a flurry of squeaky barks that played like a set of water-logged flutes.

'This fare is bland,' announced Manus' mother-in-law seated across the table.

The human gavel had arrived with her stockpile of judgements not three hours earlier, and for three hours Manus had heard naught but whines and biting innuendos.

Ballymore's cook produced an appetising meal, invariably a challenge during periods of fasting. Salted fish, delicately shaped mounds of rice baked in almond milk, and dishes of spiced vegetables, were deserving of sincere approval, but Manus refused to be baited into an inconsequential scrap. The large, pompous woman did not gift gratification liberally, and why his wife eternally cared for her mother's endorsement he could not fathom.

Yet that evening something was different.

Meg had returned from Kildea not twenty-four hours earlier, and prior to that, due to his adventures in London,

Manus had not set eyes upon Meg for many months. It came as a great surprise to discover where she had been. However, after receiving the dire news, he refrained from firing questions.

In his quiet contemplation, during his prayers for the soul of Siobhan and strength for his two dear friends, Manus noted Meg suffered her own sorrow, something he had not before witnessed in his wife. To her, grieving had always been a weakness, so too any emotion for that matter.

This night, customary indulgences were conspicuously absent from the table. No white linen cloth. No hippocras, a honeyed wine served in its stead. Meagre candles placed haphazardly cast irregular shadows. And Meg herself was not painted; no powder, no rouge. Her hair, loosely braided, hung low at her back, and she did not wear that prickly alert demeanour, that habitual edginess expectant of a tragedy of phenomenal proportions. Calm she almost seemed. Not the Meg he knew. Everything seemed suitably simple.

With those intriguing facts, Manus pondered seriously on the cryptic letter that arrived with Meg's return home; a sealed letter penned by Jarlath espousing his belief in vicissitude and a man's need for peace, and a litany of Meg's valuable assistance during her stay at their home.

As Meg's mother prattled about nothing of importance to anyone but herself, Manus tallied the other changes he had witnessed these twenty-four hours. They had been married for six years now, perhaps the longest and arduous of his twenty-five. He had only just come to notice that Meg's green eyes were flecked with sprinkles of gold when she was not coiled and ready to strike, and the hollow of her neck as she breathed slowly was somewhat – enticing. In fact, this night she

272

possessed an inner beauty, something he had not thought his wife to ever possess. Oh, he knew very well that heads turned when she walked into a room, but an ugly heart was easily hidden by a polished casing.

And she had ceased the use of multiple scents, using only oils and creams laced with jasmine; his favourite. He had caught a strong hint of its presence as he led her into the dining room this evening. She no longer spoke to the servants with arrogance, but rather, with a mild complacent tone that invariably achieved more than her previous overly wound-up haughtiness, and he did not suffer snide remarks cooked from her perception of his standing.

Intriguing indeed.

Manus was brought back to the conversation at the table.

'These spiced vegetables, what it is? I detect cumin, and something peculiar, something alien to my senses. Am I correct? Oh, dear Meg, you should not eat so fast. Exhibiting a voracious appetite is nothing short of coarse. And what is that ghastly pendant at your neck?'

'It is an Ouroboros, Mama.'

'A what?'

'An Ouroboros. It was a gift.'

'From whom?'

'Ainnir.'

'That Gael woman? Harrumph! Some pagan nonsense I suspect.' The woman placed a large piece of potato into her mouth. 'I see your fields are boasting a good supply of spring lambs, Manus,' she said as she chewed. 'It was all I could do to endure the rough roads to your home, to look out the window of my carriage and give all my attention to the beasts in the fields. I declare, I was jostled and thrown no less than a child's toy. You must give some attention to repairing those roads. And whilst we are speaking of the outdoors, Meg, as mistress of this manor you must take your gardener to task.' Another piece of potato disappeared, and more mumbling followed. 'The vines at your gates need grooming for they appear awfully wild, too much like the native barbarians of these lands.'

Manus thought the woman a toad in full song, her under-chin so bloated that her next words were likely to hit the air as a croak. And Manus found it unordinary that Meg refrained from dealing a response, whether polite or with malice. Her eyes remained downcast, and she fiddled with the silver pendant at her neck.

'Oh, I cannot fool you for one moment, can I Manus?' croaked the toad. 'I see it in your face. Full of disinterest. Well you are correct. I am here for some gossip, not to critique your lambs or your blossoms or the jewellery my daughter wears. Tell me what you know.'

'What I know?'

'Yes. What you know. Oh, first let me tell you something I learnt on my travels here. I heard that dreadful fellow, John Butler the Earl of Ormond, died whilst on pilgrimage to the Holy Lands. I'd wager you did not know that.'

'No, I did not,' Manus lied.

'Did you know Rome is in a tither over suggestions that James Keating, Prior of Kilmainham, has sold, for an undisclosed amount of coin, the remnant of Christ's Cross?'

'Nor that.' If it was true, Manus was not surprised.

'And I heard the Earl of Kildare's wife, the dear Alice,

gave birth to yet another daughter. Eleanor is the child's name, no?'

Manus juggled the prospect of pleading ignorance to that last piece of wandering chatter. 'Another daughter, yes,' he answered honestly,

She tutted. 'The Earl needs an heir, not another daughter to marry off. It is a woman's role to produce an heir for her husband. I hear—' but her words halted midair. 'Meg, what on earth ails you this night? You slouch, you look ghastly, and you offer no enjoyable conversation to your guest, your dear mama.' She did not allow for a reply, instead, grabbed at her big throat and continued on an excited indrawn breath. 'Are you about to tell your mama that you are with child, after all these years as a barren wife? Say it is true, my dear Meg, you are about to fulfil your duty and give your husband an heir.'

Of a sudden Meg stood. Her chair toppled to the floor, and she threw her knife onto the table with a rupture of clattering. Meg glared at her mother. The specks of gold were gone from her eyes. The beautiful green faded to a bland hue, an almost grey, and were suddenly veiled by a cover of moisture.

'What is wrong? Why do you look at me with such venom?'

'Wrong, Mama? I will tell you what is wrong. You can be such a bitch.'

The toad almost choked on her food, and took on the colour of a garden beet. 'How dare you?' she spluttered, frantically fanning her face. 'How dare you speak to your mother in such a fashion? Manus, I insist you take charge of your wife. Inform her immediately you do not condone such behaviour!'

Manus gave no thought to that request nor did he bother to conceal his enigmatic smile, a smile of syrupy exultance. Meg's tears flowed unchecked, spotting her collar. It was clear she had not given them permission to shed, and she sniffed angrily, attempting to pull them back. Her focus was pinned to a bowl of vegetables, as if unable to look to either her mother or Manus. Her hands gripped the edge of the table, her knuckles white. Then slowly and seemingly deliberate, her taut stance relaxed.

She lifted her chin. Manus noticed that enticing neck, that slow breath.

'If I may be excused?' Meg did not wait for permission, and walked from the room.

The flustered toad turned to Manus, arms flailing, no sound escaping her open mouth. Manus stood without saying a word and hastened from the room.

Meg's steps were slow, appeared painful as she began to climb the stairs toward her bedchamber. She turned at the sound of Manus' approach, but kept her eyes to the floor.

'If you have come to berate me, let it wait, please, I beg you, Manus. I will gladly hear you out on the morrow. But if you come in concern,' she added with a sarcastic laugh, 'I am alright, Manus. I do not need you.'

'Like Hell you don't.'

At his words her eyes flew to his face, confusion forming a sullen frown. He grabbed at her wrist and began to pull her up the steps.

'You are hurting me, Manus. Stop. What are you doing?'

276

'I am about to show you how a man and wife make maddening passionate, and all absorbing love, for it is something I should have done a long time ago.' Not a moment's rhythm was missed in his step. His stride was persistent, purposeful.

Meg's skirts gathered tightly around her ankles and she almost tripped as her feet tried to take the steps at the same pace. She lifted the hem of her gown with her free hand, and increased her stride until level with Manus on the stair landing, and together they broke into a run.

'Out now, Veronique.' Manus' order was brusque.

Veronique curtsied in her pretty French way, bobbing her head as her knees committed a short bounce of their own.

Manus did not even wait for the telling echo of the closing latch before he took his wife into his arms in an urgent embrace and devoured her lips; or was she devouring his? He could not say.

Lord on the Cross! She had never kissed him like that before. She craved his body as much as he craved hers. Desire was in her every response. Manus was in no state to wait, believed it impossible at this point to slow and bring his wife her own pleasure first. That would have to come in the second round. Oh, our dear and generous God! To think, a second round. A third round. A fourth!

His hands plucked at the lacings of her gown and to his displeasure, found his deft skill had inexplicably deserted him. Meg's hands seemed to comprehend the stumble and followed his, no less eager or fervent. Her actions stirred Manus to an even greater heat, threatening to bring him undone then and there where he stood. There was no time for niceties. He grabbed at the neckline of Meg's gown and ripped, tearing from shoulder to thigh. Meg shook the gown from her shoulders, leaving it to crumple at her feet. He lifted her in his arms and threw her onto the bed, followed her down.

Manus fumbled with his own garments and in one urgent move, he plunged. Meg threw her head back into the pillow pitching the most sensual of sounds ever to reach his ears. She arched her back and followed his wild dance, over and again.

Manus roared.

And then began the second round, and then the third.

'What is your name, sorceress, for I know you have taken the form of my wife?'

Meg watched Manus as he lay on his back looking to the roof, the smell of their coupling surpassing all other scents in the room.

'My name truly is Meg, and I am your wife.'

'You are? Then what just happened?'

Meg rolled away, suddenly afraid.

'Don't, Meg,' Manus said gently. 'Don't stop what I suspect you have started.'

She rolled back into his side and recognised honesty in his eyes. 'Oh, Manus, how can I ever apologise.'

'Do you speak of an apology to me or your mother? After what you just gave me you are totally and utterly absolved of all transgressions? As for any apology to your mother, have I ever given you reason to think I cared an ounce for her fractious sensibilities?'

'I do not speak of my outburst, but for that matter I no longer care for her either. She deserved my harsh words, and I only wish I had seared her ears long before today. What I mean is, how can you ever forgive me for the wife I have been?'

Manus didn't reply.

Meg saw his silence as an answer that she would not welcome. She raised up onto her elbow. 'Manus, for all my life it was easier to remain indifferent to anyone who had the occasion to be close to me. To be uncaring and hard of heart ensured a reliable guard that would thwart heartache clawing at me, like the talons that struck and tore at me in my childhood. My father was brutal and my mother ... well ... she was a bitch.'

'Is a bitch.'

'Yes, is a bitch.'

'Like Blanchette.'

Meg ventured a hesitant smile. 'Yes, like Blanchette.'

'And your other spaniels.'

This time a giggle escaped. 'And my other spaniels.' Her shoulders slumped and she laid back onto a pillow. 'No less than myself, I admit. And of course you were the one to be presented with the biggest front. You are the one person I perceived to have the most chance to deal pain. And well, I now see my doggedness did more harm than good.'

'Doggedness? How poetic, Meg.'

'Oh, stop it Manus. Do not tease. I am ashamed. Ainnir told me to never forget what it was like to love, and I despaired that it was too late. Then she gave me this Ouroboros.'

'And what is an Ouroboros?' Manus rolled to his side. Their naked bodies faced.

''Tis a snake devouring its tail, a symbol of re-creation.

279

The snake sheds its skin over and again to begin anew.'

His hands went to her face, pushing long errant wisps of silvery blonde from her eyes. His fingers followed the line of her jaw then just as gently traced her lips, began to pluck at them, smiled easily as the bottom lip made a wet clicking sound at each flick.

'And these sheddings, these changes, you have made them for me?'

Meg nodded. She liked his tone, liked the way his eyes consumed every inch of her.

'My wife the serpent, tempter of all that is unholy, and this here is our Garden of Eden. I think I could come to like this.'

And round four began.

In a dither, the toad ordered her servants to pack her possessions at the first sign of daylight, and she endured the pot-ridden road to leave the scathing words of her daughter behind. Veronique was at a loss for the day, had no duties to attend. Servants were admitted to their mistress's chamber only when armed with food and drink, for sustenance in plentiful was needed to keep Meg's and Manus' energy levels ripe – and rife. Yet Veronique did not worry overly, could only see the good in her hours being idle, thought she could come to enjoy such a pleasure as no doubt her mistress would.

Back at Manor Kildea, Mrs. Mulhearn with eyes tired from weeping, held her fists tight to her chest as her mistress's screams pierced the air. She doubted not that every one of the jarring shrills were heard by the Heavens.

Jarlath had delivered the news.

She looked down to the floor at her feet as the hem of her aprons swayed. She believed, just as all at Manor Kildea now believed. The young lass's soul refused to leave this earth, wanting to remain to care for everyone.

Part Three

Chapter Twenty-One

Castle Maynooth
1480

It was autumn. The night sky softened. The day made its coming known. Hues of green and pearl appeared above the height of the castle walls as the last stars blinked their light. Within the inner bailey, horses snorted and tossed their heads sensing the anticipation of their riders.

Conn Mor stared at the line of laden carts and absently rubbed at the ring upon his finger, the ring bearing the O'Neill arms. His mount shifted rearward and bobbed its head.

'I am no less annoyed than you, boy.' Conn Mor was more than miffed at being coerced into this task; travelling to Maynooth to assist in the escort of ten bathing tubs to an Abbey in Achad-finglass.

He had sought Gerald's aid to challenge his troublesome cousin Sean Buidhe O'Neill in Kinnaird, planning to ride into the northern township fully armed in the next few weeks. With his larking ways, Gerald insisted the Prince pay for the bidden favour in advance. *A ride south for a sword in the north*, Gerald demanded via missive. The words *imperative*, *clandestine* and *undisclosed purpose* painted the jaunt vital.

But here, now, the task appeared pitiful. Tubs for an Abbey! He had been abundantly misled. Or did the Earl not speak all?

'South we are heading, my lord, on this fine day,' said Harry, with a full smile. 'You are pleased?'

'You're coming too, madman,' grunted Conn Mor.

'And good it is. Have you not heard? Savages lurk in the forest, craving possession of fine craftsmanship such as these tubs. Highway robbers, everywhere. Those men crave a wash. Yes they do. They crave to be cleaned. The lands of south Kildare are perilous.'

'Perilous, my arse.'

Harry released a loud and long-winded fart. 'And it seems mine is too. Must be the excitement of the day playing havoc with my gizzards. Hah!'

'You know more, Harry. What is the Earl planning?'

'Whatever do you mean, my lord?'

Conn Mor knew he'd get no more from Beowulf. He turned his attention back to the preparations. Wainwrights made last minute repairs to cart trays. Wineskins were handed to riders and strapped to saddles. Servants hauled the last of the tubs up onto the front cart. A hooded brown goshawk, its feathers dotted with a lesser shade, was tethered to the wrist of a mounted rider. All appeared in readiness.

The men waited.

And waited some more.

Gerald walked from the hall with the Countess Joan on his arm. The woman did not appear her forty-five years. Agile in step, raven hair only faintly peppered with grey, and a face beaming with the conspiratorial look of youthful mischief as she nodded a welcome to Conn Mor.

'You have been too long from our home, Conn.'

''Tis an honour to be missed, madame,' he replied

politely.

'You refused the comforts of the castle for the night?'

'My men and I slept under the stars after a horse threw a shoe.'

'A shame,' the Countess said with lathered sincerity.

Gerald swung into his saddle, tossed an instruction to one of his captains and wheeled his horse to join Conn Mor.

'We have all missed you, Conn. Some more than others.'

'What do you play at, Gerald?'

'Wait, wait,' came a trilling voice from the steps of the hall.

Conn Mor turned to see a barefooted beauty descend the steps two at a time. Golden-red hair flew wildly. Her night gown was loosely tied, and did naught to conceal the curve of her breast and the tapering of her thin waist, nor the soft white skin of her calves. A hellion, he thought, some lucky man's bed sport.

'Are you to again leave without speaking to me?' The hellion stood with hands fast on her hips.

Gerald regarded Conn Mor with an impossible look, then inclined his head toward the steps, toward the hellion. The young woman marched through the throng of carts and horses and busy servants, and stopped at the head of Conn Mor's mount.

'Do you not recognise me?'

He made no reply.

'I am the letter writer,' she said matter-of-factly, 'in three languages. English, French and Gael. I am beginning to think you read only Latin.'

'Eleanor?'

'Yes, beloved, 'tis I, Eleanor, your future wife. An impatient future-wife. Will you ignore me so when we are finally wed? And when will you make it happen?'

Christ on the Cross, Conn Mor swore silently. When did the child blossom to this, a true beauty with an enticing brashness, and with … and with breasts? The lass's piercing eyes would have drawn blood if spears thrown by a skilled arm, but they suddenly took on the guise of a cat's; a prowling cat's. She must have smelt his astonishment, his wonder, his ardour.

'My Lord,' Conn Mor said to Gerald, his eyes not leaving Eleanor. 'Allow me a mere moment. I believe your sister has the right of things, as it would indeed be rude of me not to speak to my betrothed before we depart.'

Conn Mor could not dismount quickly enough, took Eleanor's hand in his and with long strides, caused his betrothed to break into a run if she was to keep up. He lead her inside the hall away from the many ogling eyes, eyes that gave silent and unchivalrous appraisal of her body, no less than he had, no less than he was still doing.

She was tall for a lass which was just as well for he was a giant of a man, yet she still had the need to tilt her head to look up to his.

'By all the Saints, you were a child when I last saw you.'

'I am no longer a child, Conn, I am sixteen, and soon to be seventeen. Past old enough to be a wife.'

'That you are, lass. That you are.' He lifted her hand to his mouth and placed a kiss upon her fingers. Conn Mor had been widowed for almost six years, and yes, he missed sharing a bed with the same woman night after night. Perhaps it was time to return to such an affable indulgence. And with this one, he was certain, it would be more than enjoyable. 'What say you to this betrothal of ours being honoured on my return? It seems I have deferred my obligations for too long, and only now come to comprehend my priorities have been given horrendous disorder.'

'I am impervious to the poetry of exaggeration, Conn.'

'Poetic it may be. An exaggeration it is not. And I can assure you impervious is no longer a malady I suffer.'

A small smile tugged at the corners of her mouth. 'I would like that very much.'

'Then ready your wedding gown, Eleanor. I will be gone no more than a fortnight.' Conn Mor removed the ring from his finger. 'Take this as a keepsake, a pledge of my promise. A fortnight.'

She raised a hand to his chest, splayed her fingers as if to feel the beating of his heart, measure his sincerity. 'A fortnight?'

'Aye.'

She took the ring. 'You have made me wait for a time already beyond patience, Prince of Ulster.'

'I will rush my return.' And he meant it.

'You have a fortnight, my lord.' That confident quirk at her lips suggested he stank mightily of ardour.

He placed another kiss to her hand, then gave a courtly smile and led her back out to the steps.

'You have my word.' As he made to turn, return to his horse, a hand arm grabbed at his shoulder.

Eleanor threw her arms around his neck and reached up high, her lips pressing hard against his. It was her first kiss.

He knew without a doubt. And he liked that thought. He moved his lips slowly at first, a patient teacher, showed his betrothed how a true kiss was delivered, and a true kiss returned. Whistles from their audience pierced the air.

'Less than a fortnight,' he whispered.

Eleanor giggled into his mouth. 'I believe you.'

'Are we in readiness to leave?' Gerald asked with a smirk.

Conn Mor mounted his horse. 'You have cozened me, Fitzgerald.' The two men exchanged what could be construed as half smiles. 'But you are forgiven.'

'Your allegation is only minimally deserved,' said Gerald. 'I have need to speak to you on further matters.'

'Matters?'

'Raids on the Gaels in Wicklow and Wexford, and the O'Mores in Leix.'

'You think it's time?'

'I know it is.'

'You have spoken to Jarlath?'

'I am the Earl of Kildare. I have no need to gauge the opinion of my cousin.'

Conn Mor read something in Gerald's face. 'As you say,' he allowed. 'But we now head south, no?'

'We do.'

'And south is where Jarlath lives?'

'Yes.'

'And …'

'And if time allows we shall pay my cousin a visit,' Gerald admitted.

'In Kildea?'

'In Kildea.'

'With the tubs?'

'With the tubs.'

Harry interceded. 'With the fine outstanding tubs, worldly well-crafted tubs just waiting to be poached by dangerous thieves in desperate need of a scrub. Eyes open men. Danger lurks nearby when people are desperate to bathe in luxury. Hah!'

Conn Mor stole a quick glance back toward the steps of the hall and his future wife. He kicked his mount and hoped his horse would spread wings like Pegasus.

Beside a row of thinning lavender bushes, Jarlath and old Patrick toiled without complaint, shovels digging deeper and deeper until the hole measured four hands in depth and twelve in width. An arduous task, for the autumn proved no less harsh than the summer and had baked the earth into a crust much like the face of a forest-dwelling crone past her time. A location closer to the pond or the kitchen garden would have offered more forgiving soil, but this was the location chosen by Conor, so here it would be.

'Should be enough, Patrick.' Jarlath threw his shovel to the side.

With one arm, Ainnir hugged her young babe to her hip, and with the other she guided Conor a safe distance from the men's next task. Conor failed in his endeavour to be controlled. His sniffles escaped into the air.

'Allow me, my lord,' Patrick mumbled.

'Two sets of hands will be needed, Patrick.'

'No. No. No. Can handle this on me own.' With as much care as possible, Patrick grabbed at the hind legs and dragged the dead animal into the shallow grave. The dog's head thumped onto the ground, and its swollen tongue flopped and rolled.

'Would you like to say a prayer, Conor?'

Conor looked down to the limp bluebells clenched in his fist. 'Must I?'

More sniffles came, this time from Mrs. Mulhearn and Emma.

Jarlath knelt beside his son. 'Hunter died in his sleep. He was old and it was his time. That's the way of things. And last winter, his legs hurt mightily with the joint evil. He would have suffered even more when the snows came again. We wouldn't want that, would we?'

'Grandpapa Hugh complained of the joint evil when I was in Glendalough. Will he die too?'

'It is different for people.'

'Why?'

'Because it is.'

'How do you know?'

'There is much that I know, for I am your father, so come now.' Jarlath fluffed at his son's dark hair and slipped a glance at Ainnir. 'I would tell you it is not right for a boy to cry, but I fear your mother would have me eat peppered lard for a month.'

'Peppered lard? Yuk.'

'So what say you to a compromise? One more tear, take a deep breath, find your courage and say a prayer for Hunter. I know you can do such a task, after all, you are a Fitzgerald.'

'Uncle Bradan said I am also an O'Byrne. '

'And Uncle Bradan is correct.'

From the corner of his eye, Jarlath caught a weak smile from his wife. A rarity, for Ainnir did not smile much these days. She seemed wrapped in a shawl of grief, a shawl fastened with a brooch, and fastened again. He hoped time would heal her pain, all their pain. As for Jarlath's ache, he accepted the emptiness and continued on. He could not afford the indulgence of sanctity, the pull of his childhood yew tree. No. His family was in need of him.

'Why do we not visit Grandpapa Hugh?'

'Because your grandpapa and your cousin Gerald do not see eye to eye,' explained Jarlath.

'We can make them be friends.'

'If it were only that simple. Perhaps a prayer to Saint Wilfred for Hunter. It is his feast day today.'

Conor wiped at his nose with the back of his hand then stepped closer to the grave. 'Saint Wilfred, please care for Hunter in Heaven. He likes to chase foxes and swans and he likes to chew big bones, really big bones. And scratch his belly, and behind his ears.' Conor looked to Jarlath hesitantly.

'Is there more you wish to say?'

'And … can you make sure he knows where Siobhan is so he doesn't get scared. He might worry a bit if he can't find her. Amen.'

Ainnir choked back a sob, and pressed the babe closer to her chest. The other two women turned their backs to the scene, no less emotional.

'Amen,' followed Patrick and Jarlath.

Jarlath nodded to Conor, and with that silent

instruction the boy threw the wilted flowers into the grave.

'Well done, son.'

Patrick began the task of shovelling the soil back into the hole. The tool made scrapping noises as it ploughed into the dry mound. His movements were slow, laborious. Sweat trickled from his brow.

Mrs. Mulhearn blew her nose into her apron. 'Show Patrick what you made, Conor.'

'I made a cross, Patrick.' From his belt, Conor pulled a crude crucifix created from two small sticks of kindling and twine.

''Tis a fine cross, lad. Would ya like to push it into the soil? Perhaps right here.' Patrick tapped at the edge of the dog's grave and Conor followed. 'Make sure it's in right and proper.'

'Patrick,' said Jarlath, quietly.

'My lord?' Patrick straightened.

'It was you who sent word to the Countess Joan at Maynooth, news of Ainnir's illness, wasn't it?'

Patrick nodded.

Jarlath smiled weakly. 'Good man.'

A dim clamour sounded in the distance.

'We have guests,' announced Ainnir.

A line of mounted men and carts appeared along the roadway heading toward Manor Kildea's gates.

'It's Gerald. Are you expecting him?'

'No.'

The line of carts pulled to a stop inside the gates.

'You travel with your own bathing implements?' Jarlath jested.

Gerald dismounted. 'Just paying an overdue debt.'

'On your way to Achad-finglass?'

'As father wished.'

'Thomas would be pleased.'

'Ainnir, you look well,' said Gerald with a formal nod in greeting.

'You too, my lord.'

'Your son is healthy?' he asked moving to study the child in her arms.

'Oh, that he is.'

'Could his cheeks be more red? He blushes like an apple.'

'Donal's teeth are ready to show themselves, 'tis all.'

'Donal? You named the boy Donal? Ah, with a name like that he is destined to be a good man, a great man.' The baby gripped his finger. 'And already strong.'

'Not as strong as me,' interrupted Conor.

Gerald swept Conor high onto his shoulders. 'Who said those words? Who speaks to the Earl of Kildare? Show yourself. Is it a ghost that speaks?'

Perched up high, gripping tightly under Gerald's chin, Conor laughed and laughed some more.

Gerald turned in circles, swung back and around, looked east then west, then north then south like a troubled weathercock.

'Our ghost doesn't talk,' shrilled Conor. 'She just tickles my feet.'

'What? A ghost who speaks of another ghost? Come now. Be valiant, you bold ghost. Show yourself.'

'It is me!'

'What the Devil …' Gerald placed Conor back onto the

ground. 'And who would you be, for you cannot be my cousin Conor Fitzgerald? He is only a wee lad.'

'I am Conor.'

'You are? But you are tall. How old are you now?'

'Five. Nearly six.'

'And nearly a man. Has it really been more than a year since I last saw you?'

'We are burying Hunter.'

'Oh, I see. Your father's beloved wolfhound. You loved Hunter too?'

Conor nodded.

'You did not cry, did you? Men do not cry.'

Conor bit at his lip and looked to his father.

Gerald seemed to read the child's pause, and altered his line of questions. 'Hmm. So you are nearly six?'

'Yes.'

'Well, your Aunt Joan has the right of it then. She bid me bring you a surprise.'

Gerald snapped his fingers and two stewards stepped forward, one with the hooded goshawk on his arm, the other with a small leather glove.

'Do you think you can manage her?'

Conor's eyes widened. 'Oh yes.'

'Then hold out your left arm and we shall see.'

The glove was placed on Conor's hand. With a little prompting, the bird settled her talons into the soft leather.

'You must name her,' said Gerald, and then to Jarlath, 'Walk with me.'

The two men left Conor to his new pet, and walked toward the pond, away from ears.

'I thought the goshawk rare in these parts.'

'Depends on who you are,' said Gerald with a smile.

'You have news?'

'I do. Papal approval has arrived for the appointment of a new Bishop in Glendalough. A Dominican friar. The Pope tires of the Gaels' refusal to give the church their dues. The friar is reportedly a harsh man and will take what is owed.'

'At your bidding?'

'At the Pope's bidding, but with my blessing.'

'I suspect you did not come all this way just to tell me His Holiness has signed a piece of paper and a Dominican friar is a new ally.'

'My spies tell me Kildare is to be attacked from all sides.'

'The Gaels?'

'Within the month.'

'Which clans?'

'The O'Byrne and the O'Toole ready to attack our eastern borders. And the O'Mores watch their every move readying to make their own.'

'They will move as one?'

'I cannot predict.'

'And so?'

'Do you see another alternative?'

'You are asking?'

'I want to hack and cut and slide the tip of my sword down their throats until they gurgle. I want to see their eyes glaze over at the coming of death or spurt purple blood. I want Kildare for the Fitzgeralds. But, as someone once said to me, my father listened to all counsel.'

'So you are asking?'

'Did I not?'

Jarlath smiled. 'You did. And no. No, Gerald. I do not see another alternative, although I wish it were otherwise.'

'*We* have no option. *We* Fitzgeralds of Kildare have no option.'

'When?'

'Within the week. This jaunt with the tubs is a ruse. Word of my generosity will spread, and we let the Gaels think us unaware of their plans.'

'And a week is enough time to ready men-at arms?'

'It must be. Achad-finglass is only a few hours ride from here, and I will leave the carts and the tubs at the Abbey. Travelling light will allow a speedy return home.'

'And our numbers?'

'Boosted by Scottish mercenaries soon to join us.'

'At Maynooth?'

'At Maynooth. Some of my captains remain at the castle preparing all that is necessary. We will head east, hit the Wicklow Gaels first.'

'Ainnir's family,' Jarlath said absently.

'Do you need me to offer you a choice?'

'You once said you would.'

They walked in silence for a time. Jarlath looked back to his family, to his wife, the daughter of the O'Byrne Chieftain, and to his children, the Chieftain's two grandsons. He thought of Brigid's time here, and of the O'Byrnes who cared for Conor during his stay in Glendalough. He thought of Marared, loyal, cheerful Marared who left Manor Kildea for Glendalough to be with Bradan, the man she loved; an act no different to Ainnir leaving Glendalough all those years ago to be with him.

Do you need me to offer you a choice?

What choice did he have? He was a Fitzgerald. He knew what he must do. And he could no more tell Ainnir of their plans than he could refuse to join Gerald. So, in a week he and Gerald would ride east shouting the war cry of the Fitzgeralds, Crom Abu, to devastate the place his wife once called home, bring death to some of her clan.

'I will be at Maynooth within the week.'

'Good. Now what is this ghost I hear of that tickles feet?'

''Tis nothing.'

'Your son has a great imagination?'

'He does. He does.'

The two men returned to the others.

Harry instructed Conor in the art of tethering the goshawk's jesses. The bird's hooded head swivelled left then right and tilted, taking in the sounds. Emma interrupted the instructions and fussed over Harry, her springy red hair bouncing with her exuberance. Harry spoke courteously and his hand wandered to the lass's shoulder more than once. She blushed at each touch. Ainnir chatted to Conn Mor of pending nuptials, castles in the north and O'Neill babes to come. Mrs. Mulhearn held little Donal on her hip. The baby gnawed busily on her chubby knuckle. Patrick packed up the shovels and headed toward the rear of the house. The small cross was dwarfed by the mound of loose soil, almost swallowed into the past, concealed and ready to be forgotten.

Not forgotten, never forgotten, almost twelve months had passed since the death of Siobhan, and the near-death of

Ainnir. Their home had been void of laughter for too long.

When news of their raids would return to his home …
he refused to ponder.

Gerald joined Conor and Harry. 'And does she have a
name yet, Conor?' He gifted Emma with a comely smile. The
girl blushed again.

'She's Emma,' said Conor.

'The bird, boy,' said Harry. 'The over-excited bag-of-
bile Earl here, speaks of the bird. And when he speaks of the
bird he should look at the bird.'

Emma lifted the hem of her skirt and ran off toward
Mrs. Mulhearn.

'Daft man,' said Harry. 'You're prone to spoiling
Harry's fun.'

'You frightened her, Harry. You are a frightening
sight,' said Gerald, and to the boy, 'Yes, the bird, Conor.'

'I think I should like to name her Wicklow.'

'Wicklow?' Gerald fought a sneer. 'An interesting
choice. Like we said, Jarlath, a great imagination.' He gave
Conor a curt nod, one of reticent acknowledgement, not warm
acquiescence. His voice then boomed loud enough to be heard
by the goats in the next village. 'We ride, men.'

Saddle leather creaked. Chainmail and swords and
bridles clinked and clanked. Wheels rumbled and spat stones
into the air, and churned brown clouds of dust that danced
around and around.

Jarlath mused on his son's choice of name for the new
goshawk. Words once said by Ainnir followed as an echo: *Are
Bradan and I the only two who wish this feuding to cease? Is
there not another soul who longs to live in peace?*

300

No, Ainnir, he wanted to now answer. *No. There's more than just you and Bradan.*

A warm breeze stirred at his boots. It seemed to whisper, and he believed he understood.

There are many more.

Author's Note

Melting of the Mettle is a work of fiction. Many of the characters, events and places are chronicled in the pages of history. Many are not. Thomas Fitzgerald was indeed the 7th Earl of Kildare, and the Geraldines were York loyalists who wielded power from the fortified walls of Castle Maynooth. Alliances amongst Nobles and Gaels were certainly precarious, with trickery and conspiracy often criteria. Loyalties altered, battles were rife, and power was everything.

The reason for Thomas' passing is not clear in history books. If it had occurred in battle we can assume such an instance would be noted and recorded. In the absence of any, and with records from parliament sittings immediately following his passing indicating a strong interest in pestilence, this leans to the possibility that Thomas suffered from something that resembled this horrid disease.

Many historians will question the presence of the son Maurice. I found only few sources that gave mention to this child, and only briefly. That gave breath to the possibility that this child of Joan and Thomas Fitzgerald was on this earth for a short time, and possibly shunned from public appearances. Hence, the life of Maurice is speculation on my part, sculpted from the available information. I hope you enjoy the scene with the gorgeous Eleanor and Maurice and the frog custard.

Gerald was indeed given a royal pardon to travel to England to speak to King Edward IV of his position as Justiciar. It is not known what discussion ensued, but history indicates that a surprising decision resulted for Gerald to be returned to power, and it was not expected. Combining that with information that Gerald was a prankster who possessed a great sense of humour, and was somewhat academically-wanting, (and a close ally to Conn Mor O'Neill whose children did indeed submit to the English crown), the scene at Westminster was simply begging to be told, so too, the subtle suggestions of Gerald's somewhat lagging diction.

As always, I like to inform my readers that there are many instances where my pen wanders from the conventions of a historical writer, and blends fiction with fact to bring this tale to life. Where practicable, I remain close to fact. Where accounts differ, I make choices. Where none exist, I create.

Nonetheless, I trust many of my characters will return in the next instalment of *The Chronicles-of-Crom Abu*.